I0634636

Hunting Rabbits in the Dark

S. W. Ballenger

Winnipeg, Canada

Developmental editor: Craig Gibb
Proofreader: Margaret Larson

Published July 2023 by Deep Hearts YA, an imprint of Deep Desires Press and Story Perfect Inc.

Deep Hearts YA
PO Box 51053 Tyndall Park
Winnipeg, Manitoba R2X 3B0
Canada

Visit deepheartsya.com for more great reads.

Hunting Rabbits in the Dark

Prologue

June 1987

I stared at the old yellow school bus that had been painted a dingy shade of gray and turned into a camper on wheels. The nauseated feeling in the pit of my stomach made me feel as though the hot dog I had for lunch was just moments away from being propelled out of my mouth, as if I were a parody of a cartoon character.

"Oh, come on, Hawk!" My friend Gabe stood in the doorway of the bus and beckoned.

I glanced back across my shoulder at my grandfather's house that sat adjacent to Gabe's grandparents, then back to their camper parked in the empty lot behind their garage.

For the past three years, I had been spending the summers with my maternal grandfather in Murphystown, which laid twelves miles from Pleasant. My grandfather was a tall, thin man of eight-six years. I considered him a gentle giant as he never had a bad word to say about anyone. My maternal grandmother had died on my tenth birthday. I was in the middle of my birthday party when my mother received the call that she'd been taken by ambulance to the hospital where she later died of a stroke. After her death, I felt sorry for my grandfather. Having been married to my grandmother for sixty-five years, I felt it my duty to keep him company. At first, I was bored out of my mind; until I met the boy that lived in the house next door. We became instant friends and soon spending time with Granddad meant spending time with my new friend Gabe.

Gabriel Sanchez, with his close-cropped black hair, dark skin, and skeletal-thin frame, was the exact opposite of my bowl-cut brown hair, ghost-white skin, and pudgy, twelve-year-old self. Economically, Gabe's parents lived in a much higher tax bracket than my own parents, resulting in Gabe getting just about any material thing his heart desired, from the latest video gaming system to the newest Huffy bicycle.

Three days earlier I celebrated my birthday with a small cake that my grandfather had bought from the Piggly Wiggly bakery. Granddad gave me a card with twenty dollars, his usual gift, and Gabe presented me with a cassette tape of the *Top Gun* soundtrack. Many times, we would have dance contests in his room. Although neither of us knew how to dance, we always managed to have fun moving to the sounds of Kenny Loggins.

Glancing back at Gabe, I felt my heart began to pound.

"Let's go play Battleship," I suggested, feeling the sweat beginning to collect on my forehead.

"That's boring." Gabe scoffed as he pulled off his Converse sneakers and kicked them off the lower step of the camper.

I raised my eyebrows in hopes of enticing him to a riskier excursion. "I know, let's go ride our bikes down to the sewer pond." The sewer pond was where the city's waste collected in a smelly pool of disgusting sludge where it sat awaiting treatment. With no fence or guards, being a small town, it was an enticing area to play for curious kids.

He rolled his eyes. "Quit being such a wuss and let's play Truth or Dare."

I groaned in frustration, "I don't want to."

"Oh, come on. It will be fun." He taunted me with that mischievous grin of his.

I glanced left then right and lowered my voice. "I don't like playing that game."

Gabe had introduced me to the game of Truth or Dare a few months earlier and it quickly became his favorite game for us to play. Gabe had the annoying habit of making up his own rules which usually favored him. In the case of Truth or Dare, he made the rule we were allowed only one truth per game; the rest being dares, as it was "more fun."

At first, I liked the game. From me licking the dust off the hub cap of his parent's station wagon, to him eating one of his grandmother's prize roses, it made the perfect game for two bored adolescent boys. Everything changed the week prior when we had run out of ideas for dares. While hiding in the fort we had made by covering the two bunk beds in the back of the camper with sheets, Gabe tapped his finger on his chin as he thought hard on the next task that would either cause me extreme embarrassment or leave me half-sick from eating some inedible object. As he aimed his eyes at mine, the corner of his mouth pulled upward, forming that infamous Gabe smirk, and the words that sent shock waves through my body spilled forth. "I dare you to kiss me."

Of course, I immediately refused. After all, guys didn't

kiss each other. That was disgusting. Or was it? Admittedly, Gabe fascinated me in a way that none of my other friends did. I looked up to Gabe, even though physically he was much shorter than me. He made me feel cool just being around him. Call it "cool by association" and although we didn't live in the same town and went to different schools, his cocky attitude made me wish I were more like him. He bragged constantly about different girls asking him to be their boyfriend and all of them he'd kissed. Of course, I was always taking what he said with a grain of salt, but part of me wanted to believe it. Part of me even felt giddy that he'd kissed me and that feeling is what frightened me.

"Come on, I promise, I won't ask you to do anything you don't want to do," he begged.

Knowing Gabe for two years, I knew he was lying.

I glanced at his grandmother's house that sat in the same yard as the bus and hoped by some miracle that she would come out the back door and offer us milk and cookies, but alas the screen door remained closed. We were completely alone with the blazing hot sun and the stifling summer air that made my whole body feel dirty and sticky.

The deafening silence lingered as Gabe awaited my decision.

"Please," he pleaded. "I promise. I won't make it weird."

I stared at his pouting face. How could I let him talk me into participating in this stupid game again? I wanted to sprint across the yard back to my grandfather's house and never come near that dirty old school bus ever again, but I could never say no to Gabe.

Taking a deep breath, I stepped forward and said in a low voice, "Fine, but I'm not kissing you again."

He crossed his heart and grinned liked the Cheshire cat.

Chapter One

September 1992 (5 years later)

The cold metal bleachers sent a chill up my spine as I took a seat in the overcrowded football stands for the last game of the season. The cool autumn breeze whipped my long straight hair into my eyes as I tried to check out the scoreboard with the mascot of the Murphystown's Viper angrily glaring down upon the field. I pushed my hair back behind my ears and felt it tickle my shoulders before focusing my attention on the field.

While football wasn't my first choice of sports—I preferred basketball—an occasional game, whether in gym class or an impromptu game in my backyard, was not out of the question. I had considered playing for the Pleasant High football team but changed my mind when I started working for Mr. Thompson's hardware store back in the summer and didn't have time for team practices.

My reason for attending this out-of-town game was to support the blonde girl on the sidelines in the blue and gold cheerleader uniform waving her pom-poms in the air—my girlfriend, Shelby. The mere thought of her made me feel warm all over. Most guys at school would have given their right nut to have Shelby Johnson as a girlfriend. She was by far the prettiest girl in school. Most people would assume she was your typical bleach-blonde, air-headed cheerleader based on her appearance, but they would be wrong. Shelby was smart, funny, kind, and never met a stranger. Best of all, she was mine.

We started Kindergarten together but didn't really become friends until seventh grade. That year we were chosen as maid and escort to represent our class in the Homecoming Court. The first time I held her hand, walking across the gym floor—me in my tuxedo and she in her blue sequin dress—I felt a spark. There I was, this goofy thirteen-year-old with sweaty palms, gushing over the prettiest girl in class. Shelby later told me that she felt the same way the first time she held my hand. It wasn't long after that we developed this crush on each other and soon we were officially boyfriend and girlfriend. Shelby was the first girl I ever kissed. That night at my house sitting on the sofa with our arms around each other as the credits rolled to *Dirty Dancing*, she leaned over and pressed her lips against mine. Her lips were soft and tasted like cinnamon lip gloss. In my young teenage mind, I had touched heaven.

I focused on her smile and watched as she scanned the bleachers, looking for me. I raised my hand and as soon as she saw me, she waved and mouthed "I love you." I returned the gestures.

"You two are sickening," Shelby's best friend, Melanie, who sat to my left, said.

"I know," I chuckled, "she looks good in her uniform."

Mel shook her head. "Yeah, but I just want to know one thing. Being our school colors are blue and gold, why the hell are the skirts banana yellow?"

I shrugged my shoulder, "I don't know, maybe they thought gold lamé skirts might be a little distracting?"

"Yeah, a little too eighties, I suppose," she said. "I still can't believe she even wanted to be an airheaded cheerleader."

"Shelby is hardly an airhead," I said. Earlier in the summer, Shelby began talking about signing up for cheer to meet new people. Typical Shelby, the social butterfly. While I supported her, I didn't necessarily like the thought of her being busy every weekend. Truth be told, I didn't like her being on the same bus with all those football players dressed like the girl in every jock's wet dream. While I was friends with all the guys, that didn't mean I trusted them not to make a move on her. That's when I decided that I would just have to attend every game and be *her* cheerleader. Melanie usually rode with me in my car, while Shelby rode the bus, as required, to the away games. I honestly didn't mind; Mel was like a sister to me.

"Admit it. You get off on this whole cheerleading thing." She grinned. "She told me that you asked her to put on her uniform for you the other night when you guys were fooling around."

I rolled my eyes and felt annoyed. "Jesus, does she have to tell you everything?"

Mel nodded. "Yep. I'm her best friend." We sat in silence for a moment before Mel spotted the sour expression on my face, "Oh, come on, Hawkins Keystone. Don't be embarrassed. I only *wish* I could find a boyfriend like you." She hooked her arm around mine and pulled me closer.

I couldn't help but smile, "Well...I admit, I am pretty wonderful."

She let go and shoved me playfully. "Get out of here!"

Just then, I felt a tap on my shoulder, "Hawk. Is that you?" I turned my head back to the petite lady with the long, curly black hair dressed in an oversized wool coat. Immediately, my eyes went wide at the sight of a face I hadn't seen in years.

I cocked my brow. "Mrs. Sanchez?" I asked, noticing the Murphystown Viper pennant in her hand.

She screamed as she leaned down and wrapped her arms around me in a big hug, dropping her pennant. "Oh, my God. It's so good to see you," she said in a thick Spanish accent.

I coughed, having the air squeezed out of my lungs. "It's good to see you, too."

After a long hug, she pulled back. "Look at you! You've...you've...grown up!" She flipped her hands over and lifted her palms upward.

I laughed. "Not quite an adult...yet."

"I haven't seen you since your grandpapa passed away." She tapped her index finger on her chin. "When was that, about five years ago?"

"Yes, ma'am. Just before Christmas of eighty-seven," I said, remembering that awful day when my mother got the phone call while we were busy putting up the Christmas tree that he had passed away peacefully in his sleep. I was very close my Granddad Harrison and his death hurt bad.

"Your grandpapa was such a character." She laughed. "I still miss him as a neighbor."

"Yeah, I miss him too," I replied.

Then her face brightened, "Oh my God! You should see my Gabriel." She almost bounced off her seat with excitement. I always remembered Gabe's mom as a very enthusiastic lady. Most of the time when she became overexcited, she would start speaking in Spanish, of which I did not understand a single word.

"How's he been doing?" I raised my brow, wondering what little Gabe looked like now. Still short, weighing a hundred-and ten pounds dripping wet, I imagined. My mind flashed back to all those years playing with her son, riding bikes together and getting into mischief. I quickly scanned the bleachers behind her, looking for a thin Latino boy with a buzz cut.

She pointed toward the football field. "That's him. Number nine."

I followed her finger to the field. My eyes bulged when I caught the sight of a very ripped jock pulling off his helmet. He then shook his sweat-soaked mop of curls and ran toward his team's bench.

I pointed and felt my breath quicken. "*That's* Gabe!"

"Yep." She nodded. "My pequeño mariscal del campo."

Seeing my confusion, Mel leaned over and whispered in my ear, "Little quarterback."

"Holy cow!" I swallowed, unable to fathom that the tiny twelve-year-old I knew could grow into a hunk like that. While I considered myself straight, certain guys captured my attention, just like certain girls, specifically buff guys with dark skin.

"I know he'd love to see you. Can you stay a little while after the game?" Mrs. Sanchez asked.

"Umm...yeah...sure." I turned my eyes to a grinning Mel.

I turned toward the field again and watched as Gabe put his helmet back on and ran to the starting line.

Mrs. Sanchez looked to Mel, "So, is this your girlfriend?"

"Oh. No, ma'am. This is my friend, Mel." I pointed in the direction of the Bulldog cheerleaders. "That's my girlfriend...the one with the long blonde hair."

Mrs. Sanchez followed my finger. "Muy bonita."

"Very pretty," Mel whispered in my ear.

"Thank you. I think so." I smiled. I had to admit being told I had a pretty girlfriend always boosted my male ego.

Mrs. Sanchez patted my shoulder and addressed Mel. "I swear this one and my son were always up to some kind of mischief." She laughed.

Mel pointed at me and gave me a doubtful look. "Hawk, getting into mischief?"

"I could be a bit of a troublemaker in my younger years," I said, although in the past few years, I rarely got into trouble and if I did, it was for rather minor infractions.

"The word 'troublemaker' and 'you', just don't go together." Mel laughed.

"Good Heavens," Mrs. Sanchez started. "That time you boys broke all mi mama's flowerpots all over her driveway."

"Oh...yeah." I threw my head back and laughed.

Mel lifted her eyebrows at me. "Flowerpots?"

"I'll tell you the story sometime. The game's starting again." I quickly tried to change the subject.

"Uh-huh." She looked at me suspiciously.

As we all focused back on the game, I watched as the Vipers' center snapped the ball to Gabe. As soon as he got possession of the ball, he faked a throw before tearing off down the field with the football tucked securely under his arm. Although our team tried to stop him, he plowed toward the endzone. The referee threw up his arms, signaling a touchdown. The hometown crowd roared. Admittedly, the Pleasant High football team wasn't that good. Coach Hadley always had difficulty recruiting players in such a small school as ours. He'd been working on me for two years but I would always tell him I was sticking to basketball.

The rest of the game was pretty much a blowout with the Vipers beating our Bulldogs thirty-seven to three. With a disappointing sigh, I stood up as the crowd began to descend the bleachers.

"Come on," Mrs. Sanchez said, gathering her purse. "We're going to surprise Gabriel."

I looked at Mel. "You coming?"

"I wouldn't miss this," she replied as I watched Mrs. Sanchez start down the steps in front of me. I knew the motive behind Mel's answer, she wanted to meet the Vipers' star player.

Stopping by the exit gate, I motioned across the field to Shelby, who was busily helping the cheerleading squad pack up their supplies, to join us. Just then, I spotted the hunk about my height with tight, jet-black ringlets that partially covered his dark brown eyes, running toward us. He stopped next to his mom and pushed the unruly mess back over his head triggering me to do the same with my own brown locks.

"Great game, honey," Mrs. Sanchez reached to wrap her arms around him.

Gabe grumbled as he pulled back, "Mom...please. Not in front of the team."

The sound of his deep voice took me aback. The last time I'd heard Gabe speak, his voice was that of a pre-pubescent teenager. Noticing me, I could see from the look on his face he had no clue as to my identity.

"Gabe, do you know who this is?" Mrs. Sanchez asked, smiling from ear to ear.

Gabe stared a moment before his eyes widened. "Hawk?" he said as his eyes beamed with recognition.

I couldn't help but grin from ear to ear myself. "Hey, man, how's it going?"

"Dude!" he said and leapt forward, grabbing me in a quick bro hug. The smell of his sweaty body filling my nostrils. "I can't believe it's you!"

His reaction took me completely by surprise. I expected a quick nod or a handshake, but not a hug, especially after he'd just complained about his mother's affectionate gesture.

"It's good to see you," I replied nervously as I patted him on the back once.

Pulling away he gave me a once-over. "Damn, man, you're not fat anymore!"

"Gabriel!" Mrs. Sanchez chastised him. "That's not nice."

I curled my lip at him. "And you're not a little runt anymore!" I shot back remembering how he and I used to banter back and forth as kids.

Gabe put his arms across his chest and chuckled. I noticed his light mustache for the first time. "Still the same old Hawk."

About that time, I heard footsteps come up beside me and stop next to Mel. I turned to Shelby and felt my pride swell. "Gabe, this is my girlfriend, Shelby…and her best friend, Mel." I then addressed them, "Guys, this is an old friend of mine, Gabe. He was my granddad's neighbor and we played together as kids."

"Hi," Shelby said. I put my arm around her and pulled her close. Yeah, it was a bit chauvinistic, but I liked to show off my girl. I wanted him to know that while I wasn't a football star like him, I could still score a hot chick.

Curiously, I noticed that Gabe's eyes stayed on me. "Dude, why aren't you out there on that field? Look at you all buff, damn, dude."

"Basketball is my game," I replied.

"Oh yeah. I remember when we were kids you always wanted to play basketball. You never could beat me if I recall." He pushed his chest out.

"My game has improved since then."

"Hey, do you remember the B Team?"

Shelby raised her eyebrows at me, and I laughed. "We formed our own little crime fighting team as a take-off of the *A-Team* TV show. Since the name A Team was taken, we were the B Team. B standing for best. We built our base in Gabe's backyard out of cardboard boxes."

"Yeah, one rain and our fort collapsed," Gabe added.

I recalled one of our innocent games. Gabe, of course, was the Hannibal, the leader, and I was Crazy Mad Murdock. He and our friends would act out scenes from the show using sticks as guns and his dog Obi as the hostage taken by a group of militant pet thieves. Gabe naturally took charge of the entire operation. As a kid, Gabe could be very bossy. It seemed like we always had to do what he wanted to do, and I would go along with it. I wasn't a complete push-over. A few times, he'd pushed me too far and I'd put my foot down. He would quickly back off.

Gabe continued to examine me, "I just can't get over you, dude. You look so different." He shook his head. "You know? We need to get together sometime...you know... catch up."

"Yeah, we should," I answered, knowing it probably wouldn't happen. In the South, meeting an old friend and saying "we should get together sometime" was the polite way of saying, "It's good to see you, but I'm far too busy to make the time." It's understood that the other person felt the same way; regardless, it's considered good manners.

"Hey, sweetie," Shelby interrupted, "Coach Abercrombie said I could ride back to Pleasant with you and Mel instead of on the bus."

"Good," I replied, thinking her cheerleader coach was in an awfully good mood for our team losing the game. Normally, she'd make Shelby ride the bus back to Pleasant. "Well, dude, we need to get back," I said to Gabe.

"Yeah, man, it's been good seeing you." He leapt forward, giving me another hug, taking me once again by surprise.

"You too," I replied, trying to catch my breath. Being squeezed by a one-hundred-and-eighty-pound quarterback wasn't exactly gentle.

"Bye," Mel said, looking dreamy-eyed.

A few minutes later, I unlocked the door to my mother's white Honda Prelude and the three of us piled inside, Shelby in the front passenger seat and Mel directly behind me. I started the engine and began backing out of the parking lot.

"Oh my God! That Gabe guy was so hot! I can't believe you guys are buddies," said Mel from the backseat.

I glanced at her in the rearview mirror as I shifted the car out of reverse, "Buddies? Hell, I haven't seen the guy in five years. Last time I saw him he was a scrawny little kid."

"He certainly isn't scrawny anymore. Did you check out the size of those biceps?"

I slowly shook my head, pretending I hadn't. "You need a boyfriend *bad*, Mel."

She sighed. "You have *no* idea."

"I didn't like him," Shelby spoke up.

"*What?*" we both said at the same time.

"I said I didn't like him. Yeah, he's hot, but…he's…oh, never mind." She waved her hand in a dismissive gesture.

Mel leaned forward. "No, girl. That ain't working. Spill it."

In all the years, I'd been with Shelby; I never once heard her speak bad of someone. She never put anyone down, but if she didn't like a person, she let it be known, although I'd never known her to immediately take a dislike to someone as in this case. I took a quick glance at Shelby as I pulled the car out of the parking lot and onto the street. "Babe, why would you not like him? You just met him."

"Didn't you notice the way that he kept looking at you?"

I crinkled my brow. "What do you mean 'looking at me'? Of course, he would be looking at me. The last time he saw me I was a pudgy kid with acne and braces." When I hit thirteen, I joined the basketball team, finally working up the courage to give it a try. Within a year, I lost the baby fat and gained about six inches in height. I also started working out and while I might not be quite as buff as Gabe, I could hold my own. I did have abs and pecs that Shelby enjoys immensely.

She pursed her lips. "He was practically undressing you with his eyes."

Mel and I busted out with laughter. "You can't be serious?" Mel beat me to the question.

"I am serious," she answered, "I know the look when a guy is checking me out and it's the same look he was giving you."

I could see from the look on Shelby's face she was dead serious, and my laughter stopped. "Babe. Gabe is the quarterback of the Vipers' football team and, if all the stories he used to tell me as a kid were true, popular with the girls. There's no way he could possibly be…gay."

"Just because he's a jock doesn't mean he can't be gay.

People thought the same thing about my brother J.J. *and* his boyfriend Mason, and look at them."

I had only met Shelby's older brother J.J. once at Christmas a couple years prior. He was home from college along with his boyfriend, Mason. Admittedly, I found it weird that they were a couple because neither of them acted gay. Sitting around the dining table at Shelby's house eating dinner, they acted like they were just friends. I said something to Shelby later about it and she told me they acted that way for the benefit of her father, since he still had difficulty accepting it. Everyone in Pleasant knew the "scandalous" tale of Mr. Thompson catching his son and Shelby's brother making out in the storage room of his appliance store. He fired Shelby's brother and disowned his own son. If truth be told, I avoided being at her house when her brother was home. He made me feel uneasy, not because I had anything against him, but because I was afraid he would think I was not quite straight. I mean, I had kissed a boy...Gabe, when I was twelve, and I did not find it repulsive. I've heard that gay people recognize other gay people and as crazy as it may sound, I worried he could somehow peer into my mind and see that I had kissed a boy and liked it.

"I see your point." I reached over and intwined my fingers with hers. "Either way, you have nothing to worry about, because I'm yours."

The corners of her mouth rose before she leaned over and gave me a quick peck on the cheek.

"Aww...that's so sweet," Mel said from the backseat.

"So...Mel. Are you coming over tomorrow to help

paint my room?" Shelby asked, twisting her head to the backseat.

"I...um...must help Mom with the laundry."

"That's the lamest excuse I've ever heard...at least you could have come up with something a little more original like 'I have to help Mom take the dog to the vet.'" Shelby chuckled.

"Oh, wait...laundry is Sunday. Tomorrow I must help Mom take the dog to the vet." She grinned.

"Lame, girl, lame."

Chapter Two

Leaning against the doorjamb of my girlfriend's bedroom, I felt a sense of dread for the first time. I threw my hands toward the cluttered mess. "You mean, we have to move all this shit out before we can paint?"

"Yep," Shelby said, standing next to me.

"Babe, it looks like a tornado struck, leaving no survivors," I teased.

She playfully punched me on the shoulder. "It's a little cluttered."

I stared at the piles of clothes in the corner, on the bed, on the floor and wondered if there were any clothes left in the closet. "A little!"

"Excuse me. Not everyone is a neat freak like you."

"I'm not a neat freak. I just like things organized," I said. Clothes not in their proper place drove me crazy. They needed to be in the hamper or hanging in the closet.

She looked at me skeptically. "You organize your sweaters by thickness. Who does that?"

"It's called being prepared for the season...speaking of being prepared..." I pulled the hoodie over my head revealing an old ratty white T-shirt with deep cut arm holes. I reached into the pocket of my paint-splattered jeans, retrieved a hair tie, and pulled my hair back into a ponytail. "Okay. I'm ready to search for survivors."

I caught Shelby staring at me. "What?" I asked.

"You look hot." She gave me a mischievous grin.

I posed against the doorjamb, casually pulling the shirt to the left to expose my right pec. "Do I?" I returned her grin.

She looked down the hall. "Come on." She pushed me into her room, shutting the door behind us. Shoving me down on her clothes-covered bed, she immediately attacked me with her lips. I maneuvered myself into the center where she slipped her hands into the two giant holes in my shirt and began rubbing my chest.

"What about your dad's rule?" I asked, referring to the requirement that her bedroom door always be open whenever I was over. I guess he thought that by leaving the door open it would somehow stop us from doing what all seventeen-years old couples who'd been together for three years did.

"Mom's gone to the grocery store and Dad is in his shop working on his backhoe." She looked at the alarm clock on her nightstand. "We got about ten minutes before Mom is back."

"Plenty of time." I quickly pulled my shirt over my head.

Eight minutes later, I stood, getting dressed. I gazed blissfully at Shelby, who was fidgeting with the clasp on her bra. Just then I heard her mom's car pull into the driveway.

"Perfect timing," she said as she pulled an old ratty shirt over her head.

Quickly dressing, Shelby put her hands on her hips and assessed the situation, before starting to gather the clothes on the bed into her arms. "If you want to start in the corner by the closet? Stud." She winked at me.

"Yes, ma'am." I focused my attention on the corner and the huge stack of teeny-bopper magazines. I strolled over and picked up the one on top, glancing at the photo of a smiling Corey Haim on the front. "Umm…Babe. What do you want to do with these old magazines?" I held up the one in my hand.

"Throw them out I guess." She paused a second then burst out laughing. "No wait, put them in J.J.'s old bedroom."

I lifted my eyebrows. "Huh?"

She stopped gathering clothes and sat down on the bed, "J.J. told me that he used to sneak into my room and 'borrow' the ones with Corey Haim."

I gave her a puzzled look. "Why?" She lowered her eyebrows at me, and I thought about it for a moment. "Gross!" I immediately dropped the magazine, causing Shelby to fall back on the bed in hysterics.

"That's sick." Admittedly I had done the same on occasion to a few of the *Men's Fitness* magazines I bought at the convenience store, but I certainly didn't want the love of my life to know that I found guys sexually attractive. Shelby could be the very jealous type at times, and I certainly didn't want to open up that jealousy to another gender.

"He said he liked to read the articles."

I scoffed. "Yeah right. I think I'll pick up the stuffed animals instead."

"Okay, would you go get a few garbage bags to put them in? I think I'll give them to my little cousin, Amy."

I picked up the giant stuffed gorilla with the large banana in its mouth and made a sad face at her. "You're giving away Maynard?"

She returned the frown. "Aww…you won that for me at the State Fair when we were in ninth grade." I recalled that day three years ago when I spent an hour shooting over-sized basketballs into undersized straw baskets, determined to win my girl a big prize. The result being Maynard, a name we randomly gave it on the bus ride home.

I pulled the banana from its mouth. "This thing cost me sixty bucks."

"You were so sweet." She got up, walked over, and put both her arms over my shoulders.

I pointed to my cheek, and she kissed it, then my chin, then my lips. "You were worth it." I smiled.

"Maynard stays." She dropped her arms. "So, the garbage bags are under the sink in the kitchen. Just bring the whole box. I have a feeling we'll need a bunch."

"Whatever you say, babe. Be right back," I said and headed to the kitchen.

Entering, I observed Mrs. Johnson putting away groceries and stopped. I admit I felt a little nervous knowing I had just taken advantage of her daughter while she was out grocery shopping. Shelby's mother, unlike my own, was not a very "emotionally involved" parent. Shelby had told me that her mother's discussion about the birds and the bees sounded as if she'd memorized it from a public health pamphlet. Not that she didn't try to be a loving parent, she just didn't know how, and many times came across as cold and detached. Shelby felt she did love her though and the feeling was mutual.

Just then, I caught her eye. "Oh. Good morning, Hawk. How's the painting coming along?" she asked.

"Good morning, Mrs. Johnson. We haven't been able to start yet. We're still working on clearing her room."

She grinned as she removed a can of soup from the grocery bag. "I have a feeling that you're going to be in for a long day."

"Me too," I chuckled, "Shelby said there's some garbage bags under the sink?"

She dug into the grocery bag and pulled out a new box of them. "Always be prepared." She flashed me a rare smile.

I walked over and took them from her. "Thanks."

"I'll make some tuna salad, whenever you guys are ready to take a lunch break."

"Okay, thanks, Mrs. Johnson," I said politely and headed back to Shelby's room.

Four hours later, I rolled one last strip of dark green paint over the original baby blue paint and stood back to admire our work. "It looks good."

Shelby wiped her hands on an old T-shirt we were using as a paint rag. "I like it."

"I agree that original baby blue color was butt ugly," I said.

"Yeah," she said as she sat down in the middle of the room on a paint-splatter-free section of the plastic sheeting. I sat down across from her and crossed my legs like her.

"This was originally my parent's bedroom before I was born. Dad added on to the house when I was a toddler, and I got their old room. "

I leaned over and peered into her brother's room, noticing it was half the size of hers, "I figured your older brother would have gotten the larger room."

"J.J. had that room from the time my parents bought this house. My grandmother paid to have carpet put in it because she couldn't stand the thought of her precious grandson playing on a cold hardwood floor. So, he chose to stay in the small room because it had carpet and this one didn't." Shelby had told me her brother was always her late grandmother's pick of favorite grandchild between the two of them. Sometimes her animosity toward her came to surface in casual conversations. I sometimes got the feeling she was a bit jealous of her brother as well because he did so much better than her in school.

"Do you ever miss your brother?" I asked.

She shrugged her shoulder. "Sometimes…we were never that close growing up. It was only during his senior year in high school that we became 'friends' I guess you would say."

After the "gay" talk the prior evening, I admit I was curious. I usually avoided broaching the subject of her brother's sexuality. It always made me feel uncomfortable, but I wanted to know how she might feel if one day I decided to tell her the truth about myself. Would she accept it? I would never want her to think I was gay because I wasn't gay. I loved every beautiful inch of her with all my heart. "Are you embarrassed that he's gay?"

"No, why should I be?" she snapped.

I recoiled. "I'm sorry…I didn't mean to imply you were."

She reached over and grabbed my hand. "I'm sorry…I just get angry when people judge him. You remember when I spent spring break in Texas with him and Mason?"

"Yeah. The longest week of my life." She squeezed my hand lovingly.

"It was the most amazing thing I'd ever seen. They were just like any straight couple. J.J. cleaned the apartment, Mason did the cooking and laundry. They did a budget together. They'd cuddle on the couch together like me and you. I mean, they were just as in love with each other as we are. I honestly admire them. They prove gender doesn't matter when it comes to love."

"Yeah. I believe that too. I bet they have to put up with a lot of shit from other people."

"Oh. I'm sure. I mean Austin is more liberal than Pleasant, but it is the South."

"Yeah. True."

"Austin is actually a pretty cool city. I wouldn't mind if we went to college there."

Shelby and I had talked many times over the past year about colleges. It was a given that we would be going together to the same college; although I would rather not go, get married and start a family here in Pleasant. Although I did well in school, I hated it. Going away to college was very important to Shelby, and I'd rather suffer through four more years of school than lose her, so I went along with it. "Your brother told me last Christmas they have a giant arcade center?" Love of video games was one thing her brother and I had in common.

She chuckled. "So, the quality of the college doesn't matter as long as the city has a giant arcade?"

"Naturally." I leaned over and kissed her.

After moving all of Shelby's furniture back into her room, I headed home to shower and settle in for the night. Although it was a Saturday night, and we usually cruised the town in my mother's Prelude and hung out with friends, we were both exhausted to the point that all we wanted to do was relax. I wanted to go back over to her house and hang out but I didn't want to smother her, which I sometimes had the tendency to do.

I entered through the back door of our ranch-style home and pulled off my shoes and shirt in the laundry room before making my way to the kitchen to grab a canned Coke from the refrigerator. My mother sat at the kitchen table with a red pen in one hand and cup of coffee in the other with two stacks of tests sitting in front of her.

"Hey, Mom," I greeted and sat down across from her.

"Hey, honey, just trying to get these papers graded before Monday."

"Have you got to mine yet?" Having my mother as my high school English teacher could be a bit strange at times. Being in a small school, she was the only English teacher on staff for grades seven through twelve. I had her for English for four years in a row. At school, I called her Mrs. Keystone and we maintained a "professional" student-teacher relationship, but at home she was just Mom.

"No, not yet," she answered and grabbed another paper off the top of the ungraded stack.

"Go easy on my essay answer to the question about the insanity of the narrator 'William Wilson'. That question threw me off," I said as I popped open the tab of my soda.

She patted the stack of graded papers. "Apparently, it threw a lot of people off."

"Better watch it, or you're going get a reputation as an old battle axe." I grinned.

"An F it is." She grinned back at me. "You and Shelby get finished with her room?"

"Yep. *Finally*. The painting was quick, moving all her junk in and out wasn't," I said and took a sip of my drink. "Anyway, I'm going to go get a shower, lay down, and catch *SNL* if I don't fall asleep first."

"Okay, sweetie. I'm going to be heading to bed soon myself."

"Okay. Good night," I said, standing up.

"Goodnight…oh, wait!" She held her finger up. "I have a message for you." Rambling through her papers, she pulled out a Post-It note. "Someone named Gabe called and wants you to call him back. He left his number."

"Gabe!" I raised my voice, not expecting in a million years for him to actually contact me.

She glanced at the number. "That's a Murphystown number…wait…isn't that the name of the kid you used to play with that lived next to Dad?"

"Yeah. I ran into him and his mom at the football game

last night. He said we should get together sometime and catch up, but I never expected him to actually call me."

She held the note up. "He sounded eager to talk to you. I told him that it may be late before you got in, but he said he'd be up and to go ahead and call him back."

I walked over and took the note from her. "Okay. I may call him after my shower."

"Don't talk too long. It's long distance. I can't afford a three-hundred-dollar phone bill on a teacher's salary." She smiled.

I chuckled. "I'll make it short."

Heading down the hall to my bedroom, I passed the family photos hanging on the walls, triggering my childhood memories. I glanced at the photo of me, my sister Jennifer, Mom, and my late father. I couldn't help but think about the last time I saw my father when I was five years old. He was sitting in his recliner in the living room watching a football game on the TV. I had gone to my room to get my Stretch Armstrong action figure, and when I came back, he was lying on the floor. I tried to wake him up, but he wouldn't move. I ran to get my mom and the next thing I remember was her and my sister crying and an ambulance in the driveway. Apparently, he died of a sudden heart attack. Honestly, I have very few memories of my father and I have found as time passes, even those have started to fade. It's a shame that the most vivid one is the most tragic one.

My mother remarried a few years later, but that marriage didn't last, and they divorced shortly after my sister graduated high school. I probably should have been upset about it, but Bruce was never much of a stepfather. He wasn't a bad guy per say, but he always made me feel like the relative that came to stay for the holidays and didn't know when to leave. After my sister went off to college at the University of Arkansas, it was just me and my mom.

After showering, I grabbed a pair of briefs from my bureau and slipped them on before flopping down on the bed. Grabbing the Post-It note from my nightstand, I stared at the number, debating on whether I should call. My curiosity getting the best of me, I grabbed my cordless phone and punched in the number.

The phone rang once…twice…three times. "Hello." I heard a deep voice on the other end.

"Umm…Gabe?" I asked with uncertainty in my voice.

"Yeah," came the voice.

"It's Hawk," I said with more confidence.

"Oh Hawk! Dude! I'm glad you called." He genuinely sounded thrilled I called him back.

"Yeah. Sure. What's up man?" I asked.

"I can't believe that was you last night. That was crazy!"

"Yeah, definitely!" His enthusiasm was catching.

"What you been up to today?"

"Oh…I helped my girlfriend paint her bedroom."

"Oh…cool," he replied. A moment of awkward silence passed and I tried to think of something original to say, but nothing came to mind.

"What about you?" I asked.

"Oh…me and some of the guys played football in the park."

I chuckled. "I should have guessed that one. That's all you wanted to do when we were kids."

He laughed. "Some things never change."

"Kinda the way I am about basketball."

"Something we have in common then," he said. Another moment of silence passed, "Man, I didn't even recognize you last night. You've changed so much…I mean…do you lift?"

"Yeah, I started lifting about a year ago. My boss at the hardware store I used to work at sold me his son's weight equipment that he'd left in the garage when he moved to Texas, and I turned our spare bedroom into a weight room."

"Dude. I'm jealous. I've always wanted a home gym, but Mom says we don't have the room for it, so I have to settle for the equipment at school."

"Man! When I ran into your mom in the stands and she pointed at you down on the field, it blew my mind. You were a little skinny kid the last time I saw you. What happened?" I laughed returning his question.

He chuckled. "Puberty."

"Ain't that the truth." Another moment of silence passed.

"Hey. What are you doing tomorrow?"

"Umm…hang out with Shelby I guess."

"Do you still like to fish?"

"Yeah," I answered, thinking about the last time I went fishing with Bruce at the Dam and caught absolutely nothing. One of my mother's many failed attempts to force us into some kind of stepfather/stepson bonding.

"You want to go tomorrow?" he asked, taking me aback by his invitation. "I got a boat."

"Umm," I stammered, taken aback by his invitation, "I

mean...I suppose Shelby would be okay with it," I said, even though the reasons she'd be against it did seem rather ridiculous. Gabe wasn't gay.

"I'm sure your girlfriend can spare one day without you." Gabe's sarcasm certainly hadn't changed over the intervening years.

"Yeah, I suppose." After all, it's not like her and Mel didn't go on shopping trips to Hot Springs every now and again. Oddly enough, I did not have a best friend to hang out with...I mean, the closest person to me other than Shelby was Mel, and she was Shelby's best friend, so I didn't feel like that counted. Thinking back, Gabe was the closest friend I'd ever had, but I was just a kid then and we hadn't seen each other in five years.

"Cool! If you want to meet me at my house at, say... ten...we'll head to the lake."

"Okay, I'll have to check if I can borrow my mom's car," I grumbled. Not having my own vehicle like other guys my age absolutely sucked. Anytime Shelby and I wanted to go somewhere, we had to either borrow my mom's car or her mom's car.

"Dude, you're seventeen years old and don't have your own set of wheels?" He snickered.

I felt slightly irritated, forgetting how Gabe liked to tease. When we first met as ten-year-olds, he'd hurt my feelings constantly. One day I decided to give him a taste of his own medicine. After I hurt his feelings a time or two, he backed off. From that point on, I learned to deal with Gabe by throwing his insults right back at him. "Let me guess,

Daddy bought little Richie Rich a Corvette for his sixteenth birthday."

"Ouch. And it wasn't a Corvette. It was a Jeep."

"Douchebag." I laughed.

"God, I forgot how fun this used to be," he sighed. "Anyway, I'll see ya in the morning around ten."

"Maybe or maybe not…" I teased.

"Don't be late," he commanded.

"Still like ordering people around, I see."

"You know you missed your old buddy, Gabe." I could picture that trademark smirk on his face on the other end of the line.

"Not hardly." I laughed.

"Uh huh."

I hung up the phone and laid back on my bed, folding my arms behind my head. What am I doing hanging out with Gabe again? Yeah, we used to have fun as kids, and he helped pass away countless hours at my grandfather's house when I'd otherwise be watching TV all day. He was always getting us into trouble. Like the time he dared me to break a window in Old Man Alquist's storage shed. What possessed me to pick up that rock and hurl it at that glass pane, I'll never understand. Once I threw the first stone, he threw the second and then it became a contest to see who could break the most windows; which ended up being every one of them. His father grounded him for a month and my mom grounded me for a month and a half. I had just gotten a Sega Genesis for my birthday and had to stare at it for weeks, not allowed to play it. Gabe spelled trouble, but, funny enough, those times with him were the best memories of my childhood.

Chapter Three

Sunday morning, I managed to talk Mom into letting me borrow her Prelude. Thankfully, she still had tons of papers to grade and would be stuck at the kitchen table most of the day. I pulled up Gabe's driveway approximately twenty minutes later, where I parked beside a shiny red jeep with a boat and trailer hitched up behind it.

I spotted Gabe in the garage dressed in a pair of red shorts and a sleeveless white Murphystown High Vipers T-shirt. I looked down at my Pleasant High Bulldogs T-shirt and chuckled. Not seeing me drive up, I hopped out of the car and heard ice being shuffled around in a large red cooler.

He looked up, having just iced down a twelve-pack of sodas. "Hey, dude!"

"Hey." I stopped a few feet from him.

"Hope you like Dr. Pepper…it's all we had," he said as he closed the lid.

"I do."

Just then he spotted my T-shirt. "Dude, the Bulldogs suck."

"If that fumble you made the other day was any indication, I'd say the Vipers suck more," I teased, even though I knew Gabe was a damn good football player and basically won the game for them.

We both laughed. Just then I spotted the brand-new

Yamaha four-wheeler sitting next to the big jet ski. "Yours, I suppose?"

He stood up straight and stuck out his chest. "The way I look at it is if my parents are going to have a kid as wonderful as me, I deserve to be spoiled."

"Still full of shit too, I see." I laughed.

"I'm kidding, dude. Those are my dad's toys. So is the boat. I had to beg him to let me borrow it again. Last time I accidentally dented the side of it trying to back the trailer into the lake. I'm terrible at driving in reverse, especially towing a boat." I knew his father owned several car dealerships in Southern Arkansas; obviously his business had been doing well for them to afford the boat, the new automobiles and the man-toys.

"Oh, I see."

"If you could grab the fishing rods and tackle box, I'll grab the cooler. Then I think we'll be ready to hit the water."

Doing as he said, I grabbed two fishing rods leaning against the wall of the garage. I turned just in time to see him lifting the heavy cooler onto his shoulder, noting how his muscles flexed as he lifted it. *Damn, he's fit. I wonder what he looks like under that shirt,* I quickly shoved that thought out of my head.

Getting into his jeep, I glanced to my left. "I've never seen your hair long before," I said.

He shook his shaggy mop of tight ringlets before flipping them back over his head, "Yeah, my hair has always been a lot of maintenance. As a kid, my mother thought it easier to just to keep it buzzed."

"It looks good on you. I wish mine were curlier," I said,

shaking my straight hair forward and running my fingers through it.

"Don't be, it takes me two solid hours to get it like this."

"Seriously?"

"Yep, they're called finger coils and it's a tedious process to do them."

"There's a couple of black guys on my basketball team that have those," I said.

He chuckled. "Yeah, funny story, when I started growing my hair out, I had no idea how to take care of it and it looked like shit. My buddy, Charlie, who's black, took pity on me and showed me some ways to care for my type of hair. You know I'm a quarter black?"

"Really?"

"Yeah, my mama's father was from the Dominican Republic and his parents were from the Sudan in Africa. My dad, of course, is from Mexico. My dark skin"—he held up the back of his hand and showed it to me, his light-colored fingernails contrasting the deep rich brown skin around his fingers—"and, of course, my hair are my African roots. My abuela...grandmother...says I looked just like my grandfather when he was my age."

"I never knew that." Gabe's maternal grandmother lived right behind them, but his grandfather died before I met Gabe.

"My brother and sister are lighter skinned like my papa's side of the family. Just by looking at me, most people wouldn't know I'm Latino. Believe me, more than one teacher has been surprised when they see my name is Gabriel Sanchez."

"I can see that," I said. The first time I met Gabe, I assumed he was a black kid and of course had black parents, until I met them and learned that he was Hispanic. I did wonder why he was darker-skinned than the rest of his family.

"I'm Afro-Latino," he said proudly.

On the ride to the lake we spent a little time reminiscing about old times. For some reason, though, Gabe kept steering the conversation back to mine and Shelby's relationship, asking questions about how long we had been together, our plans for the future, etcetera. I did manage to squeeze in the question if he had a girlfriend, to which he responded with a quick "no," but did not offer any more information. I wanted to do more digging into his past relationships but ran out of time, deciding to save it for the boat.

As we pulled into the boat ramp area, my eyes widened at the number of people.

"Oh, great!" Gabe sighed. "Just what I need."

"It won't seem as crowded once we get on the water."

He groaned in frustration. "It's not the people, it's the vehicles. I told you I'm terrible at backing this boat into the water and I need a lot of room to do it. I can't back in this thing with a dozen other trailers right beside me."

I surveyed all the vehicles, boats, and trailers turning the entire area into one big traffic jam. My eyes zeroed in on the one open spot in the middle of the ramp. While it would be difficult to maneuver the trailer into the water, I felt confident in my own driving abilities. "You want me to do it?"

He turned his head to me. "Have you ever done it?"

"Umm, no, but I can get into the toughest parallel parking spots, so I'm sure I can handle this," I said with confidence, even though I had never backed up anything on wheels hitched to a vehicle.

"Just be careful. My father would kill me if I dented his boat again," he said as we got out of the vehicle and exchanged places.

Once secure behind the steering wheel, I maneuvered the jeep forward into the open spot between a guy backing in a party barge and another with an old aluminum fishing boat. Lining up my vehicle to fit in the tight spot, I shifted the jeep into reverse, careful to keep the steering wheel straight. I noticed that just a slight twist of the steering wheel resulted in a sharp turn of the trailer. The last thing I needed to do is ram the trailer into the side of another person's vehicle or, worse yet, the tongue of the trailer into the side of Gabe's jeep. I instructed Gabe to get out of the vehicle and let me know when I had the trailer sufficiently submerged in the water so that we could release the boat.

After some intense focus, I manage to back the trailer down the ramp perfectly. I watched in the rearview mirror for Gabe to give me the signal to stop. In a few moments he held his hands up, so I hit the brake and threw the jeep into park. Getting out of the Jeep, I helped Gabe unhook the boat.

"Dude, that was perfect!" he said as I started releasing the straps that held the boat in place.

"Not bad for my first time, I suppose." I laughed.

"I know who will be doing this from now on." He returned the laugh.

Hmmm…obviously, he assumes that we'll be doing this again, I thought to myself as I released the final strap holding the boat on the trailer. Gabe hopped in the boat and steered it to the dock while I parked the jeep and empty trailer. I then walked down the dock and hopped in the boat with Gabe.

Taking control of the wheel, he sped the boat to an area of the lake he claimed was the best fishing spot. For mid-September, it was a typical early autumn day in Arkansas—sunny with highs reaching the mid-80s. I stuck my finger into the water. It immediately sent a chill through my body.

"Woah!" I exclaimed. "The water is freezing!"

"Yeah, we're in a very deep spot close to the mouth of the dam, the hydroelectric pumps are stirring things up and the cold water at the bottom is rising to the top."

"I wouldn't want to swim in this water," I said. Deep water gave me the creeps ever since I'd seen the movie *The Abyss.*

"Oh, I don't know. Would probably feel pretty good," he said as he stood up and pulled his shirt off. "Maybe we can swim later in a shallower part."

My eyes went immediately to his ripped, deep brown torso. No more ribs showing through his taut skin, instead there was a pair of nice sized pecs resting just above a very defined six-pack of abs. His smooth chest narrowed down to a V-shaped waist, and I could see the prominent oblique muscles rising above the waistline of his shorts. His triceps and biceps were huge. The rays of sun on his chest made his flawless dark skin sparkle, absolutely mesmerizing me. Little Gabe had grown into one *very* hot Afro-Latino guy. Despite my best efforts to control my own body's reaction, my heartrate increased.

He cut his eyes to me and immediately I shifted mine to the water.

"I saw you checking me out." He grinned. "Now, off with yours."

I lifted my eyebrows. "Huh?"

"The shirt. It's my turn to check *you* out," he said, very causally.

I shook my head not comprehending his words. "Excuse me?"

"Oh, come on. Don't tease me I know you got a hot bod too, so let's see it."

"*What?*" My jaw dropped.

"Come on, dude. I've been fantasizing about what's under there for three days now."

"*Dude!* What the—" I started.

Gabe interrupted me, "Come on Hawk. I can't believe you didn't figure it out when we were kids...I'm gay." He said it as if it were plainly obvious.

"*What?*" He was openly admitting that he was gay. If the dam had broken at that moment and sucked us down the river in a torrent of death-churning rapids, I wouldn't have been more shocked. I sat in stunned silence.

He frowned. "Too forward, wasn't I?"

"I...I...I..." I stuttered.

"Yep," he nodded, "sorry, I thought telling you while

we're stuck out here on the lake, it would keep you from running away in case I was wrong about you."

I crossed my arms over my chest protectively, feeling the need to somehow stop him from undressing me with his eyes.

"Oh, come on, dude, don't be like that. I'm not going to jump you out here in the middle of the lake…unless you want me to?" He winked.

I stood up and yelled, "What the fuck, Gabe? I'm not gay!"

"You're not?" He gave me a suspicious glare. "You could have fooled me by the way you were checking me out."

"I…I…I…" I stammered again. I hadn't expected to get caught. "I…I…wanted to see how much you changed from when we were kids."

He lifted his arms and flexed his biceps like some sort of Hercules. "Impressed?" He turned his head and examined each of his muscles.

"Your unbelievable!" I screamed. "Take me back to the dock. *Now!*"

His cockiness began to fade as my reaction began to convince him he was wrong. He calmly sat down. "You're really not gay?"

"No! I'm not! I've got a girlfriend. You're fucking nuts!"

"Oh man," he shook his head, "wow. I totally got that wrong."

"Take me back to the dock…now!"

"I'm sorry, dude, I shouldn't have come on to you like that. I assumed you were hiding it too… I was so sure the way you looked at me the other night. I convinced myself you were and I went a little crazy. You know how I get. Remember the flowerpot incident?"

I recalled the time when Gabe got the bright idea for us to steal clay flowerpots out of his grandmother's garden shed, climb to the top of her roof and roll them off only to watch them burst into a million pieces on her concrete driveway. That one cost me three weeks without my bicycle. "Yeah, I remember, but that doesn't give you an excuse to lay something this…huge…on me…like that."

He gave me his best sad eyes. "I know. Honestly, I haven't been able to stop thinking about you ever since I saw you the other night. I mean…I've always had a crush on you."

I shook my head in disbelief. "You what?"

"Had a crush on you. Why do you think I was always trying to talk you into playing Truth or Dare? I liked kissing you and I had the feeling you liked kissing me too."

"Jesus, Gabe. We were kids! Kids experiment. I'm not gay…I like girls. I have a girlfriend I've been with…like forever. Hell, I plan on marrying her one day!"

"And she's like your real girlfriend and not a girl you're pretending to be with just for show?"

"No, Gabe! She's my real girlfriend and for the last time *I'm not gay!*"

He hung his head, "God, I'm so stupid. I thought I had found someone that *finally* understood. Do you know how hard it is pretending to be interested in girls, when I have no attraction to them whatsoever. Hell, I'm still a virgin. Not that I haven't had plenty of opportunities to have sex, but the thought of having sex with a girl…well, it makes me sick to my stomach."

This "defeated" side of Gabe was something I'd never seen before and I couldn't help but feel sorry for him. "Dude. I know it must be tough and I'm sorry. Does anyone else know?"

He looked up at me. "No. You're the only person I've told. I always trusted you when we were kids and—" He shrugged his shoulder.

"I appreciate you feeling you can trust me, and I'll keep your secret, but I'm not interested in you in *that* way." I really did feel for him.

"I know it was stupid of me to come on to you like that, but seeing you after all these years…I worked up all these fantasies in my head. Can we please just forget all this and be friends?"

I turned my head. "I don't know, Gabe. It's going to be awkward now." Truth be told, knowing Gabe was gay brought out my own insecurities about the fact that I had same-sex attraction. I'd never been around another gay teenager, especially one that I was attracted to…and one that was attracted to me. Being friends with Gabe again would be like trying to be buddies with a hot girl. Not that I would *ever* cheat on Shelby, but I know she would *never* approve and the temptation would always be there.

"I promise you I won't make a move on you," he pleaded.

"I don't know Gabe." I honestly didn't know how it would work, but I certainly didn't want him to think that being gay was a bad thing. It's not like I couldn't relate to some of his feelings. I hated my feelings of attraction toward guys. It made me feel ashamed of myself as well as guilty for not sharing that information with Shelby. Gabe, at one time he'd been my best friend and I guess I owed him a chance. "Let's just see how the rest of the day goes. Okay?"

He nodded. "Okay. I'll be on my best behavior. Scout's honor."

I nodded. "We came to fish, so let's fish."

Gabe reached into the cooler and grabbed a cellophane-wrapped package of some kind of meat. I cringed at the site of the bloody pieces. "Chicken livers," he said as he started tearing open the package. "Always the best bait. Good eating too, if they're cooked right."

"Dude, chicken livers are nasty." I scrunched my face as I thought about the last time, I sampled some Mom had fried up for supper. The sharp flavor of the meat was certainly an acquired taste.

I watched Gabe fold the bait onto his hook. Handing me the container, I did the same. Pressing the button of the reel with my thumb, I cast my line into the water and watched as the bobber floated to the surface. I looked around at the beautiful oaks and pine trees that lined the banks of the quiet lake. The leaves of the sweet gums and maples glowed in a myriad of colors. I tried to maintain my focus on the water and the bank, rather than on Gabe.

After an hour of fishing and hardly speaking, Gabe moved the boat further up the lake to another fishing spot he said he had good luck in. Unfortunately, this spot was not shaded and the temperature by lunch easily reached into the nineties. I was absolutely frying under the hot sun but felt reluctant to take my shirt off. Finally, I couldn't stand it any longer and pulled it over my head. Immediately, I shot my eyes to Gabe to make sure he wasn't checking me out. With a sense of relief, his eyes were glued to his cork, which he playfully bobbed up and down by raising and lowering his fishing pole.

"I've got some ham sandwiches in the cooler if you're hungry," he offered. "I know I am."

"Yeah, I am getting hungry. Do you think we could move the boat to the shore to eat? I'm about to bake in this sun." I said, wishing I had thought to bring a cap and sunglasses like Gabe.

"Sure," he said as he got behind the wheel and moved us toward the bank.

Gabe hopped out of the boat into the knee-deep water and tied the rope to a large rock on the shore to tether the boat. I grabbed the cooler, hoisted it on my shoulder and stepped ashore. Finding suitable shade, I gently lowered it down under a large oak tree. I then sat down beside it and glanced around, noticing there wasn't a sign of civilization.

After rinsing his hands in the water, Gabe came over and sat down on the other side of the cooler. He opened the lid, reached in, grabbed a sandwich sealed in a plastic storage bag, and offered it to me. I took it, and he retrieved one for himself. I couldn't help but compare myself to him, I noticed that he and I very much had the same physique, and while I had a nice tan, I couldn't hold a candle to Gabe. His skin was dark perfection and with those long black curls...I struggled not to stare.

"Your granddad was quite the character, wasn't he?" he

remarked, taking his sandwich from the bag, shaking me from my trance.

"Yeah, he was." I did the same.

"Remember that time he took us to swim up here on the lake and the brakes of that old '63 Dodge Dart gave out right before we got back to his house?" He chuckled. "Did your granddad panic? Nope, he just calmly killed the engine, threw it in neutral and did circles in his lawn until the car came to a stop."

I laughed. "Thank God granddad never drove above thirty-five miles per hour, or we'd been in *real* trouble."

"I know, right. I tell you, there wasn't much that could rattle that old man."

"Yeah." I smiled. "I really miss him."

"How come we stopped being friends after he died?" he asked before taking a bite of his sandwich.

I shrugged my shoulder. "I wouldn't say we stopped being friends, it was just harder for us to hang out. I mean...it's not like you weren't welcome to come to my house. I know we lived in different towns, but still."

He swallowed. "I know. I just assumed it was because of what happened between us in the bus." He turned his head to me.

Immediately, I felt a cold chill run over my body as my mind flashed back to those encounters in his grandparents' camper. "That had nothing to do with it," I lied.

He pursed his full lips and frowned slightly. "Somehow I don't believe that."

"Maybe it did...I mean...it was wrong. I know we were just kids, but it was wrong."

Gabe locked his eyes with mine. "It didn't feel wrong to me."

I let out a long sigh, "Listen, Gabe, I'm trying to be your friend but you're not making this easy."

"I'm sorry, Hawk. It's just…those memories of all the fun we used to have together…they were some of the best ones of my childhood."

"Mine too, but that was the past. We're not kids anymore."

"Obviously." He eyed me like a piece of meat. "I never dreamed you'd grow up to be this hot."

"Gabe!" I shouted and stood up. "See…that right there is why we can't be friends."

His face became panic-stricken. "I'm sorry, Hawk. It was a joke. Fuck…damn…I did it again."

"I can't do this. I'm sorry, Gabe. This isn't going to work. You're a good guy, we had some good times together, but I can't tolerate you coming on to me. It makes me very uncomfortable. Believe me, it has nothing to do with the fact you're gay. I'm happy for you, but I love Shelby."

He jumped up. "I promise. I'll never make jokes like that again."

"I want to believe you, but I can't. Take me back to the boat dock. I mean it this time," I said, as I walked back to the boat to retrieve my shirt.

Gabe stood speechless.

As soon as we arrived back at Gabe's house, I immediately got in my car and left. After the third time Gabe apologized,

I told him not to speak to me again. Maybe I was overreacting, but the whole situation just made me not want to be around him. He knew I had a girlfriend, but that didn't stop him from coming on to me. Part of me felt guilty for checking him out. Idle curiosity, that was it. It didn't mean that I was interested in making out with him, like he obviously wanted. At least, I assumed that's what he wanted.

I needed Shelby and decided to stop by her house before going home.

Knocking on the door, Mrs. Johnson opened it.

"Oh, hi, Hawk," she said. "I thought you were going fishing with a friend today?"

"I was, but we weren't catching anything, so we called it a day," I lied.

"Oh, I see." she nodded.

"Is Shelby around?" I asked.

"Yeah. Her and Mel are in her room…supposedly organizing the closet, but there's probably more talking being done than work." She chuckled.

"Probably." I smiled as she ushered me in.

I headed down the hall and heard Mel's laughter. Standing in the doorway of Shelby's room, I spotted Mel trying on one of Shelby's old straw hats from when she was in our eighth-grade production of *Huck Finn*. None of the boys could act, so Mrs. Gruber gave the part to Shelby.

"Oh my God, I can't believe I wore that in front of people," Shelby said, before Mel saw me.

"Hey, hot stuff," Mel said. I rolled my eyes, that's not what I needed to hear at the moment.

Shelby turned her head to me. "Hey, babe. What are you doing back so soon?"

"Fish weren't biting." I tried the lie on her, planning to tell her the truth later when it was just the two of us, but she saw right through me. Of course, the rattled expression on my face probably gave me away.

"What happened?" Shelby asked. My eyes went to Mel, indicating that I needed to talk to Shelby alone.

"Oh…well…gotcha," Mel said, "I'll be in the living room."

As she started to leave the room, I stopped her. "Oh, fuck it, Shelby's going to tell you everything anyway."

"Really. I'll leave if you want me to," she said in a sincere voice.

"Na. Just stay," I said and turned to close the door. Mel took a seat on the bed.

I walked over and sat down on the edge of the bed between them. Packed like sardines, a moment of silence passed as I didn't know exactly how to begin. I flopped back on the bed and groaned loudly in frustration. "Babe, what happened?" Shelby leaned back on her side and rubbed my forehead. I locked my eyes with hers.

"You were right about Gabe."

Mel put her hands over her mouth and gasped. "He's gay?"

I looked at her and slowly nodded, "Oh yeah. And guess who he has the hots for."

"Oh my God. No way!" Mel giggled.

I lowered my eyes at her. "It's not funny."

Shelby pushed my hair out of my eyes and over my

head. "I'm sorry, Babe. Do you want to talk about it?" she asked in a sympathetic voice.

I thought about the little Truth or Dare game I played with him back when we were kids. I had never told anyone about it, not even Shelby. I let out a long sigh. "I've never told you, but when Gabe and I were kids, we used to play Truth or Dare. On more than one occasion he dared me to kiss him and because I did it a couple times…he thought I was gay too."

"Seriously?" Mel interjected, "I've kissed Shelby before on a dare. It's not a big deal."

"It's a big deal when the other person admits they've always had a crush on you." I propped myself up on my elbows.

"So, what exactly did he do on the lake?" Shelby asked as she stroked my hair over my head.

I shrugged my shoulder. "Kept checking me out…coming on to me…told me I was hot."

"He isn't wrong," said Mel.

"Please don't make this day any weirder for me," I begged her.

"I'm sorry. I don't know when to shut up."

"What did you do?" Shelby asked.

"I tried to be supportive of him being gay, but he came on to me strong…like *really* strong. I finally told him we couldn't be friends."

Shelby frowned. "I'm sorry, babe."

"I liked Gabe. He was my friend for a lot of years. It makes me sad." I stared into her eyes.

"Not interested means not interested. Apparently even *gay* guys don't get it." Mel crossed her arms in front of her.

"That's right!" I nodded at her succinctly. "Do you know what it feels like to be stared at like a piece of meat?" Both her and Shelby howled with laughter. "Okay. That was a really stupid thing to say."

I couldn't help myself and started laughing with them.

"Come here, my juicy piece of steak." Shelby leaned down and kissed me.

Chapter Four

October 1992

Weeks flew by and September had turned into October. With Halloween came the Pleasant High School tradition of the annual Halloween Carnival held on the Pleasant School Campus after dark. The Senior class was always put in charge of running the hayride, which usually sold the most tickets out of all the games and booths. All money collected would be used to fund our senior class trip at the end of the year. All the guys wanted to be one of the actors whose purpose was to frighten the riders. Scarers, as we called them, were the guys that dressed up in a costume, hid out of sight along the path of the hayride, and jumped out, frightening the passengers. Of course, it was strictly forbidden to throw water balloons at the passengers, but no one ever obeyed the rule. Unfortunately, there could be only a limited number of scarers, and to make it fair we drew tickets for our job assignments. Much to my disappointment, I drew the job of a ticket seller, meaning I was stuck behind a table all evening collecting money and handing out tickets. The only classmates that had it worse than me were the ushers, whose job was helping passengers on and off the back of the flatbed trailer. At least I wasn't stuck holding the sticky hands of candy-stuffed children all night. Shelby drew an usher position but was able to talk her friend Megan into trading her ticket-collecting job so that we could work the table together.

Getting into the spirit of the holiday, Shelby came up with the idea that she and I would dress as Zach and Kelly from *Saved by the Bell*, only with a twist. Shelby would dress as preppy boy Zach and I as his cheerleader girlfriend Kelly. At first, I balked, but as usual through a little feminine persuasion I gave into her. Shelby wore a blue polo shirt, khakis, and a pair of penny loafers and tucked her blonde hair under her baseball cap, while I dressed in a cheerleader outfit complete with a low-cut blouse, a skirt, and panty hose. A temporary black hair dye job, make-up, and Shelby's pom-poms completed my costume.

We'd been sitting behind the ticket table for an hour, and needless to say, I wasn't in the best of moods. "This job sucks," I said to Shelby.

"Oh, it's not so bad," she said after just handing a ticket to a mother and her daughter, who was dressed as Ariel from *The Little Mermaid*, "Some of these costumes are just precious."

I looked down at my padded bra, "I feel ridiculous in this costume. I can't believe I let you talk me into this."

"You look so good." She laughed. "Mel did a great job with your make-up."

I gave her a sarcastic grin, "Remind me to never thank her."

I leaned back in my cold metal chair, folded my arms in front of me, and sulked. The table was placed in the lit area away from the location of the ride itself, so I didn't even get to see the ride for which I was selling tickets for. "Not only do I feel ridiculous, but I am bored out of my mind. We should be out there having fun scaring people. Not stuck behind this stupid table all night."

"You just want to throw water balloons." She grinned at me.

I shrugged my shoulder. "Like I say, having fun."

She leaned over and hugged my arm, "Oh, come on, it's a gorgeous evening…the stars are out…and just look at that harvest moon." She pointed to the sky.

Always like Shelby to find the positive side of any situation. I lowered my eyebrows at her. "Please don't say you think this is romantic."

"I wasn't going to say that…grumpy."

I soften. "I'm sorry. I just want you and I to at least get one hayride together. Look," I reached under the table, "I even brought a blanket for us to cuddle under."

"Aww…you're so sweet. Don't worry, I think I can persuade your mom to take over for us for a little while," she said.

Not only was my mother my English teacher, but she was also our class sponsor. Her job was to assist our class in raising funds to pay for our senior prom and graduation class trip. My mom absolutely loved Shelby, and I knew she wouldn't have to do much arm twisting to get her to agree to watch the table for a us to have one ride.

Just then I looked up and spotted a familiar face heading my way. I groaned loudly. "Oh great! Just when I thought this evening couldn't get any worse."

"What?" asked Shelby before she spotted Gabe heading my way.

"Is that—" she asked.

"Yes, it is," I interrupted her. "What the hell is he doing here?" Just then I remembered my costume and began to panic. "Oh, fuck, I can't let him see me dressed like this."

I bent down under the table and started rummaging through a paper bag full of tickets, pens, and other desk supplies, hoping he'd quickly get his ticket and leave. "One ticket, please," Gabe requested in that deep voice of his.

"That'll be five dollars," Shelby said as I continued to rustling the paper bag, thoroughly scrambling the supplies.

"Wait, your Hawk's girlfriend. Right?" he asked.

"Yes, I'm Shelby.

"Oh. Nice to see you again," he replied. *Liar, you tried to steal her boyfriend.*

"Is Hawk…?" he started.

Please, go away, please go away.

"Hawk, Is that you?"

"I can't seem to find it," I said in the worst high-pitched feminine voice imaginable. So much for my acting skills.

"Hawk?" he said again as my eyes met his staring back at me from under the table. "What are you doing under there?"

I lifted my head, accidentally bumping it on the underside of the table causing Shelby's empty soda can, to roll off the table.

"I can't find it," I said to Shelby in my normal voice, then turned my head to Gabe. "Oh. Hi,"

Gabe began laughing, "Well, well, this is something I *certainly* wasn't expecting," My face turned fifty shades of red. He pointed his finger at me and then Shelby. "Kelly and Zack?"

"Very good." Shelby smiled.

"What are you doing here, Gabe? Doesn't Murphystown have its own Halloween Carnival?" I asked in a very snarky voice.

"We do, but your mayor and his wife invited our family to dinner, and I got bored after we ate, so I decided to come check out your little carnival," he said.

"Lucky us," I mumbled. Shelby kicked me under the table.

"Huh?" he asked.

"Nothing…it's five bucks for the hayride." I held out my hand for the money.

"Oh…okay." He reached into his back pocket and pulled out his wallet.

Laying the bill in my hand, Shelby tore off a ticket and handed it to him. Just then, my mother walked up behind us and put her hand on my shoulder. "Hi, honey, I've got an emergency I need your help with. Chris Owen's mother called the school looking for him. Apparently, his grandmother has fallen, and they've taken her to the emergency room. Chris is out along the hayride route somewhere dressed as Jason from *Friday the 13th* and I need you to find him and tell him he needs to go home and stay with his little sister."

"No problem. Where're your car keys?" *Anything to get out of sitting behind this table for another hour.*

"They're in my purse in my classroom. It would be

easier just to take the hayride. Tell Mr. Evans what's going on and have him stop when you see Chris."

I turned my head to Gabe and my stomach sank.

I turned back to my mother, "I think it would be quicker if I take your car...I mean that hayride goes what? About twenty miles per hour...this is an emergency you know."

"You won't be able to drive any faster in my car on those gravel roads," she said.

"Oh, you'd be surprised how well those little cars handle on rough terrain. I mean those Preludes were built—"

"Hawk," she interrupted me, "take the hayride."

"But, Mom—" I whined.

"Hawkins...please do as I say." Calling me Hawkins, I knew she meant business, which meant I had one last card to play.

"Can Shelby come with me?" I asked.

"No. I need her to watch the table. Mrs. Trumbole needs my help with the seventh-grade cake walk."

"Yes, ma'am," I said as she walked away. With my shoulders slumped, I glanced at Gabe, who stood grinning from ear to ear. I lowered my voice to Shelby. "I'm sorry about the romantic hayride,"

"I know." She laid her hand on mine and squeezed.

I glanced at Gabe then leaned over and gave Shelby a long, deep kiss for his benefit. "I'll see you afterwhile. Love you."

"Love you too," she said, as I got up to head down the hill to board the hayride.

As I started my march, Gabe came up alongside me. "Care if I walk with you?"

I kept my head down, focused on the task at hand. "Yes," I snapped.

"Look, Hawk. I'm sorry. I really am. I should have never—"

"Just stop, Gabe," I cut him off. "We've had this discussion."

Stopping at parking area for the hayride, I heard Mr. Evans' farm tractor coming from up the road pulling a trailer full of passengers. I sighed with relief that I didn't have to wait long for his return...with Gabe by my side. As soon as he came to a stop, I ran up to him and told him the situation. By the time I was finished, the previous group of passengers had unloaded, and the new group had boarded. I climbed onto the trailer and searched for a bale of hay on which to sit. The trailer was absolutely packed with people. Spotting one available seat, my shoulders slumped at the person to the right of it. Raising my chin defiantly, I marched over and sat down next to Gabe, making sure to cross my legs so that I wouldn't accidently flash everyone with my underwear.

The tractor engine roared to life and the trailer jerked forward as the hayride began. I kept my eyes forward and my mouth shut, ignoring Gabe, as the tractor sped up on the paved part of the road. About ten minutes into the ride, Mr. Evans veered the tractor onto the gravel road that led off into the woods, and I began feeling the effects of the cold wind blowing against my heavily exposed skin. In all the excitement, I didn't think to grab the blanket from under the table. A cheerleader's uniform wasn't exactly designed for cold weather.

I bent forward and wrapped my arms around myself. Glancing around, I caught mean old Mrs. Latch giving me the evil eye. I gave her a sarcastic grin to which she just shook her head. *Closed-minded bigot.* I felt sure my costume would be the subject of the next Women's Bible Study group—The sexual corruption of today's youth.

"You cold?" Gabe asked.

"What do you think?" I refused to look at him.

"You want my coat?"

"I'm fine," I snapped, trying to keep my voice low as not to bring any more attention to myself.

"No, you're not. You're freezing." He started removing his coat. "Here, I don't need it, I got a sweater and T-shirt on."

I turned my head and bored my eyes into him. "I don't need your coat…*Gabe!*"

"Suit yourself," He pulled the coat back on.

A few minutes later, I reached down and began rubbing my legs, attempting to warm them. I felt a peck on my shoulder and turned my head to see Gabe holding out his coat to me.

"I said I don't—" I started.

He cut me off. "Would you quit being a dick and take the damn coat?"

"Fine!" I reached out, grabbed it and put it on. I shimmied in the warmth of the thick wool coat.

Several moments of silence passed before he spoke

again. "Jesus. How long is this ride?" he asked as the trees around us thickened.

"About forty minutes," I answered.

"Think you guys made it long enough?" he asked rhetorically. I refused to give him the satisfaction of conversation.

Just then, we hit a bump and I jolted to the side, my shoulder colliding with his hard chest. I immediately jerked back. "Sorry."

"It's okay," he replied. "So...um...was this costume your idea?"

I huffed. "No."

"Didn't think so," He paused, "You must see the irony of this situation."

I couldn't help but smile a little on the inside, "Is this how I'm dressed in one of your little fantasies?"

He turned his head the opposite direction, but I couldn't help but notice his smile. "No comment."

As much as I tried to keep up the cold shoulder act, I felt it beginning to thaw. "Thanks for the coat," I said.

"You're welcome...so, does this mean you're talking to me now?" He turned his head back to me.

"For the moment," I answered.

A few more moments passed. "You remember that Halloween we dressed up as Doc and Marty?" He asked, referring to the characters from *Back to the Future*.

I chuckled. "My wig kept falling off." I remember we argued back and forth as to who would be Doc and who would be Marty. Of course, we both wanted to be Marty, but, as usual, I let Gabe talk me into being Doc. We hit so many houses that night we had candy until Valentine's Day.

"You remember when Obi grabbed it and ran off with it and we had to chase him for two blocks?"

"Yes! And by the time we got it back he'd chewed it all up."

"It looked like you had a dead racoon on your head." Gabe laughed.

"It didn't help when you banged it against that tree trying to fluff it back out. How is Obi?" I asked.

"We had to put him to sleep a couple of years ago. He was old and got where he couldn't walk. I cried for weeks." His eyes revealed his sadness.

I felt for him. "I'm sorry. Obi was a good dog."

"The best. My parents offered to get me another one, but no dog could ever take the place of Obi."

Just then a water balloon came flying through the air, landing directly in Gabe's lap. People jumped from their seats as several other water-filled missiles made contact with other passengers, with fallout splashes hitting my bare legs.

Gabe hopped up from his seat, "Fuck!" He yelled. Mrs. Latch's jaw dropped at the use of profanity, while a couple of kids gasped. It's then I noticed that Gabe's jeans and the lower half of his shirt were completely soaked.

A little girl wearing a princess costume cried at her water-soaked pink dress. "Umm…maybe the water balloons were a bad idea," I lamented.

"You think?" he fumed.

"Here." I dug my hand into my bra and began pulling out wads of rolled-up toilet paper, handing them to him.

Seeing me unstuff my bra, the corners of Gabe's flipped in a grin. "Thanks," he said as he tried to soak up some of the water from his jeans.

Just then I caught sight of a guy in a hockey mask running toward the trailer with a plastic machete in one hand and a water balloon in the other, "Hey, that's Chris!" I pointed.

I stood up and yelled for Mr. Evans to stop the tractor and started waving my arms over my head indicating for all the monsters heading our way to stop. "Chris!" I yelled, "Stop!" Immediately, everyone with a water balloon in hand stopped moving. I jumped off the hayride and ran to Chris to explain the emergency. He thanked me and I got back on the trailer. Mr. Evans started moving us once again. Taking my spot next to Gabe, I looked down at his wet pants and pulled my borrowed coat tighter around me. I felt rather bad for him. I looked at my own cold, bare legs before addressing him, "I would offer you my skirt, but I think you would be the only one on this ride that would appreciate seeing me in my underwear."

He howled with laughter.

The rest of the ride back we talked and laughed about old times. By the time we got back to the school, I agreed to give him another chance, but only time would tell if he would stay true to his promise and respect mine and Shelby's relationship.

Monday morning at school I sat in the lunchroom cafeteria

feasting on meatloaf and mashed potatoes. Shelby sat to my left and Mel across from me.

"I wouldn't trust him," Mel said, attempting to coat every leaf of her salad in low-fat dressing.

"He promised he'd respect mine and Shelby's relationship," I said, taking a sip of milk from the small cardboard container. After a long discussion with Shelby the prior day, she agreed to put her dislike for Gabe aside and trust my judgement. The whole situation reminded me of some clichéd teen television drama where the star football player tries to steal his former best friend's girlfriend, only with a twist. An alternative reality where the love that dare not speak its name speaks, or rather shouts, in Gabe's case.

She looked to Shelby. "What do you think?"

Shelby wrinkled her nose as she picked a cherry tomato from her cafeteria salad and placed it on a napkin. "I trust Hawk."

"That doesn't mean Gabe won't try something or try and convince Hawk to do things." She then lowered her voice to a whisper, "I've heard that most guys don't have a problem doing things to themselves in front of other guys, even if they're straight."

"Ha! That is the biggest crock of shit I've ever heard in my life!" I said louder than I intended.

"So, you're saying it doesn't happen?"

"Hell, I don't know. Maybe. *I've* never been in that situation." Even though Jason Gregory joked one time in the locker room that he and Larry Cox used to climb up in the tree behind his house and have jerk-off contests. Both of them are straight as far as I knew.

"Would you have a problem with it?" she asked me pointedly.

I hesitated for a moment, caught off guard by the question. "Of course, I would…That's sick!" Even though, if Jason asked me to scale up an oak tree with him… *No, Hawk! Get your mind out of the gutter!*

"Why did you hesitate? Huh, Hawk?" she teased.

I set my fork down on the table. "You know, Mel, sometimes I wonder why we're friends."

"I was only joking, babe, no need to get all worked up about it."

"From now on, only Shelby is allowed to call me babe." I picked up my fork.

"If Hawk wanted to do it, I wouldn't object," Shelby said.

"*What?*" Mel and I shouted at the same time.

"I know Hawk loves me and I know he'd never do anything to betray our love. It's just taking care of a biological need. I trust him." She reached across the table and placed her hand on mine.

I gave her a loving smile, "I love you."

"I love you too," She squeezed my hand.

Mel sighed, "God, I need a boyfriend."

Later that afternoon, I had just finished an intense basketball practice and stepped out of the locker room shower. I wrapped my towel around me and pitter-pattered over to my locker to retrieve my clothes. Just as I reached inside for my shirt, a voice behind me startled me.

"Hey, man. Can I talk to you a minute?"

I turned around to a very naked Eddie Davis, one of our all-round athletes that no matter what the sport season, he played it: baseball, football, and basketball. Football season was winding down fast with only a few weeks left, but basketball was just winding up. Eddie played a linebacker for the football team and a point guard for the basketball team. At six-four, he towered above my five-eleven frame. My eyes aimed directly for that part of him just below his waist. Though bigger and taller, I still had him beat in one area, like I did with all the guys on the team, which I took enormous pride in. "Sure, what's up?" I asked, my eyes shifting to his massive pecs.

"You're friends with Melanie Minsk, right?" he asked, my eyes discretely memorizing the striations of his abs.

"Um…yeah…Mel," I said.

"Is she single?" He asked, stretching his arm out and placing his hand against the locker.

"Yeah. She is." I noticed how the shape of his triceps were perfectly proportioned to the size of his biceps. *I wonder what it would be like to wrap my hands around that arm. I bet those muscles are hard as rocks.*

"So, do you think maybe she'd be open to going out with me sometime?" He reached down and scratched himself and while I should have been disgusted, I somehow wasn't.

My face suddenly felt flush. "Well…um," I stammered, "I don't know. Probably."

"Cool," he said, "I may hit her up for a date tomorrow. Thanks, man."

"Sure," I replied. He turned and walked away; I couldn't help but stare at the roundest set of globes in the locker room. My imagination ran wild. *I like a nice ass.* I felt myself getting excited and quickly reached for my underwear.

An hour later, I was forced to ride the bus home from school. With Mom having to stay after school to tutor some of her students, I had no other way home. Living in the country sometimes sucked. Forty-five minutes of snotty-nose kids, dusty dirty roads, and the smell of exhaust fumes, had put me in a shitty mood. As I strolled down the long drive-way to our house I spotted my older sister Jennifer's Chevette in the driveway along with a late-model blue Audi. Immediately, I picked up my pace. Jennifer being home outside of the normal college breaks was highly unusual. Hitting the front door, I hurried inside.

Not seeing her anywhere in sight, I hollered, "Jenn!"

Just then, she came running out of the kitchen, "Little brother!" she yelled, her arms wide open. I opened mine and we hugged each other in a warm embrace. "I've missed you!"

"I missed you too," I said, my arms wrapped around her.

When we broke apart, she looked me up and down. "You've grown since August."

I looked down at myself and then at her with skepticism. "It's only been two months. I couldn't have grown that much." I chuckled and paused. "What are you doing here?"

She stood back, lifted her left arm and showed me the

back of her hand. On her finger, a sparkling gold ring with a *very* large diamond sparkled under the ceiling fan light.

My eyes widened. "You're engaged?"

She nodded her head giddily. "Yep."

"Holy shit, Jen!" I laughed. "That's…great!"

"I know!" She was almost jumping up and down.

I cocked my head. "So…umm…who is the groom?" When she left for school in August, she was most certainly single, now two months later she was engaged to be married? My sister's pickiness when it came to guys was well-known. In her almost four years in college, she'd only brought home one guy for a weekend. His name was Oscar and all he did was complain, mostly about the government. One morning he cornered me at the breakfast table and forced me into listening to his two-hour rant on Reaganomics and President Bush's failures with the U.S. economy. At one point, I consider spilling hot coffee on myself just to escape; it would have been less painful.

"So, his name is David and he's finishing up his pre-med degree this year."

"Went and bagged yourself a doctor huh?"

She laid her hand on my shoulder and giggled. Looking back over her shoulder, she shouted, "Honey, come here." A few moments later, a very handsome guy with glasses, blue jeans, and a navy sports jacket entered, eating a sandwich. "David. I want you to meet my little brother, Hawk." He certainly looked like a future doctor with his professionally-styled hair and perfect posture.

He stuck out his empty hand. "Nice to finally meet you, Hawk. Your sister talks very highly of you." I shook it.

I grinned at my sister. "Nice to meet you," I said to him.

The room fell awkwardly silent for a moment, and I felt as though the pressure were on me to say something to him. Not exactly a natural for making small-talk, I said the first thing that came to mind. "Is that your Audi in the driveway?"

"Yes. It belongs to me."

"Nice car," I said.

"Thanks. I just bought it last week." I glanced out the living room window at his very expensive new car and contrasted it with the ten-year-old piece of shit sitting beside it.

Jennifer rolled her eyes, "I know what you're thinking, little brother. I know you too well."

"I wasn't thinking anything," I said with a wry smile.

Jennifer reached in her pocket, pulled out her keys and held them out. "Here. It's your piece of shit now."

"*What*?" I screamed. "You're giving it to me?"

She hooked her arm with David's. "David's got a Land Rover as well, so I'll be driving it."

"Seriously?" My eyes widened.

"Yep." She grinned from ear to ear. I immediately grabbed her in an embrace. "You are the best sister *ever*!"

She shrugged her shoulder. "I know it."

Like a toddler who'd just received a new tricycle for Christmas, I sprinted out the door to check out my new beat-up Chevy Chevette.

"Hey!" Jennifer yelled out the door, "David and I want to take you and Mom out to dinner tonight in Hot Springs. I thought you might want to invite Shelby."

"Okay. I'll call her when I get back," I yelled back as I hopped into my car to take it for a spin.

After an expensive dinner at a fancy steak house in Hot Springs, courtesy of David; Shelby and I laid on my bed with her head on my chest and my arm around her.

"David seems like a nice guy." Shelby played with one of the buttons on my shirt.

"Yeah. I like him. He actually seems normal. Not like the last guy she brought home."

"Oh, you mean Oscar the Grouch?"

I laughed. "Yeah."

"It sounds like David's family has money. I mean, they own a villa in Italy." She stuck her finger through the space between the buttons and rubbed my bare chest.

"They go skiing in Aspen every year. Isn't that where all the big celebrities go?"

"Yeah," she confirmed.

"Can you believe he's going to be a plastic surgeon?" I chuckled.

"I bet he's already got a list of rich female friends lining up for boob jobs." She laughed and looked down at herself. "I wonder if he offers free services to friends and family?"

I glanced at Shelby's blouse. "You don't need any work. Those babies are perfect."

She hit me on the chest with a limp wrist. "Oh. Stop it."

A few moments passed and Shelby let out a contented sigh.

"I never knew how good of friends Jenn and your brother were until she asked about him," I said.

"Yeah, did you know they once went out on a date together?"

I looked at her. "You're kidding right. Your brother is gay."

"He wasn't always out." She went on to explain, "J.J. told me the story about when him and Jennifer went to a party together as a couple. He thought it would make Mason jealous. Apparently, he and Mason had some sort of fight and weren't speaking. My brother got drunk and started making a fool out of himself. Somehow, before the night was over, he and Mason ended up making out in the woods and Jennifer caught them."

"Uh-oh."

"Yep, your sister was the first person to know that J.J. and Mason were gay. Actually, Mason is bi." She shrugged her shoulder.

"Mason is bi?" I asked, finding it interesting that Mason and I might have something in common.

"Yep, of course, he hasn't been with a girl since he's been with my brother. Honestly, I think if gay marriages were legal, they'd be married."

"I don't know. It's hard for me to believe that a gay couple could be just as happy as a straight couple. What about kids?" I asked, digging into some of the questions I sometimes pondered.

"Seriously, babe, you never heard of a surrogate mother?"

"Oh. Yeah. I didn't think about that. I know I want us to have a bunch of kids."

Shelby laughed. "Not too many. Three max."

I began tickling her. "Or four...or five...or six..."

She giggled loudly. "Stop. Stop," she yelled in between laughs.

I stopped. "So, when are we getting married?" She flipped over onto her back and I pushed myself up on my arms over here where our faces were mere inches apart.

"I don't know. We need to graduate high school first." She smiled.

"I know. Let's get married next summer," I said half-jokingly.

"Is that a proposal?"

"Do you want it to be?" I couldn't tell if she was joking or was serious, but as her smile faded, I could see she was dead serious. I flopped down on the left side of her and lifted my head on my elbow. "For real?"

She shrugged her shoulder.

"Holy shit!" I gasped, slung myself onto my back, and folded my hands over my forehead. My emotions overwhelmed me, I started crying and laughing at the same time. She was ready to commit to spending the rest of her life with me.

She flipped toward me in a panic. "Babe, are you okay?"

I threw my arms in the air. "Yes! God, yes! I'm so happy I could piss my pants!" I practically yelled.

"Don't do that. It would kind of ruin the moment." She winked.

I grabbed her in an embrace. "I love you so much, Shelby Johnson."

She squeezed me. "I love you so much, Hawk Keystone."

Chapter Five

November 1992

Over the next couple weeks, I felt as if I were walking on air. After Shelby told me she would marry me, I told her I wanted to do a proper proposal, as in presenting her with an engagement ring and made plans to do that on Christmas Day. Sure, we hadn't done much planning for the future, but it didn't matter. After all, my parents married young and were together for fifteen years before my father died. Shelby's parents married when they were both eighteen and they had been together for even longer. If they could make it, I knew we could. By selling my coveted Nintendo, I had just enough money to buy a ring I knew Shelby would love. Thanks to my upcoming nuptials of my sister and her rich fiancé, I finally had a ride, thus a way to go shopping for a ring without anyone knowing.

My rekindled friendship with Gabe, continued to grow. In fact, it was starting to feel like old times. We'd been playing scrimmage football in the Murphystown Park the past couple of Saturdays with a bunch of his friends. Most of the time after the game, I'd accompany them to the Murphystown Dairy Barn and throw back some burgers and fries. All of them were his teammates on the Vipers football team. My blue Bulldogs letterman jacket stood out among the sea of red ones at the table, but any school rivalries were set aside. In fact, his friends were very welcoming to me and they even invited me to hang out at their houses after our games a couple of times. I began looking forward to Saturday Mornings.

The Saturday before Thanksgiving, I was once again at the Murphystown park playing football.

"Go long!" Gabe yelled as I ran toward the two trash barrels that served as markers for the end zone. I looked back over my shoulder, waiting for him to throw me the long pass. A few moments later, he hurled the ball in the air. I kept my eye on it as it spun my way. Leaping into the air, I caught it in my arms and came down just inside end zone. "Game!" he yelled, throwing his arms in the air in celebration.

We ran at each other, jumped up and knocked shoulders. "Dude!" we both said simultaneously. Sure, it was just an amateur game on a makeshift field in the city park, but, to us, it felt like we'd won the state championship...for about three seconds.

"You guys coming to the Dairy Barn with us?" asked our friend Charlie.

I pointed at Gabe. "If he's buying," I said as I turned out the empty pockets of my sports pants.

Gabe chuckled. "I got it covered."

"Cool, we'll see you there," Charlie said.

As Charlie walked away, Gabe bent down and rubbed his knee, grimacing. "What's wrong?" I asked.

"Twisted my knee a little when I made that last pass," he said.

"Can you walk?" I asked, feeling genuine concern for

him. I'd hate for an amateur football game to ruin his ability to play for the Vipers.

"Oh, yeah." He waved his hand dismissively. "I'm fine. Done this before, it's no biggie."

"Okay, I'll meet you at the diner," I said.

He nodded.

I drove my car from the park to the diner and after stuffing myself with a double-cheeseburger and fries, I walked out the restaurant with Gabe in tow. Once outside, Gabe came up behind me and playfully jumped on my back. I laughed as I stumbled forward.

"Apparently, your knee is okay," I said as I pitched the toothpick in my mouth on the ground.

"Oh yeah, I'm tough," he said without hesitation.

I stopped and turned around. "Thanks for lunch."

"Sure, man, no problem," he said, as I pulled my keys from my pocket.

I put the key into the lock of my car and turned it. "What you doing the rest of the day?" I asked.

"Play video games…might rent a movie. I don't know. What about you?" he asked leaning against his jeep that was parked beside me.

I shrugged my shoulders. "Don't have anything planned. Shelby went to Hot Springs to find a Homecoming dress. She asked me to go with her…but—"

"You told her you'd rather play football." He grinned, finishing my thoughts.

"I didn't come right out and say that…I just suggested that Mel would be a better choice than me for helping pick out a dress." I smiled.

"Smooth." Gabe nodded.

"Let me guess, Shelby is the queen?"

"How'd you know?" I laughed.

He pursed his lips, "Lucky guess...and you're the king?"

"Technically I'm her 'escort'."

"You guys are disgusting." He shook his head.

"Mel's always saying that too."

"I kind of gather you and Shelby don't spend much time apart?" he asked.

"Not really...well...we're not together *every* night...but we do talk on the phone," I said, deliberately not saying "for hours". I knew we probably spent too much time together, but that's just the way we were and had been for years.

"Wow," he said. "Have you guys always been that way?"

"Yeah, pretty much. I was thinking...you wanna come back to my place and hang out. I mean if you're not busy."

His eyes went wide. "For real?" His voice went high.

"Dude. It's not a big deal," I lied, trying to play it cool. It *was* a big deal. I was beginning to enjoy having a male friend in my life again. The connection Gabe and I had as kids had remained and honestly that's what scared me. Perhaps I also had a little crush on Gabe like he had on me. Maybe that's the reason I always gave into him when he wanted to play Truth or Dare and why I ended up kissing him more than once.

"It *is* a big deal. You finally trust that I'm not trying to get in your pants."

I quickly looked around making sure there was no one

within earshot. Luckily, there wasn't. "You had to go and make it weird, didn't you?"

"I'm joking, dude. Remember, it's me, Gabe, I make stupid jokes. Sorry," he attempted to backtrack.

He was right about that, Gabe "open mouth, insert foot" Sanchez. I pointed my fingers at my eyes and then at him to indicate that I was watching him. "Do you want to follow me or do you need to go home first?"

"Hmmm…follow me to my house and I'll drop my jeep off and I'll ride back to Pleasant with you. You don't mind taking me home later, do you?" he asked.

"Na. It's no problem. As long as you buy the gas." I smiled.

"No problemo!"

I followed him to his house he parked his jeep and hopped into my car. I put the car in reverse and started backing down his driveway. I noticed him looking at the coffee-stained backseats and the torn headliner above his head. "Dude, this car is a piece of shit."

"Agreed, but it's a set a four wheels and beats the hell out of having to borrow my mom's Prelude all the time," I said as I threw the car into drive.

"True." He leaned toward me and sniffed. "You smell like ass."

"No shit, Sherlock, I'm sure you don't smell like a bouquet of roses either," I huffed, even though the temperature was around sixty-degrees, I still sweated a lot on the field.

He puckered his lips and fluttered his eyelids. "Only when I wear my mom's perfume."

I threw my hands up. "I give up."

"Dude. Joke. Do I look like a guy that's into wearing perfume?" He threw his arms opened and looked down at himself.

"Hell, I don't know what you're into," I said.

"I'm not into drag. Not that I have anything against people that are, but it's not me. Honestly, man, I'm basically like you only I like dudes instead of chicks."

Since Gabe and I rekindled our friendship, I never questioned him about his sexuality beyond the fact that he was gay. "So, you don't find girls attractive at all?"

"Of course, I do, I admire their beauty, but I have no interest in having sex or a relationship with them. A naked girl does nothing for me."

I glanced at him, "But a naked dude does?"

"Not just *any* nude guy does it for me, only a certain type," he said as he checked the pocket of his jogging pants, I assumed for his wallet.

"And that type would be?"

He cocked his head at me. "Why are you asking me all these questions?"

"I don't know. I'm just making conversation," I raised my voice. "Just call it curiosity."

"Jock types…fit…lots of muscles. Don't like chest hair, but happy trails, *dude*." I gave him a confused look, having never heard the term. He lifted his shirt showing me his stomach. "Hair that starts here and goes to here. I don't have any. But it's a huge turn on for me. As far as personality, I like a guy that'll be there for me."

"I suppose we all want that in a partner," I said.

"Okay, it's my turn." He cracked the window to let in some fresh air. "Tell me something about you that I don't know."

"Um. I don't like banana pudding," I said.

"And I don't like chocolate pie," he retorted. "Dude, come on, I want to know something about you that no one else knows. Not even Shelby."

I thought for a moment. I debated whether I should tell him my secret, but I had been dying to tell someone. "Open the glove box." I nodded toward it.

"Hmmm…okay." He reached forward and released the latch, revealing an owner's manual and a small felt-covered black box. He looked at me.

"Open the box."

Gabe reached in, pulled out the box and slowly opened it. His jaw dropped and his eyes shot to me. "That's an engagement ring! You're going to propose to Shelby?"

I nodded.

"Holy shit!" His eyes stayed as big a golf balls.

"Giving it to her for Christmas," I said proudly.

He turned his head, slowly shut the lid and remained speechless for a few moments, before looking at me evenly. "Hawk. Are you sure about this? You guys are only seventeen."

"I've never been surer of anything in my life. I love her, man. I've been in love with her since I was thirteen. I want to spend the rest of my life with her, and she feels the same about me."

"I mean…if that's what you want…I'm happy for you," he said, but I sensed sadness in his voice.

"You don't sound like you are."

He shook his head, "No. It's not you. I really am happy for you. It's…nothing." He turned his head to face his window.

"What is it?" I pushed.

He shrugged his shoulder. "I don't know. It's just I wonder sometimes if I'll ever find a guy that loves me as much as you love Shelby. I want to marry and have a family just like you, but I can't because I'm gay. Even if it were possible, my family would never accept it. Hell, no one in this town would." He hung his head.

"I don't live in this town, but I would accept it," I said.

"Yeah, one guy out of what? Three thousand?"

"You could always move away…somewhere that's more gay-friendly."

"I don't want to move. This is my home. I want to be partners with my dad in his car dealership business. You know what would happen if anyone found out I was gay. I'd lose my family, my friends…basically my entire life. Believe me, I've thought about it more times that I care to admit. My entire future depends on how well I can keep acting like I'm straight."

"Does that mean you're going to keep dating girls?"

"Probably. Hell, I've been doing it for the past two years."

"How does that work?"

He shook his head. "I go out with a girl a few times and when I see she's wanting to get more serious, I deliberately sabotage things. I hate doing it, but it's all part of this 'wonderful illusion' of the straight jock football player," he said with bitterness in his voice.

I wanted to give him words of comfort, but I knew he was right. I had the same thoughts about myself. Thankfully, I would be marrying Shelby soon and would never have to deal with those kind issues. "I don't know what to say."

He locked eyes with mine. "Because you know I'm right,"

I hesitated a moment before I nodded.

"Oh well." He sniffled and pulled his chin up. "I guess I'd better keep a good supply of hand lotion, tissues, and *Men's Fitness* magazines on hand."

Seeing Gabe reveal his true feelings was a side of him that I'd never seen before. For as long as I had known Gabe, he always had this air of confidence about him and kept his emotions hidden within himself. "Shelby's brother is gay." I tried to offer him hope.

He gave me a wry grin, "Is he hot?"

"He's got a boyfriend; they've lived together for three years."

"Good for him," he said, although I couldn't tell if he was being sincere or sarcastic.

When we got back to my house, both of us took turns showering. I loaned Gabe a pair of shorts and a T-Shirt while we ran his jogging pants and hoodie through the washer and dryer. We rented *My Cousin Vinnie* and *Encino Man* from the Pleasant video store. Mom had gone out for the evening, and we had the living room to ourselves. I sat on one end of the sofa and Gabe on the other. We made lots of jokes throughout Encino Man about how annoying Pauly Shore was. In one scene, Gabe made a sexual comment about Brendan Frasier and what he'd like to do to him. It planted a thought in my head that didn't disgust me.

As the credits rolled, Gabe glanced up at the clock on the wall.

"It's nine, I should probably be getting home." He stood up, still wearing my open-sided T-shirt, giving me a nice view at his perfect physique. I had grabbed the first shirt out of my dresser drawer, which just happened to be one of many I had taken a pair of scissors to. Admittedly, I did like seeing his body, although I'd never want him to know that.

"Yeah. I thought Shelby would have called me by now to tell me if she found a dress." I felt a little concerned, but knowing Mel's love of shopping, she probably dragged her to every clothing store in town to find *the* perfect dress.

"Yeah, you know how girls love shopping." He folded his arms behind his head and yawned, revealing the only hair on his upper body, which looked perfect on him.

"That's true," I said. Being that it would take at least forty-five minutes to drive Gabe back to Murphystown, drop him off, and drive back, I really wanted to make sure Shelby was home safe before we left. "Are you in a hurry? I'm a little concerned that Shelby hasn't called and I'm afraid I'll miss her if she tries."

"Dude, I got all night, just didn't know if you went to

church or something tomorrow morning and needed to go to bed early," he said as he sat back down.

I gave him a slight grin, "I haven't gone to church since I was ten, so I think I'm good."

"Cool…you got any other movies to watch?" He looked toward the VCR.

"I got a fuzzy copy of *Ghostbusters* I recorded off the TV a few years ago," I said.

"Eh." He shrugged a shoulder. "Video games?"

"Sold it to buy the ring." I glanced at the hole in his shirt again.

"Board Games? I know you have some of those." He moved his arm to the back of the couch causing his left nipple to be completely exposed. The contrast between the white shirt and his dark skin were like day and night. *Quit staring, Hawk!* I chastised myself.

I quickly averted my eyes. "Umm…Scrabble or Monopoly?"

"I am *king* of Monopoly." He grinned.

"Okay," I said before going to my bedroom to retrieve the game and setting it up on the kitchen table.

An hour later, Gabe had me on the verge of bankruptcy. Of course, looking at the clock on the wall every five minutes and becoming more worried certainly didn't help with my concentration. I tried to disguise my worry, but Gabe easily read my face.

"You're really worried, aren't you?" He laid the dice in his hand back on the table.

"Yeah. This isn't like Shelby." I glanced up at the clock again.

"Maybe you should try calling her?" he suggested.

"Yeah, I'll do that," I said as I got up and walked to the phone hanging on the wall. I lifted the receiver and dialed the number to her parent's house. The phone rang once...twice... "Come on," I said with impatience. On the third ring, I got the answering machine. Not wanting to leave a message, I hung up.

I wrinkled my forehead. "Something is wrong."

"Calm down, buddy. It's probably nothing...they may have had car trouble or something. I'm sure she'll call soon."

Not finding comfort in his words, I felt my anxiety growing. "Do you think you could just stay here tonight?"

"Umm...yeah...sure." He looked as though he were searching for what to say. "Can I get you a soda or something?"

"No. I'm good." I sat down on the stool next to the phone, wishing for it to ring.

Over the next hour, the phone still did not ring. That's when I started calling her house every five minutes only to get the answering machine each time. Shortly before midnight, I reached my breaking point. "Fuck this shit! We're going over there." I grabbed my keys from the counter. "Come on."

As Gabe and I started toward the door I heard the garage door opening and knew my mother had made it home from her "teachers' night out" bowling event. I glanced up at the clock and noticed she was getting in over an hour later than she had originally informed me. In fact, with all my worry over Shelby, I hadn't noticed that my mother had not returned home. I decided to wait a few moments for her to come into the house to tell her where I was going. Just then I saw two more sets of headlights pull into the driveway. Having visitors at our house, way out in the country, late at night, was highly unusual. I felt a knot in my stomach. "What the fuck is going on?" I looked to Gabe as if he had the answer.

I waited impatiently for my mother, who seemed to be taking longer than usual to enter the house. Finally, the door from the garage opened, and my mother entered, I barely had time to focus on her when Principal Anderson and Mrs. Abercrombie, Shelby's cheerleading coach, filed in behind her. My eyes went to the tears rolling down my mom's and Mrs. Abercrombie's face. The knot in my stomach tightened and a wave of panic swept over me.

"Mom…Mom," my voice trembled. "What's going on?"

"Oh, Hawk," she began to sob uncontrollably.

Principal Anderson stepped forward and put his hand on my shoulder and locked his eyes with mine. "Hawk, son, let's go sit on the sofa."

I jerked away and turned back to my mother. "Mom! Mom! What going on?" I felt as though my stomach was lodged in my throat.

Principal Anderson grabbed my shoulder and spun me around to face him once again. "Hawk. Son. I need you to be strong."

Suddenly, the dead seriousness of his voice caused my entire body to start shaking. Uncontrollable tears began to pour from my eyes. "It's Shelby. Isn't it? Oh, God, no…please just tell me." I said in a childlike voice.

Principal Anderson started, "This evening around eight p.m., Shelby and Melanie were travelling on Highway 7 from Hot Springs and Arkadelphia and they were hit by a drunk driver coming in the opposite direction." He paused and his eyes moistened. "There were no survivors."

"No! No!" I screamed angrily and looked to my mother. "It's not true!" Mom nodded, unable to speak, her sobbing uncontrollable. "No…no." I felt my knees give way as I fell to the cold tile floor and curled into a ball.

Moving shadows flickered in and out of my vision as the sound of footsteps surrounded me, I pleaded for my mind to paint this reality as a nightmare. The worst nightmare imaginable. Muffled voices fell on my ringing ears as hands were laid upon my body. I lifted my eyes and desperately searched to latch onto something, capturing two desperate pools of brown mere inches from my face. "Help me, Gabe. Please help me," I cried in the voice of a five-year-old boy who found his father dead on the floor. Everything went black.

My eyelids lifted and through the strands of my own hair, the sight of my sixth grade basketball trophy came into focus.

"Mrs. Keystone!" I heard a desperate voice yell. "He's awake." I heard quick footsteps coming closer. "Hawk. Can you hear me?"

I then felt a hand push the hair from my eyes and I focused on the boy in front of me squatting beside the bed. I nodded.

"You're going to be okay," Gabe said in a gentle voice.

I felt movement on the bed from behind me, "No, I'm not," I managed to whisper as my mother's arms pulled me into her embrace.

"Shh…baby…shh…" My mom began rocking me. "It's going to be okay." I just wanted to be held.

I began to sob. "Please, Momma, please tell me Shelby isn't dead."

She squeezed me tighter. "I'm so sorry, baby."

I cried out in pain.

I awoke, sunlight beamed through my bedroom window, hitting me in the face. Feeling a little disorientated, I spotted Gabe laid back in my desk chair asleep, his feet propped up on the desk itself. I lifted my head slightly and peered at my alarm clock which read 9:03 a.m. *It must be daylight*, I thought. I'm not sure how long I cried in my mother's arms the previous night before the sedatives she gave took effect. My mind felt numb. Feeling the need to take care of a basic body function, I sat up and threw back the covers. Looking down at myself, I noticed I was still wearing the T-shirt and shorts I had worn the previous evening. Just to confirm I hadn't dreamed it all, I glanced at Gabe again and saw he too was dressed in the previous night's clothes. *Must be Sunday*, I said to myself.

Standing up in my bare feet, the soft carpet filled in the gaps between my toes. Just then, Gabe's eyes shot open.

"Hey," he quickly sat up in the chair, "are you okay?"

At that moment, my brain began coming out of its fog

and I felt as though I had the worst hangover in history. "Yeah, gotta pee," I said just above a whisper as I stumbled toward my bathroom.

"Do you need help?" he asked.

"No, just a little dizzy," I responded.

I entered my bathroom and closed the door. Lifting the toilet lid, I stared straight ahead in a state of shock as I tried to piece everything together. Like a zombie, once finished, I dragged myself to the sink and washed my hands. Staring into the mirror above the sink, I focused on sad, swollen eyes. My disheveled hair hung below my chest in a frizzy mess of tangles. I swept it over my head in a quick motion with my hand.

Gabe knocked on the door. "Are you okay?"

My voice strained to answer. "Yeah. Be right out."

Robotically, I stepped to the door and pushed it open. Standing on the other side was a very worried Gabe. Many distant voices from outside my bedroom door captured my attention. I tried to contemplate my next move, but my mind felt incapable of making decisions. *How many people are here? Are they here for me? Should I make an appearance to show everyone I'm okay.*

"Where's my mom?"

"She's taking care of the...guests." I could see he struggled for the right word to call them. "Do you want me to get her?"

Again, my mind processed in slow motion, delaying my response. "No...why are those people here?"

"For you," he answered.

A sudden wave a grief washed over me again and I began sobbing. "Shelby's gone."

Tears began flowing down Gabe's cheek. "I know." He stepped forward and grabbed me in an embrace as I cried on his shoulder.

"I'll never see her again," I blubbered.

"You will again one day," he said, telling me the same words that I heard many times growing up in the church. Even if I believed it were true, it would be an entire lifetime for me before that happened.

"What am I going to do, Gabe? I can't live without her," I cried.

"I know it feels that way, buddy, but she'd want you to go on."

I jerked away and snapped at him, "No, she wouldn't!" I could see that my anger took him by surprise.

"I'm going to go get your mom," he said, but before he could move, I lost it again. This time grabbing him in an embrace. I put my head on his shoulder. "I'm sorry. I didn't mean to snap at you."

He rubbed my back. "It's okay."

A few minutes later, I attempted to gather myself. I pulled back from his comfortable embrace, suddenly feeling the need to be around people. "I want to go out there."

Gabe didn't attempt to argue with me. "Okay. You want to change clothes?"

I looked down at my lounge shorts and my Bart Simpson T-Shirt with the caption, *Don't have a cow man*. It certainly wasn't appropriate for the situation. "Yeah," I answered.

He ran to the closet and grabbed a pair of jeans and a blue button-up shirt. I automatically began undressing as he removed the clothing from the hangers. He handed me the jeans and I pulled them over my underwear. The shirt came and I struggled to button it, my fingers uncooperative.

"Here," he said, as he started at the top button and worked his way down. I felt like a helpless toddler. After he finished the shirt, he picked up the sneakers beside my bed. I sat down and he got down on the floor and proceeded to put them on me, while I stared straight ahead as if in a trance. Just then I began to feel another wave of grief building as another reality hit me.

"Mel's gone too," I cried.

Gabe had just finished tying my last shoelace, and sat back on the floor, looking up to me and nodding slowly.

"Oh God. Poor Mel." I sobbed and slid off the bed onto the floor facing Gabe.

"Buddy, I think you need to get back in bed. You're not ready to go out there yet." He tried to help me up from the floor.

I looked up at him. "I need to be around people."

"Hawk, please don't force yourself to do something you're not ready to do," he pleaded.

"I can't just sit in here thinking about it. I can do this."

He sighed. "Okay." Reaching out a hand, I grabbed hold as he hoisted me up. Quickly, he changed into some of my jeans and one of my nicer shirts and brushed my long hair. Opening the bedroom door, he led the way down the hall.

Approaching the living room, the voices became

louder. As soon as I stepped into view, everyone's head turned to me. Suddenly, I did not like being the center of everyone's attention. I scanned the room. Somehow, the entire Bulldog basketball team had squeezed into my living room, along with several teachers from my school, my mom, and our minister. Eddie Davis was the first to step forward and grab me in a hug. "I'm so sorry, man." I felt a few drops of water on my shoulder, but I refused to let myself break down in front of everyone. I needed to remain strong. It was my duty.

"Thanks, Eddie." I patted his back.

One by one, I repeated the ritual with all my teammates until my mother approached me and signaled for me to join her in the kitchen. Entering, my eyes beheld casseroles and desserts covering the table, countertops, and even the stovetop. I never understood the Southern tradition of when a loved one dies, the entire community feels the need to bring food to the survivors, when eating is the last thing they feel like doing.

Mom turned to face me. "You need to eat, honey."

"I'm not hungry."

"Hawk. You've got to eat." She stood in front of me and tucked my hair behind my shoulders.

I started crying again, "I don't want to eat."

She grabbed me in an embrace. "Okay, baby. You don't have to right now."

She held me in her arms for a few minutes until I stopped crying. "Why don't you go lie down?"

I shook my head. "I want to be around people."

She pulled a tissue from the box on the counter next to us and handed it to me. "Honey. Please don't push yourself."

"I'm not," I said.

The rest of the day was a continued influx of people attempting to comfort me with the same clichéd words. "She's in a better place." "God had a purpose for her." "The Lord took her home, honey." I thanked them for the kind words, as I was supposed to, while mentally cursing the "all powerful" god that did this. I nodded along not really listening to their stories about how they knew me, or her, or my mother and eventually they drifted along, like ghosts roaming in and out of our newly haunted house.

Daylight soon turned to dusk, and all the people had left. I sat at the kitchen table with my mother and Gabe. For the moment, I was holding myself together as I ran my eyes over massive amount of food.

I said the first thought that came into my mind. "We're never going to be able to eat all this."

"I've never seen so much food in my life," Gabe said, picking up an olive from the enormous vegetable platter courtesy of the Pleasant Lions Club. In all honestly, I never knew so many people cared about me as Shelby's boyfriend. I could only imagine the amount of food that Shelby's family received.

"We'll just eat what we can," my mom said.

The room went silent again before Gabe spoke up. "I need to call my parents to come get me."

"No." I panicked, knowing that as soon as my head hit the pillow, my thoughts would turn to Shelby. I refused to feel the pain. "Stay another night."

Mom reached over and grabbed my hand. "Hawk, honey, Gabe has school tomorrow."

"He can miss." I cried, "Mom. Please. I don't want to be alone." I gazed desperately into her eyes.

"It's okay, Mrs. Keystone. If Hawk wants me to stay, my parents will understand," Gabe said.

She nodded. The thought occurred to me to sleep in my mother's bed, like I did for two years after my father died, but back then I was only a child. Now at seventeen, the idea just felt too weird to me, despite my grief.

Just then, the phone rang as it had been doing most of the day. Mom got up to answer it.

I heard lots of "yeses" and "okays" but had no idea who was on the other end of the line. After a few minutes she hung up. "Who was that?" I asked.

"That was Mrs. Johnson, they would like to see you tomorrow."

The thought of walking into Shelby's house without her there filled me with overwhelming sorrow. I felt my eyes begin to water and gave her my immediate answer. "No. I can't Mom."

She nodded. "It's okay. They'll understand."

The rest of the evening, the three of us sat in the living room watching TV, not really paying attention to it. My mind would occasionally flash with a memory of Shelby and I'd feel myself tearing up. In those moments, I would shift my attention to flashing pictures on the TV until it passed.

Mom, exhausted from the long twenty-four hours without sleep, retired to her bedroom around nine, leaving

Gabe and I alone on the couch. Most of the evening we'd all sat in silence. My eyes began to droop around midnight.

"Are you ready to go to bed?" Gabe asked.

I nodded.

"Do you have some blankets that I can make a pallet on your bedroom floor?" he asked as we entered my bedroom.

"My bed is big enough for both of us," I said, and he nodded.

Preparing for bed, we both stripped down to our underwear and climbed in. As I stared at the rotating blades of the ceiling fan, I willed my thoughts away from Shelby only for them to return a few moments later. I needed conversation.

I turned my head to Gabe, "What are you thinking about right now?"

"The Algebra test I'll miss tomorrow," he answered.

"I'm sorry. Will your teacher let you make it up?" I asked.

"Yeah. It's no big deal."

With more silence, my mind started going to Shelby again. I needed more. "What age did you know you were gay?"

He gave me a puzzled look.

"I'm sorry. I'm thinking out loud…trying to keep my mind from thinking about—"

"I understand." He stopped me from having to say her name and I returned to staring at the ceiling "Ten."

"How did you know?" I wanted to understand.

He turned his head back to me. "Could we talk about anything but this, right now?"

Obviously, I hit a nerve; the room went silent. *Stop thoughts...stop thoughts...another subject...another subject. Shelby's dead. Shelby's dead. Shelby's dead.*

He sighed. "That day you and I played in the mud and my mom had us shower together."

"Oh," I said. *Shelby's dead. Shelby's dead. Another subject. Shelby's dead. Making mudpies. Me and Gabe. Showering.* My mind was a jumble of thoughts, and I said the next one out loud. "You felt tingly all over, didn't you?"

His flipped his head to me wide-eyed. "Yes. How did you—"

Shelby's dead. Shelby's dead. I put my palm over my eyes, interrupting him. "How am I going to get through this Gabe? She was everything to me." I started crying again and curled myself into a fetal position.

Gabe started rubbing my back. "You will, Hawk, you'll get through this. I know you will."

Chapter Six

Three days later, reality sank in. The entire town of Pleasant was filled with sorrow. Two innocent teenagers died at the hands of a drunk driver. The story made the front-page news of the Murphystown Courier and was soon picked up by the state media, igniting a firestorm of criticism regarding sentencing guidelines for repeat D.U.I. offenders. Apparently, the man that murdered the love of my life and her best friend had been arrested six times prior and each time the judge had let him off with just a fine. In an interview on Channel Four with the state president of Mothers Against Drunk Driving, the lady used the word "murdered" instead of "killed" because the intoxicated driver deliberately made the choice to use his truck as a weapon for murder when he got behind the wheel. In another interview, Arkansas Governor and Present-Elect Bill Clinton vowed to strengthen drunk driving penalties.

Even so, it offered little comfort. Nothing would bring back Shelby.

Life without Shelby was my new reality, but it didn't stop my mind from creating delusional reasons as to why I hadn't seen Shelby in four days. *She's gone to cheerleader camp. She and Mel have gone on vacation to Florida with Mel's parents for the week. She's home sick with the chicken pox and is too contagious for me to be around.* The human mind is very adept at creating ways to avoid emotional pain.

Gabe spent only the one night at my house and his mother came and picked him up the next day. He returned to school on Tuesday but came to my house afterward each day and stayed as late as possible for the rest of the week. Honestly, I don't think I could have made it through those days without him. Principal Anderson told my mother and I to take as much time off as we needed. The thought of returning to school filled me with an overwhelming sense of dread. It's funny how the brain focuses on the most insignificant things like who I'll sit with at lunch. The Johnsons' world, the Minks' world, and my world had been ripped apart, and I'm thinking about who I'll be eating cafeteria burritos with. It seemed so stupid.

Over the week, I came to some frightening realizations. I had no close friends from school. Since that first day, no one called or came to my house to check on me, not even my teammates. It made me realize that I had centered my entire world around Shelby for so many years, I never took the time to make other friendships. Sure, I had "acquaintances", as I called them, the ones that you call friends but who you know almost nothing about. Hell, I had enough of them to be chosen as the queen's escort, but only because I was Shelby's boyfriend. Everybody loved Shelby. No, in my time of need, I had to turn to my best friend from my childhood.

On the fifth day after her death, I finally felt able to meet with Shelby's family. Pulling into their driveway, I glanced toward her bedroom window and felt my stomach twist into a knot. I had to stay focused on not breaking down.

With trepidation, I got out of my car and walked to the door. Mrs. Johnson opened it, anticipating my visit. She immediately pulled me into her arms.

"She loved you so much, Hawk." Her voice quivered.

"I loved her too, Mrs. Johnson." I knew my tears would start flowing, if there were any left in me.

She held me in her embrace for several minutes in an unusual display of emotion for her. "We're all in the kitchen," she said before leading the way.

Sitting around the table were Mr. Johnson, and a very muscular twenty-something-year-old with shoulder-length black hair that I recognized as Shelby's brother, J.J. Like me, both looked as though they were cried out. Mr. Johnson stood up and shook my hand and J.J. grabbed me in a hug.

Mr. Johnson pointed to the only empty chair in the table, "Have a seat, Hawk." He looked at me with soft eyes and his voice was gentle. "How you doing, son?"

I felt myself starting to lose it and swallowed, pushing my grief into the pit of my stomach. "Not good, sir."

His eyes filled with water. "I know, Hawk. She was the light of our life."

"Mine too." My composure hung by a thread.

"Hawk," said Mrs. Johnson, "you know we all consider you like family. You knew Shelby better than anyone and we would like to plan a funeral that celebrates her life. Do you feel up to helping us?"

"Of course. Anything," I said.

She picked up the pencil from the table and pressed it

against a sheet of notebook paper in front of her. "What was her favorite flower?" she asked.

"Lilies," I answered.

"Her favorite colors?"

"Green and yellow." It felt almost cold to know Shelby's vibrant life was now being summarized in a few short questions.

"Any special songs you think she would have liked played at her funeral?"

A memory from when we were both thirteen popped into my head and suddenly this talk didn't seem so cold anymore. For the school talent show that year, Shelby, Mel, and their friend Megan decided to do a dance routine to Cyndi Lauper's *Girls Just Want to Have Fun*. A few days before the day of the talent show Megan came down with a bad case of the chicken pox. Feeling that the act wouldn't work without a girl trio, Shelby charmed me into donning a green spiked wig, a short leather miniskirt, and a sleeveless leopard-print blouse and taking Megan's place. Learning the dance routine came easy, having copious amounts of makeup applied to my face was not. Our act was a success and only a few people know to this day that it wasn't three girls performing the routine.

Of course, that song was completely inappropriate for a funeral. I realized I was smiling; I quickly pushed the thought away. "I'm sorry. Just something I remembered."

"You're thinking about that Cyndi Lauper song, aren't you?" J.J. smiled at me.

"Yeah. I am." I smiled back.

He turned to his mother. "Mom, we're playing *Girls*

Just Want to Have Fun." He pointed at the paper. "Write that down."

After a few more basic questions and shared memories, Mrs. Johnson laid her pencil down. "I think we got everything we need. Thanks, Hawk, this really means so much to us."

I looked to her and then to Mr. Johnson. "Can I please have a request?" I could barely hold back the floodgates.

"Sure, Hawk, anything," Mrs. Johnson said.

I reached into my pocket and pulled out the small felt-covered box. I placed it on the table and opened the lid. "Can she…be buried…with this? It…it…was going…to be her Christmas present." With those words, I covered my eyes with my hands, hung my head and bawled.

J.J. jumped up and wrapped his arms around me. I heard Mr. Johnson lose control of his emotions and that only made me cry harder. I remember slipping from my chair and after that, everything went black.

I opened my eyes to surroundings unfamiliar to me. I moved my gaze around the room, focusing on the posters on the wall of a curly-headed man with a floppy hat and extra-long scarf around his neck, some sort of robotic creature that resembled an oversized pepper shaker, and a poster of Janet Jackson. It hit me then I was lying on Shelby's brother's bed.

"Hey," I heard J.J.'s voice come close to the bed. He reached out his hand that held a wet washcloth. "Put this on your forehead."

I reached for the cold rag, pushed my hair back and

placed it just above my eyebrows. "What happened?" I asked in a barely audible voice.

"You passed out and I brought you in here." I ran my eyes over him. He looked even bulkier than the last time I'd seen him.

"How long have I been out?" I asked, focusing on his eyes that mimicked Shelby's.

"About an hour." He grabbed his desk chair, pulled it to the side of the bed and sat down. "Hawk, when's the last time you ate anything?"

I had to think on it for several seconds. "I...um...I ate a piece of fried deer steak for dinner...on...um...Tuesday. I think."

"That was two days ago, Hawk! Give me your arm," he ordered. Lifting it, he pressed his thumb against my wrist and looked down at his watch. A few seconds later he nodded. "Just as I thought. Your pulse is racing. You're dehydrated. Don't move."

He left the room and returned in a few moments with a large tumbler full of ice water. "Drink this slowly." He handed it to me.

Taking the plastic cup, I sat up, put it to my lips, and began draining its contents. I felt him grab the cup. "Slowly, I said." He pulled it back slightly.

I nodded and began drinking more slowly. It took me a couple of minutes to drain the contents. "Thank you," I handed him back the empty cup and he sat it on the desk.

"Listen, I know this is hard for you, but you've got to take care of yourself."

"I need to go," I said as I started to get up. Being in that house, just across the hall from Shelby's room was way more than I could handle.

He reached over and pushed me back down. "You're not going anywhere until I see you eat something."

"I'm not hungry."

Just then, the door opened and in stepped an equally buff blond guy with a buzz cut, carrying a plate full of food and a glass of tea. J.J. took it from him. "Thanks, babe."

"Sure," he answered, leaning against the doorjamb.

"Mrs. O'Dell's homemade chicken spaghetti. You're not leaving here until I see you eat at least half of it." J.J. shoved the food and drink at me.

"I'm really not hungry," I said. My stomach growled upon getting a whiff of the garlic toast resting on top of the pile. I attempted to get up again.

"Hawk," he gave me a threating look, "eat this or Mason and I are going to tie you to that desk chair and feed it to you like a baby."

I couldn't help but size him and his partner up and knew they out-muscled me about four to one. "Fine!" I glared at him.

Pulling myself up against the headboard, I took the spaghetti and dug in, taking small bites. Mrs. O'Dell, the town librarian, made the best chicken spaghetti in town and always brought it to any church or community potluck. It had always been one of my favorite dishes. He laid a napkin in my lap and nodded to Mason, who headed back down the hall.

He hmphed. "God, you're as stubborn as Shelby."

I thought about the few times she and I had arguments.

Some of them would last for days because neither one of us was willing to be the first to apologize. Usually, I would be the one that would end up apologizing because I couldn't handle the tension. "I…mmm…don't know 'bout that," I said, my mouth full of food. I pointed to one of the posters with my fork. "*Star Trek*?"

Turning his head to the poster of the pepper shaker, he gasped. "*Star Trek*? I'll have you know that's *Doctor Who*. The greatest sci-fi series ever made." He grinned at me.

I shrugged my shoulder and wrinkled my nose, "Sorry…mmm…not a sci-fi fan," I said, while trying to chew.

"Oh yeah, video games. Right?" he said.

I nodded then swallowed. I then focused on a photo on his bureau of a very chubby teenager standing next to a grey curly-headed gentleman in a cloak. The autograph on the photo read "To J.J., Jon Pertwee '87".

I cocked my head and pointed with my fork. "That's you?"

He turned his head to the photo and chuckled. "Yeah, I liked to eat back then."

"I did too," I said. "What did you do to get in shape?"

"Diet. Exercise…that's how I met Mason. He was my trainer in high school."

"Cool. I lost weight when I started playing basketball," I said, finishing off the last bite and setting the plate beside me.

J.J. picked it up. "Polished that off in a hurry," he said as I grabbed the glass of tea from the nightstand and downed it.

"Can I go now?" I wiped my mouth, "I don't like being in this house."

His face became serious. "Listen, Hawk. I'm worried about you. You're dehydrated, not eating and you look like you've had almost no sleep."

I felt myself start to tear up again and stared deep into his eyes. "Do you know what it feels like to have your whole world taken from you?"

He grabbed me in a hug. "I'm so sorry, Hawk."

Before I left, I promised J.J. I'd take care of myself; basically telling him what he wanted to hear to get out of that house. I got into my car and glanced down at my watch, which read 2:00 p.m. Honestly, I did not know what to do with myself. I just knew I didn't want to be alone. Mom had returned to work and although Gabe planned on coming to my house after school, that would be another couple of hours. The thought of going home to my dark and depressing bedroom filled me with dread and I couldn't wait another two hours for Gabe to be at my house, so there was only one thing to do.

I turned the key in my ignition and headed to Murphystown. The normal twenty-minute trip took less that twelve minutes. With each thought about Shelby, my foot became heavier on the gas pedal. I hated being alone with my own thoughts.

I pulled onto third street and drove past several houses until I came up on the empty lot next to Gabe's house, where I stopped my car. Staring out my windows at the empty plot of dead grass where my grandfather's house once stood, my mind took a trip back to my childhood when I spent weekends and summers with him. Even back then, the century-old home was in poor condition. Granddad didn't have much money, so most home repairs went unattended. I remembered areas in the dining room where the hardwood floor had rotted to the point that he placed ashtrays on the floor to mark spots where not to step, for fear of falling through the floor. It often felt like walking through a mine field to get from the kitchen to the living room. Many nights I'd lay in bed and pull the covers over my head with every pop and crack of the ancient structure convincing me a ghost haunted the place. More often than not, I'd end up sleeping in the same bed with Granddad on stormy nights. Even though his house could be creepy at times, it was still filled with love. Grandad loved me to the moon and back and of all the grandchildren I was the closest to him. His death hurt me, but Granddad was ninety-five, and I knew he wouldn't be around for many more years. Even with that knowledge, it still came as a surprise when he suddenly passed away in his sleep. But he led a long, full life and Shelby's life had just begun. We had our whole future together. It wasn't fair!

Before I had another break down, I started the car again and drove to the next house, pulling into the Sanchez's driveway. Hoping anyone was home, I desperately rang the doorbell. A few moments later the door opened to a beautiful Hispanic lady dressed in a sweater and slacks with a dish towel in her hand. I let out a sigh of relief. Mrs. Sanchez gave me a startled look. "Hawk?" Immediately, she dropped the towel and threw her arms around me. "I am so sorry. Gabriel told me everything."

"Thanks, Mrs. Sanchez. I appreciate it," I replied when she released me, but not before my emotions started to get the best of me once again.

My voice trembled. "I'm sorry to intrude...I just can't...be by myself right now."

"Oh, bebé," she ushered me inside, "come into the kitchen with me. I was just finishing up some dishes."

As we walked through the living room, I noticed it hadn't changed much over the years. A new sofa had replaced the old worn leather couch. A large rear-projection television had replaced the old wood-cabinet-styled console one. Entering the kitchen, I felt a sense of déjà vu. Many hours had I spent in their kitchen as a kid eating her deliciously prepared meals.

"Have a seat." She pointed to one of the kitchen chairs. "Would you like a Coke?" she asked.

"Yes, ma'am. Thank you," I replied and sat down in one of her very ornate oak chairs.

She pulled a can from the refrigerator and filled a glass with ice before setting both in front of me and taking the adjacent seat. I poured the drink into the glass and took a sip before resting my hands on the table.

Immediately, she placed her hands over mine. "Bebé, if there's anything I can do, please ask."

"Thank you, Mrs. Sanchez. I'm okay. Really," I lied.

She looked at me with skepticism, "Gabe had planned on coming to your house after school."

"I know. I just didn't want to be alone. My mom offered to take another day off work, but she's already missed so many days because of me. I don't want her to get in trouble, so I told her to go and that I would be okay," I neglected to tell her that I planned on meeting with the Johnsons today because I knew she would have insisted on staying with me.

Mrs. Sanchez nodded. "Are you sure you're okay?"

I nodded and she patted my hand.

"I am so happy you and Gabriel are getting close again," she said, changing the subject.

"Me too."

She shook her head slowly. "It was so hard for Gabriel growing up. He was so shy when he was little. Kids teased him because of his small size and mixed race and never really had a friend until he met you."

About that time, the door between the garage and the kitchen opened and in walked a boy and a girl that looked around nine or ten years old. They looked at me with trepidation.

"Do you remember Maria and Miguel? The twins?" Mrs. Sanchez asked me.

I recalled the last time I saw Gabe's brother and sister they hadn't even started kindergarten. A memory flashed in my head of me and Gabe playing blocks with them on their living room floor when they were toddlers. "Oh, wow, they've gotten big." I smiled at them.

"Maria, Miguel, this is Hawk. He's a friend of your brother's," she said.

"Hi," they both said in unison, as they hung their coats and backpacks on the two wall pegs just inside the door.

"Mama," Miguel said, "can I go play at Blake's house?"

"As long as it's okay with his mama," she said.

"It is," he said before tearing down the hall to his room.

"You two stay away from that sewer pond. Comprenda?" she yelled, an order I'd heard many times when I was his age.

"Yes, Mama!" His voice echoed from down the hall.

"Mama. Can I have a snack?" Maria asked.

"Sure, bebé, what do you want?" she asked.

The little girl placed her index finger on her chin and looked up. "Fruity Pebbles."

"Okay, a small bowl, I'm making tamales tonight," she said.

At one time I could eat a dozen of her delicious corn-wrapped pieces of heaven. Sadly, at the moment, not even those sounded good.

About that time, I heard a vehicle door slam and a few moments later Gabe came through the door wearing a pair of jeans, a Nirvana T-shirt, and a blue-jean jacket. His eyes widened at the sight of me. "Hawk. What are you doing here?"

"I needed to get out of the house," I said, not wanting to say too much in front his little sister.

"Oh," He wrinkled his forehead and hung his backpack and coat next to the door.

"You have a good day at school, mijo?" his mother asked him as she pulled the milk from the refrigerator.

"Sí," Gabe answered in Spanish.

Gabe mouthed the words "You, okay?" to me.

I nodded.

"Mama, Hawk and I are going to my room."

"Sí, bebé," she answered.

I followed Gabe to his room. As we entered, I noticed he had gotten new bedroom furniture. The room was very neat and tidy, just as I remembered it. Gabe had always been a stickler, like me, for everything being in its proper place. After we would finish playing with his Atari, he'd always ask me to re-stack all the game cartridges under the television cabinet. The blue sheet rocked walls were void of any adornments. The one nightstand had a lamp and alarm clock sitting on it, the dresser, two watches and a bottle of cologne. Other than those few items, the room was very minimalist. Certainly, a contrast to the room I remembered filled with toys, games, and posters. "Where's all your stuff?" I asked, still trying to hide the pain I felt inside after my visit with Shelby's family.

"What do you mean?" he asked, closing the door behind us.

"This room used to be full of stuff."

He ran his eyes around the room. "Yeah. I got rid of all that years ago."

He kicked off his shoes before opening the closet door and neatly placing them inside next to a pair of dress shoes. I noticed his clothes fill only half the closet.

"Is that all the clothes you have?"

"Yeah. How many pair of pants does one person need?" he asked as he sat down on the bed next to me.

"The Gabe I knew always had to have everything," I said.

"I used to be that way, but one day it occurred to me that I never used even half those things, so what's the point in having them?"

"That's a good way of looking at it I suppose." I turned my head away from him, feeling my tears building as another wave of grief washed over me. *Keep it in, Hawk. Don't break down.*

"Hawk, are you okay?" I could hear the concern in his voice, but refused to look at him knowing I'd lose it.

"I went to see Shelby's family earlier and, umm…it was bad."

"I know it was," he said as he placed his hand on my shoulder.

I shook my head. "I can't do this, man."

"Listen, Hawk. You can. You're going to get through this." He rubbed my shoulder.

Slowly I turned to face him, my eyes filled with tears. "I should have died with her."

His face became ashen. "Don't say that, Hawk, please don't say that."

"It's true, Gabe. I was selfish. I wanted to play football instead of going with her that day. Me living is God's punishment."

"Oh God, Hawk. You can't think that way." His brown eyes stared deep into mine.

"I want to die, Gabe. I don't want to live like this." I shook my head as his eyes moistened.

"Please don't say that." He sniffled.

"It's the truth."

He placed his other hand on my shoulder and turned his body toward mine. "You're going to get through this, Hawk. I know it seems like right now you're not, but you are. I'm here for you."

We both stared at each other as a moment of silence passed before I collapsed into his arms. "Please just hold me."

I didn't cry or speak, I just let the warmth of his embrace shield me from my pain as he comforted me. Slowly, I closed my eyes and drifted off to sleep.

A few hours later, I found myself waking up in a dark bedroom that wasn't my own. Muffled voices in the hall became clearer as I tried to shake the grogginess away.

The voices became clearer. "Mama, I'm really worried. There's something seriously wrong with him," I heard Gabe's voice.

"He's grieving, bebé," Mrs. Sanchez said.

I heard Mr. Sanchez's voice. "It's normal, son."

"No, Papa. It's not normal. He's saying he should have died with Shelby and that living is God's punishment for not being with her that day. I'm really worried that he might…" Gabe lowered his voice, "try to hurt himself."

"Teresa, go call his mother," his father said. I heard footsteps scurry down the hall. "You stay with him. Don't let him out of your sight," Mr. Sanchez said to Gabe.

In the darkness, I felt the mattress shift as Gabe sat down on the edge of the bed. My eyes searched for him, and I spoke. "I'm too afraid to kill myself."

His voice quivered. "I'm here for you, Hawk."

"I'm sorry." I pulled my knees to me even tighter. A hand laid gently on my shoulder and began rubbing down my back. I reversed my position and laid my head in his lap. He then began stroking my hair, running his fingers through the strands and down my back. "Please don't leave me alone."

"Never," he said as I felt one of his teardrops fall on my face.

Chapter Seven

Late November 1992

Another week of living in my own personal hell passed. For several days, I stayed at home under my mom and Gabe's watchful eyes. Mom took some more time from work to stay with me during the day and Gabe relieved her every day after school. I repeatedly told them it wasn't necessary and that I wasn't going to try and harm myself. Mom relented only after I agreed to see a psychologist who specialized in helping people who have suffered a traumatic loss in their lives. I found the visit utterly useless, other than her assuring my mother that, in her professional opinion, I was no danger to myself. I told everyone that from the beginning, but no one believed me. Not that I hadn't thought about it, but I knew what it would do to my mom. While I had few memories of the aftermath of my father's death, Jennifer told me that it completely devasted Mom. In fact, there were many days she would not get out of bed. With the psychologist's recommendation, my doctor put me on Prozac. The pills didn't make me feel any better, only sleepy, and sleep is all I did most days. By the time Thanksgiving rolled around I missed almost two weeks of school and skipped Thanksgiving dinner at my grandmother's house, much to my family's disappointment. Most of my time, I spent in my bedroom becoming accustomed to the smell of soured milk from the partially-eaten bowls of Frosted Flakes that cluttered my bedroom floor. In the past, I would have never been so disgusting, but now, honestly, I didn't give a fuck.

In my fragile mental state, my mother felt that I shouldn't attend Shelby's or Mel's funerals. At least that was one thing we both agreed on. I could not bear the thought of seeing my precious Shelby lying in a coffin and having that memory etched into my brain the rest of my life. Shelby's family said they understood and from what my mother told me of the funeral service, the church in which it was held could not fit all the mourners, forcing many to stand outside in the cold to pay their respects.

I don't know what day of the week it was, but I awakened from my deep slumber by the sound of footsteps marching into my bedroom.

"Rise and shine!" I heard Gabe's chipper voice grating on my ears.

A few seconds later, sunlight came beaming through my window, searing my eyes. "What the fuck, dude?" I groaned and pulled the comforter over my head.

"Nope." He walked over and jerked it back, leaving me lying in just my underwear. He pinched his nose. "Damn, dude, how long's it been since you showered?"

"Fuck off." I buried my face in my pillow, which even that wasn't safe from his onslaught, as he jerked it from under my head.

He walked over to the wall and flipped on the overhead light. "We got a party to go to."

"I said fuck off," I pulled the comforter back up over

my head. He quickly yanked it off the bed and threw it to the floor.

I curled up in a ball and felt him grabbing my wrist, pulling me off the bed. My fall landing me in a curdled bowl of milk. "Uh oh, I guess you're gonna have to shower now." He grinned at me.

I wrinkled my nose in disgust as the smell hit me. "What the hell, man." I sat up and rested my back against the edge of the bed.

"Your mom's made your favorite chocolate chip pancakes with rainbow sprinkles. Now. Get up and get in the shower."

I picked up a dirty sock and tried to wipe the spoiled milk off my leg. "I'm not hungry."

"Yes, you are. You're wasting away and that body of yours is too gorgeous for me to let that happen."

I pursed my lips at him.

He pointed toward my bathroom.

"Go away, Gabe," I huffed.

"I'm not going away. You're getting out of this house if I have to drag you out in your underwear."

"I'd like to see you try." I eyed him up and down from my position in the floor.

"Oh, I can do it." He stared me down. I could fight him, but wasn't in the mood to argue.

"Fine!"

He gave me a satisfied grin. "I thought so."

"What party?" I asked.

"My brother and sister's. They invited you."

"I'm not in a partying mood," I replied, reaching for another dirty sock to wipe more milk off my foot.

"Too bad. You're going anyway. Now go shower. You stink."

I moaned some more and held onto the bed to pull myself up, "I'll get a shower but I'm not going to no party."

He ignored my last statement. "I'll lay out your clothes on the bed for you."

"I can pick out my own clothes. Thank you."

Feeling groggy from the effects of that damn antidepressant, my hand slipped, and I fell back on the floor. "Here," Gabe extended his hand.

"Thanks," I said, grabbing his hand and pulling myself up. After gaining my footing, I reached down and slipped off my underwear. Gabe's eyes went as big as golf balls before turning his head as if he were embarrassed.

"Come on, dude. You play sports. It's not like you haven't seen a naked guy before," I said before turning and walking toward the bathroom. I couldn't help but smile a little as I closed the door behind me. *That'll teach him to pull me out of bed.*

A half hour later, I dragged myself into the kitchen, wearing a pair of jeans, a red plaid flannel button-up, and my Doc Martens boots. Mom stood over the stove flipping a pancake and Gabe sat at the kitchen table pouring syrup over the flapjacks on his plate. Mom looked up. "Good morning, honey."

"Good morning," I mumbled, pulling out the chair across from Gabe and flopping down in it.

He sniffed the air. "Is that teen spirit I smell?" He

smirked in reference to the Nirvana song and my choice of Grunge clothing.

I shot him a dirty look, "The old Gabe is back, I see." Over the past couple weeks, I saw a side of Gabe I'd never seen before—supportive, caring and attentive. He may have started out on the wrong foot with me, but he'd more than proven that he just wanted to be my friend and right now that's what I needed the most.

"Yep. Haven't you missed him?" He took a bite of pancake and pointed toward my feet with his fork. "I like those boots by the way."

"No," I said.

My mother brought over a stack of pancakes and a cup of coffee and sat them in front of me. "Here you go." She patted me on the back. "Your favorite…with sprinkles."

"Thanks, Mom," I said, picking up my fork and digging in. For some reason, that first bite tasted like heaven, the second bite even better, and within a couple of minutes I had shoveled down the entire plate. "Got any more?"

"Damn, dude!" Gabe said, obviously still working on his first stack.

"Sure, honey, coming right up."

Eight pancakes later, I sat back in my chair and rubbed my stomach. "Did you add something new to those pancakes?" I asked my mom, who sat in the chair adjacent to me eating.

"No. The same as I've always made them. I read that Prozac increases your appetite and causes some changes in the taste of food."

"Yeah. I don't like the way these make me feel so groggy," I said.

"The doctor said it takes a couple of weeks for the medication to get in your system, then those groggy feelings should go away."

"I hope so."

Gabe jumped in, "I need to run by the store and get a birthday bag. Hey, this will be your first traditional Mexican birthday party."

"Why is a Mexican birthday party so special? Do you guys like throw plates or something?" I asked.

Mom patted my hand gently. "That's the Greeks, honey."

"Oh," I said.

"Anyway, you ready to go?" Gabe asked.

"Not really, but I don't have much choice, do I?"

"Nope."

Driving up to Gabe's house, I scanned the street; it was lined with at least two dozen cars. "Are all these people here for the twins' birthday party?" I asked.

"Yep."

"Dang, dude," I said, wondering if the neighbors were accustomed to the Sanchezes having such large parties.

"Most all of them are relatives. Birthday parties are traditional family gatherings for us."

"My last birthday, me and—" I stopped, not wanting to say her name. I rubbed the St. Christopher medal cross hanging from the chain around my neck recalling the night she gave it to me. She had taken me to my favorite Italian restaurant for my birthday and handed me a little box with a little blue bow on top right after dinner.

Gabe turned to me. Obviously, he saw where I was going and why I stopped. "Wait until you see the enormous piñata my dad got!" he said, deliberately pulling my mind from the past.

"Cool," I said, my voice reflecting my overall sadness.

Walking into door of the Sanchezes' house, my brows rose at the number of people crammed into the home. Gabe led me through the crowd and into the kitchen, where I heard a guitar being played in the backyard. Continuing through the sliding glass door to the outside, I beheld balloons, steamers, and the largest donkey piñata I'd seen in my life hanging from the limb of the old oak tree near the swimming pool. *Swimming pool?*

"When did you get a pool?" I asked Gabe.

"Dad had it put in last year. You'll have to come over for a swim when it gets warmer."

As we walked up to Gabe's mom, she spoke Spanish to an old woman. Upon seeing me, she stopped talking and grabbed me in a hug. "Hawk. I'm so glad you could come," she said.

"Thanks for inviting me." She let go.

"Hawk, you remember my grandmother?" Gabe addressed me. The memories of the flowerpot incident flashed though my head. He then turned to his grandmother, "Abuela, este es mi amigo, Hawk."

"Encantada de conocerte, Hawk," she said to me.

My puzzled gaze fell upon Gabe, "She said it's nice to

meet you." He lowered his voice, "Her memory is getting bad so she probably wouldn't remember you."

"Nice to meet you too," I said in a loud voice. As if raising my voice would help her understand English.

Gabe began having a conversation in Spanish with his mother, grandmother, and a couple other family members, while I stood looking around at the decorations, my eyes finally landing on two folding tables piled with birthday gifts. Feeling lost in the conversation made me wish I had taken Mr. Denny's Spanish class more seriously.

Gabe tapped my arm, breaking me out of my trance. "Do you want some punch?"

"Sure," I said, letting him lead the way to the table filled with a couple of Hispanic foods I recognized—churros and sopapillas.

He pointed to the plates. "Help yourself."

"Dude, I'm still stuffed from breakfast, but I will take a couple of those churros."

As I snacked on my churros, I spotted the twins, Miguel, or as everyone called him, Miggy, and Maria playing with some other children. As I scanned the crowd, I noticed everyone was speaking Spanish. I leaned in close to Gabe. "I have no idea what anyone is saying."

Gabe laughed and pointed to a group of men. "They're talking about my cousin Jose joining the military." His cupped his ear toward a group of ladies. "Those ladies are talking about my aunt Angelica having a new baby."

"I know casa means house," I offered up.

He widened his eyes and he slowly nodded, giving me a sarcastic grin. "Impressive."

I elbowed him playfully and chuckled. "Shut up."

"Come on, the party is about to start," he said as we moved toward an empty table surrounded by chairs. Miggy and Maria took their place as Mrs. Sanchez marched out of the house carrying a birthday cake with sparkling candles. They laid the cake in front of them and began singing a song in Spanish that was not "Happy Birthday". Gabe looked at me and grinned as he sang the song as if he knew it by heart. I shrugged my shoulders, smiled, and began humming to the very long tune. "It's called 'Las Mañanitas'," he told me after they were finished singing.

Then in my amazement they tied Miggy and Maria's hands behind their backs. He then told me to shout the word "mordida" along with the crowd, on cue. Watching in surprise, two of the guests shoved both their faces into the cake shouting the Spanish word three times.

Stunned, I turned my head to him. "What the hell was that?"

"All part of the fun, my friend." He laughed.

Next, everyone lined up for the striking of the pinata. Gabe insisted I join the queue. When it was my turn, Gabe handed me the stick and blindfolded me. His little brother Miggy spun me around. I swung and felt the stick make contact with something, hoping it was the donkey and not a human being. Everyone shouted in celebration, and I untied my blindfold to the site of the donkey's leg hanging by a thread and several pieces of hard candy on the ground. I bent down and picked up a few pieces and stuck them in my pocket.

Later, with the guests starting to leave, I volunteered to help clean up. Admittedly, for the first time in two weeks I felt my spirits somewhat lifted. Feeling a little joy, if even for a brief moment was a nice change.

Gabe grabbed a garbage bag, and we began pulling down the streamers. "Did you have fun?" he asked as he pulled a strand of paper from one of the limbs of the oak tree.

"Yeah. You guys certainly know how to throw a birthday party." I held the plastic bag open for him. "Are all your birthday parties like this?"

"Oh, no, the milestone birthdays are even bigger. Just wait until my eighteenth one next year. Now, *that* will be a party." He grinned.

"I'm looking forward to it," I said as I pulled down another streamer.

A few moments later, Miggy ran up to me. "Hawk, can you come help me build my C3P0?"

I looked to Gabe. "Go ahead. I can get this."

Miggy grabbed my hand and dragged me to the house. Halfway to the door, I turned back to Gabe and smiled. Although I hadn't seen either of the twins in five years, they warmed back up to me very quickly. Gabe and I played with them quite often when they were small. Perhaps they hadn't forgot.

After two hours of helping Miggy with his *Star Wars* Lego set and playing with Maria and her new Barbies, I was ready for a break. I left the twins and headed to Gabe's room. Entering, I spotted Gabe sitting against the headboard of his bed watching *Wheel of Fortune*, clad in a pair of green shorts and no shirt.

"Hey," he said as he spotted me. "The twins finally give you a break?" He chuckled.

"Yeah," I said, checking out his abs. "Been playing with Maria's Barbies in the dream house." I laughed.

"Maria loves for me to play dress-up with her. She likes to put her princess crown on me and pretend I'm Princess Gabriella. Funny enough, I kinda enjoy it." He winked.

"You're too much." I shook my head.

"Clash of the Titans!" He yelled at the TV. A few moments later, the contestant shouted out the answer. Gabe pumped his fist. "Boo-yeah!"

He patted the bed next to him. "Remember when we'd watch this with your granddad?"

"Yeah, he loved this show. I think he had a thing for Vanna White."

"I think you're right," Gabe said as I sat down, paralleling his position on the bed. My eyes automatically glanced to the right, studying the muscular striations on his torso. "You have killer abs," I said.

"You think?" He looked down and pointed to an area of his upper stomach. "Wish I could get this area here more defined and make this six-pack into an eight-pack."

"Crunches, I've found, are best for that area. See?" I said and lifted my shirt up just below my pecs and pointed.

He moved his finger to just above my stomach and stopped. He looked at me questioningly. "May I?"

I shrugged my shoulder. "Go ahead."

He rubbed his index finger over the bumps and ridges

of my skin, "Yeah, your muscles are definitely harder than mine." He then moved his finger to the thick brown hair that grew below my navel down to the top of my jeans. "I'm more jealous of this than the abs."

I suddenly felt a familiar tingle that ran through my body like a lightning bolt straight to the area just below his finger. I felt myself getting excited, which in my case is *very* noticeable. And, of course, he did notice.

He pointed. "Woah, looks like somebody likes that."

I shoved his hand away. "You just had to say something, didn't you?" I glared at him.

"I didn't mean anything by it."

"It wasn't funny. You can be such a jerk sometimes!" Immediately, I realized I overreacted. It wasn't his fault. I invited him to touch me. What in the hell was I thinking? Shelby hadn't been gone three weeks. Had I absolutely lost my mind? "Dude, I'm sorry. I'm so fucked up right now."

"No, it's my fault, I shouldn't have said what I said. I don't know why I say shit like that...it's like whatever pops in my head comes out my mouth."

"It's okay. Let's just forget it," I said and moved back to the bed, sitting on the edge away from him this time.

"Are you spending the night?" Gabe asked.

"Is that okay?" I asked, confident of his answer.

"Yeah. Sure."

"Thanks."

The next night, back in my own bed, I had a dream. I was

sitting on the edge of my bed when Shelby sat down beside me.

"What are you doing here?" I asked.

Her hair shimmered like gold and her eyes were piercing blue. "Why weren't you there?"

I gave her a puzzled gaze, "What do you mean?"

"You weren't at my funeral." A silver tear trickled down her cheek.

My own tears began to flow. "I couldn't, baby, I couldn't see you like that. It hurt too bad."

"You didn't even say goodbye to me," she cried.

I reached out to hold her. "Oh God, Shelby. I'm so sorry. I love you so much."

Then she disappeared.

My eyes flew open and I set up in my bed. Immediately, I covered my eyes with my palms and began bawling. A few moments later, I heard footsteps tearing down the hall. My door opened.

"Honey, are you, okay?" asked Mom. I shook my head, unable to speak. She rushed over and grabbed me in a loving embrace. I melted into her. "Shh...shh...it's okay." She began rocking me.

"I should have gone to the funeral," I cried. "Shelby wanted me there. She told me."

"Oh, honey, it was just a dream. It wasn't real. Shelby would have understood why you weren't there."

I dropped my hands and held her gaze. "Every time I close my eyes, I see her. My mind repeats 'Shelby's dead, Shelby's dead' over and over. It never ends. If I smile or laugh, it feels like I'm somehow…betraying her. What right do I have to go on living when she can't?"

"Honey, listen to me." She put her hands on either side of my face, "You *can't* stop living. When your father died, I felt the same way, but I finally realized he would not want me to stop living because of him. He loved me too much, just like Shelby loved you."

"I know, Momma. It's just I don't know if I can. I'm so scared to go back to school. Shelby and Mel's…ghosts are going to be everywhere. I'm going to be so alone."

"You won't be alone, baby. You can come pull me out of my classroom anytime you need me. You have the other teachers, your friends, and even Principal Anderson there if you need to talk. They understand."

I lowered my head. "I know."

"Honey, you can't hide in here forever," She stroked my hair.

"I know I can't. It's just…Shelby was my world. It's like I don't know what to do without her. I feel…lost."

"I know, honey. But that's why you have friends."

I shook my head and started to tear up. "I don't, Mom. Gabe is the only friend I have."

"I don't believe that. You have your friends on the basketball team. What about Eddie Davis?"

"He's the only one. Have you seen any of the rest of them around here since that day after the wreck?"

"No." She grimaced. "I don't understand that. I felt sure more of them would be coming around to see you."

"It's because they don't care."

She wrapped her arms around me, "Oh, honey, there

are lots of people that care about and love you." I laid my head on her shoulder.

The previous day, Mom kept me busy decorating our house for Christmas, and although I certainly was not in the Christmas spirit, going all out on decorations was a Keystone family tradition. The tradition required our home to be the most decorated in town. To quote Chevy Chase from *Christmas Vacation*, "Two hundred fifty strands of lights! One hundred individual bulbs per strand for a grand total of 25,000 imported Italian twinkle lights!" While we didn't have quite that many, I'm sure our house could be seen from space. Honestly, I didn't mind the work. It kept me from dwelling on my returning to school the next day. Gabe came and helped, which made the decorating go much faster than prior years. Just like he did when we were kids, he had to take control of the entire operation. When I'd call him out on it, he'd back off; but within ten minutes he was barking out orders again. Finally, I gave up and let him have his way. Admittedly, the display looked the best it ever had.

In my almost two-week absence from school, I had missed countless basketball practices and at least three games, but, honestly, I couldn't have given two shits about basketball. In fact, I had made up my mind to quit the team. Only one of my teammates came to check on me over my two weeks absence: Eddie Davis. Megan Cartwright, one of Shelby and Mel's friends, called me once to see how I was doing. The conversation was rather short because the mere mention of Shelby or Mel's name would cause both of us to break down in tears. It was basically a fifteen-minute crying marathon. The sadness of Shelby and Mel's absence at school was difficult enough to face, but the bitterness I felt for my so-called friends made me want to never go back to Pleasant High. Hell, even Gabe's friends on the Murphystown Vipers football team sent me a sympathy card. If I weren't graduating in a few months, I'd been transferring to Gabe's school in a heartbeat.

Monday morning, I pulled my car into the student parking lot and killed the engine. I stared at the high school building, dreading everything in front of me. I ran my fingers down a long strand of my hair, remembering the last time Shelby and I had walked from the main building to the cafeteria together sharing her tiny umbrella. She kept trying to hold it over my head. "Your hair is so much harder to fix than mine if it gets wet," she said to me in the downpour. "I'm a guy. I don't care how mine looks. You're more important." I'd push it back over her head. A sudden tapping on my window startled me. I turned my head to the beast of a guy standing outside.

"Hey, man, you okay?" Eddie's voice was muffled by the window.

I nodded.

Grabbing my backpack, I opened the door and stepped outside. Immediately, he grabbed me into a quick bro hug, almost squeezing the life out of me. "It's good to see you, man."

I coughed, trying to catch my breath. "Thanks."

I could see him struggling with what to say next, but he

then eyed my backpack. "Here, let me get that." He yanked it off my shoulder.

"Um...thanks," I said as he slung it over his shoulder, and we proceeded to the building.

"We missed you on the team," he said in that deep baritone voice of his.

"*You* may have, but no one else did," I snapped.

"Umm..." he said. I could see that I caught him off guard.

"You're the only person on the team that came to check on me. Hell, I didn't even get a phone call from any of the other guys," I said, not hiding my anger.

He stopped and turned to me, his face flushing red. "Are you kidding me?"

"No...I'm not."

"I told them...those fucking assholes. That pisses me off."

I shook my head. "Just forget about it. I just don't want to be here. I'm angry, sad, and just want to go home."

"I understand, dude," he said.

Entering through the dual metal doors, the hallways were packed with students from seventh to twelfth grade. Suddenly, conversations stopped and everyone turned to gawk at me with sad looks of pity on their faces. I couldn't do it. I turned around to leave and felt Eddie's huge hand on my shoulder. "Ignore them and stay behind me," he said.

He gave me a look of encouragement and I nodded. Like Moses parting the Red Sea, Eddie led the way to my locker.

As I turned the knob of my combination lock, Eddie

acted as my own personal bodyguard, folding his arms and glaring at the passing students. A few moments later, I felt arms grab me from behind. Turning me around, Megan pulled me into a hug.

"I'm so glad to see you back, Hawk," she said as tears rolled from her eyes. It was exactly what I *didn't* need at the moment.

"Meg, please don't start crying. I'm barely holding it together right now."

She pulled back and sniffled, wiping her tears away with her fingers. "I'm sorry."

"It's okay." I gave her a soft smile.

I felt a pat on my shoulder. "Good to see you, man," said Tom Price as he walked by.

"Glad to have you back," said Chris Lamb, doing the same.

Eddie seemed to take on the job as my own personal bodyguard and walked me to my first period science class, I had about a dozen or more people come up and give me words of encouragement and soon my bitterness began to subside.

I struggled through my first three classes, being unable to focus on anything my teachers were saying with my mind filled with thoughts of Shelby and Mel. Every one of the teachers, except Mr. Groover, my social science teacher told me I didn't have to make up any of the work I had missed. Of course, Mr. Groover, whom everyone hated, gave me a three-page list of assignments that needed to be completed by the end of the semester.

In fourth period Algebra, my class just before lunch, I

completely lost it. Sitting behind Shelby and Mel's empty desk, I made it all of about three minutes before I had to excuse myself to the men's room. Luckily, the restroom laid empty.

I ran to the sink and splashed my face with water several times and then stared at myself in the mirror. "You can do this, Hawk. You can do this." I tried to pump myself up to make it through the rest of the day.

About that time, the door opened and in walked Caleb Foster, one of the "smart" kids that always sat in the front row of every class I ever had with him. I honestly didn't know him that well, but he seemed like a nice guy. "Umm...you okay? Mrs. Steen sent me to check on you."

I glanced at his jeans and *Back to the Future* T-shirt. "Yeah...I'm okay."

He nodded and pushed up his wire-framed glasses. "Umm...the yearbook staff voted to dedicate this year's book to Shelby and Melanie."

"That was nice of you guys," I said, knowing he was the editor.

He looked down and shuffled his feet as the room fell silent. "Umm...if you don't have anyone to sit with at lunch, you're welcome to sit with me and my friends."

"Thanks, man, I appreciate that."

He lifted his head and gave me a timid smile. "Cool."

Somehow, I managed to make it through the rest of Algebra. After the lunch bell rang, I dragged my feet to the cafeteria. Coming out of the lunch line with my tray filled with two corn dogs, French fries, corn, fruit, and milk, I stared at the table that me, Shelby, and Mel usually sat at.

Memories of us talking, laughing, and gossiping came flooding back to me and my eyes moistened.

Just then, Eddie came up behind me. "Hey, dude, come sit with me and the guys." He motioned with his head toward the table on the opposite side of the room. I glowered at the table filled with my so-called friends, before shifting my eyes a few tables down to Caleb and his four friends. "Thanks, dude, but Caleb invited me to sit with him and his friends."

Eddie regarded their table. "Oh, yeah, dude. I get it." He glared back at our teammates.

"Thanks, man."

"Later."

I strode over to the Caleb and his friends' table. "Hey, Caleb. Is this seat taken?" I asked.

He glanced up at me. I noticed the look of surprise on his face, before he broke into a welcoming smile. "No. Have a seat. Hey, guys," said Caleb, "I think you all know Hawk." I immediately noticed the puzzled look on their faces. Obviously, Caleb hadn't told them I might be joining them and suddenly I felt very self-conscious.

"Hey," I said, willing myself not to feel completely out of place.

"Hawk, I'm not sure if you know Roger, Cameron, and Blaine," Caleb went around the table.

"Hey, guys." While I knew who they were, I'd never actually spoken to them.

"Thanks for inviting me to sit with you guys," I said to Caleb, letting the others know I didn't just take it upon myself to invade their little group.

"We were just debating who's the better Captain—Kirk or Picard. What's your opinion?" he asked as I pulled my chair up to the table and laid a paper napkin in my lap.

"Umm…that's *Star Trek*, right?" I asked.

"Yeah," he chuckled, "I guess you're not into it?"

"Nah. Not really," I said, tearing open the little packets of mustard for my corndogs. I noticed the blank looks around the table.

"That's cool. Nothing wrong with that. My brother is more of a *Star Wars* fan," he said.

"Shel—" I started, but stopped myself. "I rented one of those *Star Wars* movies one time. I remember those teddy-bear looking creatures were funny."

"Ewoks," Roger grinned, not quite sure if he was amused by my description or lack of knowledge. I felt it was the latter.

"Umm…so…what kind of movies do you like, Hawk?" Blaine asked.

"My friend Gabe and I rented *Encino Man* a few weeks ago, that was funny," I said, picking up my corndog. "You guys seen it?"

"Yeah," said Cameron, "I thought it was kinda far-fetched. I mean, two idiots finding a frozen caveman buried in their backyard in Encino, California?"

"It's Pauly Shore. It not supposed to be taken seriously. You know…'weee-asel'," I mocked his famous catchphrase.

"I thought it was funny," Roger jumped in.

Seeing that I wasn't having much luck connecting, I turned the questioning around, "So, you guys into video games? I'm pretty good at *Street Fighter II*."

"We all play *Dragon Quest*," said Blaine.

"Heard of it, but never played it," I said before taking a bite of my corndog.

"So, what other hobbies do you have, Hawk?" Caleb asked.

"Hmm," I laid my corndog down. It was plainly obvious I had nothing in common with these guys. I'm sure telling them that I enjoyed repairing broken household appliances wouldn't endear me to their little group. I thought back. "When I was younger, I liked to write short stories?"

Suddenly, all their eyes lit up, "Really?" asked Blaine. "What kind of short stories?"

"Action/adventure stories...like treasure hunts...pirates and stuff like that," I said.

"Oh yeah!" Caleb's eyes sparked with recognition. "I remember in sixth grade you won that contest Mrs. White had for the best short story. You wrote one about a bunch of kids that travel the country looking for a treasure using clues they found at famous U.S. historic sites."

I chuckled. "Yeah, *An American Adventure*, I called it. Looking back, I could have come up with a more creative title I suppose."

"I like to write short stories too," Blaine said.

Roger pursed his lips at him. "Your elf erotica stories don't count, Blaine."

I wrinkled my nose. "Seriously?"

"Blaine has this weird *Lord of the Rings* fetish," Roger said.

"He whacks off while he's writing," Caleb said in an aside to me that everyone heard.

Blaine narrowed his eyes at him. "That is a lie," he paused then grinned, "I do that afterward."

The other guys moaned and threw French fries at him. I found myself laughing for the first time that day. "Maybe we could exchange stories sometime," I joined in.

"You guys are sick." Roger shook his head.

Although I had little in common with the group, I somehow found enough to talk about to keep my mind off the current situation.

By basketball practice, I had made my mind up. I marched directly into Couch Hadley's office, bypassing the locker room altogether. All day, I had been planning my resignation and by the time sixth period arrived, my grief had manifested itself in feelings of intense rage toward my teammates.

Stomping through his open door, I slammed the resignation letter I had scribbled down during sixth period study hall on his desk. "I quit!" I yelled and turned to leave.

Coach stood up from behind his desk. "Keystone! Wait!"

I turned and pointed to the letter on his desk. "Everything you want to know is in that letter. Now, I've had a really shitty day and I'm going home." Even though there was still an hour of school left for the day, I honestly didn't care. Let them put me in detention for skipping class.

"Hawk, listen. Eddie Davis came to me this morning and read me the riot act about the team's behavior in this situation and how much we'd hurt you. It's all my fault. I told the guys to give you space and that when you're ready to talk, you would reach out to them. It was a bad decision on my part and I take full responsibility. I'm to blame for this, not your teammates."

I felt myself becoming emotional. The grief I had managed to keep under control throughout the day began to surface, "I've been through hell these past two weeks. Do you know how it feels to think my friends don't even care?"

He hung his head. "I'm sorry, Hawk. I thought you needed time to yourself."

"Well, you were wrong!" The tears started flowing again.

"I know and I sincerely apologize. Come in, close the door, and let's sit down and talk," he said.

I considered it for a moment, but my heart wasn't into it. With only two games left in the season and the fact I'd be graduating in the spring, I no longer cared about some stupid sport. "You know, Coach? I think I'll pass. I was never that good at it anyway."

"We need you, Hawk," he begged. "Come on, let's sit down and work this out."

I paused for a moment, giving his offer consideration. "Nah. I think I'm done," I turned and walked out the door before he could say anything more.

Beelining it to my car, I sat behind the wheel and had a good cry. After several minutes, I began thinking about how my entire life had been turned upside down. I wanted someone to blame and the only person that I could blame had died in the wreck along with Shelby and Mel. Suddenly, I felt a new emotion on this rollercoaster ride of grief—rage.

It was easy enough to blame some omnipotent being for my loss, that is, if I truly believed in such a being, which lately I had come to doubt. No, my rage became directed at the person I loved most in the world and who'd allowed me to build my world around her. I looked skyward and screamed, "You let me do this, Shelby, and now you leave me all alone!"

I started the engine, threw my car in reverse, and then peeled out of the parking lot, dirt and gravel creating a thick cloud of dust. I started to head home but decided to drive around awhile. I started thinking again about the future with Shelby that would never be. If I hadn't have wanted to play football that day of the accident, I could have saved us. I'm a good driver. I would have seen the truck coming at us and avoided it. Shelby wasn't the best driver in the world. If I'd never given Gabe a second chance after he came on to me, I would have been there, where I *should* have been. Had Gabe been playing me all along? Was his so-called "caring friend" all a plan to make me want him? I let him run his fingers over my abs, sleep in my bed, see me naked! That fucking sneaky bastard! Aiming my car in the direction of Murphystown, I stomped the gas.

Making it to Gabe's house in less than ten minutes flat, I pulled into the driveway; parking behind his Jeep. I got out and rang the doorbell.

A few moments later, the door opened with Mrs. Sanchez standing on the other side. "Oh…hi, Hawk."

"Hi, Mrs. Sanchez. Is Gabe here?" I tried to sound calm and rational even though my rage swam just below the surface.

"He just got home and is in his room," she said, inviting me in.

"Thank you." I entered and proceeded to march down the hall, my anger in complete control of my actions. With his bedroom door being closed, I burst in without knocking.

He twisted around having just pulled his shirt off to change out his school clothes. Fucking bastard teasing me again like some cheap whore "Hawk! What are you doin—"

Before he finished his question, I shoved him hard, causing him to stumble backward.

Immediately, his hands came up and he shoved me back. "What the fuck are you doing?" He stared at me, his face reflecting his disbelief.

Irrational and completely out of control, I confronted him. "I figured out your little plan…now that Shelby is out of the way…there's no one stopping you from getting what you want."

"What the hell are you talking about?"

"Me! This pretending to be my friend…I'm here for you, Hawk…I care, Hawk. It's all part of your little scheme to get into my pants."

He slowly shook his head. "You've lost your fucking mind."

"Oh yeah." I shoved him again.

He pointed his finger at me. "Hawk. I'm warning you. Don't do that again."

I gave him another shove.

His face flushed red. "You asshole!" He lunged at me, tackling me to the bed. A right hook across my chin stung like hell. I wrestled with him to gain control, but he outmuscled me. We rolled off the bed and hit the floor, my foot taking his nightstand lamp with us.

I got in a quick punch, striking him in the stomach, which he easily shrugged off. Just then I heard Mrs. Sanchez's voice. "Boys! Stop it! Gabriel! Hawk!" she screamed.

"What is wrong with you? Why are you acting like this?" he yelled, sitting on my chest and attempting to hold my arms down.

"Her death is all your fault." I squirmed.

"*What*?" He tightened his grip on my wrists.

"If I hadn't been so fucking selfish and wanted to play football with you, I would have been there that day and would have seen that truck coming."

His grip on my arms relaxed. "You don't know that, Hawk."

My eyes filled with tears. "I could have saved her. I know it."

"You don't. You could have died too."

"What if I did? Nobody would have cared." I began to sob.

"That's not true. A lot of people care." He let go of my wrist.

"No, they don't. I have no friends… Shelby was all I had in the world and now she's gone forever." I cried.

"Hawk. You've got friends. I'm your friend and I really do care for you. I always have and I would never do *anything* to hurt you," I gazed deep into his moistening eyes and could see he was telling me the truth. It was then I realized how crazy I had been.

"I'm so sorry Gabe. I didn't mean any of that."

"I know, buddy." Tears fell down his cheeks.

I grabbed him in a hug. Placing my head on his shoulder I cried. "I'm sorry Gabe. It's just been an awful day."

"I know." Mrs. Sanchez came around to the side of the bed where we sat hugging on the floor. "We're okay, Mama," he said to her.

I heard her sniffle before she left the room, closing the door behind her. Gabe held me until I finally managed to pull myself together.

"You want to tell me what happened today?" he asked me.

I nodded as he rose from the floor and sat down on the edge of the bed. I did the same, sitting next to him. "It was awful. No matter where I went, a memory of Shelby or Mel would flash through my head. Do you know hard it is to sit in class and stare at their empty desks, knowing they'll never sit in them again?"

"I can't imagine, buddy." He put his hand on my shoulder.

"Everybody stared at me. Giving me their looks of pity. The guys on my basketball team barely spoke to me, so I just quit the team."

"You quit the team? You love basketball!"

"I just don't care about it anymore. In fact, the basketball team, school, all of it can just go to hell. Fuck everything!"

"Hawk. Look at me," I turned and locked eyes with him, "I didn't know Shelby, but from everything you've told me, she loved you with all her heart. Do you think she would have wanted you to stop living because of her?"

I paused to think about what Shelby would say to me. "She'd tell me to get up off my ass and start living again."

He gave me a slight smile. "That's what I thought."

Shelby and I used to ask each other that stupid question that couples sometimes ask one another: "If I died tomorrow, would you go on without me?" Of course, we would always deny we would, but we both knew the truth. We were both a couple of seventeen-year-olds, of course we would.

"There's only one problem, Gabe. I don't have a life."

He furrowed his eyebrows. "What do you mean? Of course, you do."

"No, Gabe. I said it before, I built my entire life around Shelby. I neglected making new friendships, finding new hobbles, because she was all I needed to be happy. The only reason I went along with her plan for us to go to college was to be with her. I would be just as happy if we'd gotten married, got us a place together, and started a family, and never leave Pleasant. When I said she was my world, I meant it."

"Wow, Hawk. I'll be honest, that's kinda scary."

"You see why it's so hard to move on? I feel…absolutely lost. I don't even know how to start building a life without her."

"Okay. We can fix this," He stood up and began pacing in typical Gabe problem-solving mode. "First thing we're going to do is find you some new hobbies…and, secondly, some new friends."

"I like your friends that we played football with," I said.

"Yeah. They're good guys. We'll start having more scrimmage games since season is over. What else do you like to do?"

"I like to work on vacuum cleaners."

He stopped pacing and gave me an amused grin. "Seriously, dude, that's just sad."

I kicked at him with my foot. "Shut up." I smiled. "It's more fun than it sounds."

"Okay, Mr. Maytag Repairman." He laughed.

Chapter Eight

December 1992

Over the next few weeks, I fought with bouts of depression, denial, and anger. Even though I agreed with Gabe that I needed to move on, it certainly wasn't easy. Grief is such an odd beast. Although I knew Shelby was gone, my mind continued to deny it with explanations for her absence. Sometimes I'd have these mini fits of anger and start cursing the name of the drunk driver that killed her. The saddest part about him dying, is there was no way for him to be punished for murdering two innocent people. Yes, I said murdering because in my mind, driving a vehicle under the influence of alcohol was the same as shooting a gun at someone. Although I did drink on occasion, I never drove. Shelby was *always* my designated driver when we went to a party.

School life improved a little. I did not rejoin the basketball team. Coach's advice to the other players to give me space, had to be the "dumbest piece of shit advice I'd ever heard"—those words quoted directly from my mother. Within a week, Mom said it came down from the school board that all faculty and staff would be required to attend a half-day class on grief counseling. Although all my teammates apologized for following his advice, I still held a grudge against the coach. As far as my lunch hour, I found myself slowly drifting to the jock table as my teammates seemed sincere in wanting to make amends. I tried to eat with Caleb and his friends a few more times, but I ended up being bored out of mind and not able to contribute much of anything to their conversations. While the jocks could act stupid and immature, they did make me laugh and all laughter to me was a blessing.

Outside of school, I started hanging out in Murphystown with Gabe and grew closer to his friends. I'd even attended my first MHS party at our friend Chad's house. I met several new people that night, but generally stayed close to Gabe, and I certainly didn't drink. When I observed a few people that I knew were too drunk to drive getting behind the wheel, I told Gabe I was ready to leave. I pointed out a few of them, and while some of our friends went over and took their keys, I began to feel like I was policing the party, which was not my job. Not to mention the fact that I'd become extremely angry knowing that their recklessness could take someone's loved one away, which pretty much ruined the party for me.

The Friday night before Christmas, we were hanging out in Gabe's room playing *Street Fighter*. I glanced over at Gabe in his lounging attire—barefoot, shorts, and no shirt, his hair falling freely on his naked, muscular shoulders. While I always appreciated the view, it had been well over a month since I had any sort of relief, and it was getting much more difficult at times to hide that fact. Honestly, I hadn't really been in the mood, but it didn't mean I'd become asexual. Shelby and I had a *very* active sex life.

"Hey," said Gabe, his eyes glued to the game, "do you remember those kids that lived across from the school that we used to have rock fights with?"

I had to think for a moment before recalling these "fights"; I guess you would call them, with this family of four brothers and one sister. While I'm not one for name calling, they could best be described as poor white trash. We tried to be friendly with them, but things went sour when the sister took a liking to me. At ten years old, girls were icky, and no way did I want to be her boyfriend. So, when she popped the question, my refusal was met with name calling and being chased by her brothers and their pit bull, Happy. After that, we were in a constant feud with the McCoy family. No kidding, their surname was McCoy. Like the infamous feuding Hatfields and McCoys from Kentucky.

I chuckled, sweeping Gabe's character's leg. "Oh man, Cyndi McCoy. I haven't thought about her in years."

"Today her and her brother, Don, got busted at school for possession of drugs." Gabe hit my character with a chop to the stomach.

"Seriously?"

"Yeah. The police came with drug sniffing dogs and everything. Evacuated the building. It was quite the shit show." He gave me a wink. "Just think, buddy, she could have been yours."

"I can see us now, married and living in a trashy mobile home with a bunch of filthy kids in dirty diapers playing in the front yard." I smiled.

"Next to an old Chevette on blocks," he added.

I faked a gasp. "Are you implying that my car is trashy?"

He cocked his eye at me. "I don't know. Am I?"

I grabbed the pillow behind me and threw it at his head. "Asshole." I laughed.

Just then, the computer voice came through the television speaker. "Round over."

"Hey! You made me lose." He stuck his bottom lip out.

I playfully mocked him. "Poor baby."

"Hmmm...looks like I'm going to have to teach someone a lesson," he said before he leapt at me, tackling me to the floor. We began wrestling on the floor once again, only this time for fun. It didn't take long before he had me pinned once again. Admittedly, I purposefully allowed him to get the upper hand. Holding my arms down over my head, I pretended to resist. I looked up at him, his face mere inches above mine. His deep brown eyes and those luscious lips smiling down at me. The smell of his cologne with a slight mix of his body odor pleased my senses. *God, he smells good.* "Now what you going to do?" He laughed.

"Let you win as usual." I laughed. He let go of my hands and sat up, straddling my legs. Flexing his arms, he kissed each one of his biceps. "Pfft...showoff."

The view of a shirtless Gabe, sitting on me flexing caused an uncontrollable stirring in my loins. My jeans began to rise. My smile faded. "Get off me."

"I think I like it here." He continued to joke around, still oblivious as to what was happening to me.

"Seriously. Get off," I said evenly.

Just then the bulge in my jeans caught his eye and his face dropped. "Oh…sorry."

He immediately leapt off me and my face went twelve shades of red as I sat up, trying to hide my problem. Why I felt I needed to explain myself, I don't know. "Sorry man, it's been a long time…since…umm…you know?"

"I get it," he said before picking up his game controller from the floor and sitting back down in front of the television, "You want to play another game?"

"Yeah…I guess. Give me a minute." My mind began racing. Should I just come right out and tell him that I was bi and that he was right about me liking to kiss him when we were kids. I couldn't though. What would that do to our friendship if he knew? I certainly couldn't tell him I found him *extremely* attractive. I felt like shit after that day I falsely accused him of manipulating me into having some sort of sexual relationship with him. That wasn't Gabe. Never once since that day on the lake all those months ago had he made a pass at me. He was a true friend—my best friend. That being said, shouldn't I be able to talk to my best friend about anything? Would he suddenly think that he had a chance with me if I told him the truth about my sexuality? God this was so confusing.

"You okay over there," Gabe asked, repeatedly flipping the controller in his hand while he patiently waited for me.

"Yeah," I replied, before getting up and taking my seat by him once again.

"Do you want to switch characters?" he asked.

"Na. I'm good." Gabe started to press the button to

start the next game, but I reached out my hand to stop him. "Wait."

He focused his gaze at me. "You okay?"

I cast my eyes to the ceiling as I struggled to find the courage to say the words out loud. "Fuck!"

"Hawk?"

I'm just going to say it. I'm just going to say it. I turned my head to face him. "Gabe. I'm bi."

"You're...what?" I could see the confusion on his face.

"You're going to make me spell it out, aren't you? Fine. I'm attracted to girls *and* guys."

He sat stunned for a moment before the corners of his mouth lifted and he pointed his finger at me. "I knew it! You sneaky bastard! I fucking knew it!"

I pursed my lips at him, "Well, fuck you too! I just came out to you and this is what I get. Some best friend you are," I huffed.

"I'm sorry." He stopped smiling and placed his hand on my shoulder. I brushed it off. "It's just...you never acted like all my other guy friends. The kissing thing in the bus when we were twelve...none of the other guys would do that. Believe me, I tried after we stopped seeing each other. Hell, I got my first black eye trying to trick one of them into kissing me. Glad his family moved before school started and he could tell everybody."

"Now you know my secret. I didn't want to tell you because I didn't want this to affect our friendship."

"It's not. Believe me when I tell you that I would never do anything to jeopardize our friendship, especially after all you have been through. You're the best friend I've ever had, and I don't want to lose you for a second time."

"Me either."

"Good. You want me to make us some popcorn?" he asked.

"Sounds good to me."

"Be right back." He jumped up and sprinted out of the room. I hoped telling him was the right move.

Christmas 1992

Christmas Day had arrived. The day I dreaded the most because it would have been the day I formally proposed to Shelby. Jennifer and David were home and Mom planned on preparing a big family Christmas dinner. Gabe had invited me to spend Christmas with his family, but I knew it would break my mother's heart if I didn't spend it at home.

I rolled out of bed Christmas morning, slipped on some pajama pants, and made me way into the living room.

Jennifer ran to me and slung her arms around my neck. "Merry Christmas, little brother."

I chuckled. "Merry Christmas to you too, big sis." Jennifer always turned into a kid on Christmas morning, no matter her age.

I spotted Mom in her recliner drinking her morning coffee and David sitting back on the couch in his pin-striped pajamas, robe, and slippers. I found it amusing that David always seemed to dress the part of a future doctor; I half expected him to be smoking a pipe.

"Stockings first." Jennifer ran to the fireplace that held a warm crackling fire and pointed to my stocking that hung on the mantle.

"Okay." I walked over and dug into it. Feeling around, I pulled out an orange, an apple, several chocolate bars. and a very nice pocketknife. I held up the pocketknife and joked, "I feel like I'm playing the 'one of these things is not like the other' game," in reference to the *Sesame Street* song.

Jennifer smiled at her fiancé. "That was David's idea."

I flipped out the blade and ran my finger along it, checking its sharpness. "I like it. Thanks, David."

"You're welcome." He nodded, taking a sip from his coffee mug.

"Okay, okay." Jennifer jumped up and down excitedly. "You have to open the one from all of us."

"What about you guys?" I asked, feeling I had become the focus of the gift opening.

"We can open ours gifts later. You're the baby of the family," Jennifer said, almost giddy.

I pursed my lips at her. "I'm almost eighteen, I'm hardly a baby."

She walked over to the tree and picked up medium-sized box wrapped in paper covered with Santa Clauses and handed it to me. Sitting down on the floor, I ripped the paper from the box and my eyes widened. "A Super Nintendo!"

"We heard you sold your other one, and we know how much you loved it," Jennifer said from her spot on the sofa next to David.

A vision of Shelby popped in my head, but I promised

myself I wasn't going to lose it on Christmas. "I appreciate it, guys."

Making our way around the room, each one of us opened our presents. In addition to my gaming system, I received a pair of jeans, some new sneakers, and a box of haircare products, which I found rather amusing. Jennifer joked that if I insisted on having hair longer than hers, then I needed to take proper care of it. My hair had grown almost to my waist and needed a trim, but I absolutely hated sitting in a barber's chair making small talk. It was much easier just to let it go.

With wrapping paper and bows covering the floor, Mom grinned at me. "Okay. Santa has one more gift for you that he insisted on delivering it himself."

I gave her a puzzled look. Just then I heard a "Ho! Ho! Ho!" coming from the kitchen. "What did you guys do?" I laughed.

She pointed to herself. "We didn't do anything. This was all Santa's idea."

"Ho! Ho! Ho!" I heard the voice again, coming my way. Just then, my eyes beheld the sight of an Afro-Latino Santa dressed in a Santa suit, complete with the hat and white beard carrying a small red toy sack. He stopped mere inches in front of me. "Ho! Ho! Ho! Santa heard you've been a good little boy this year."

I rolled my eyes and grinned from ear to ear. "What are you doing?"

"I got a special delivery directly from the North Pole," he said, as he placed the sack on the floor and reached into it, pulling out a Border Collie puppy with a big red bow tied around its neck. My heart melted as Gabe held her up to me, and she stretched her neck up, licking my face.

"I can't believe you," I gushed at both the puppy and the fact that Gabe cared enough to surprise me on Christmas morning.

"Ho! Ho!—" He started again in a deep voice before switching to his normal voice. He looked down at himself. "Oh…shit. She just peed on me."

Everyone in the room started laughing at the sight of his now wet Santa suit. Gabe wrinkled his nose.

"I guess she doesn't need walking then," I said, petting her between the licks on my face.

"We need Christmas music!" My mom jumped up from the couch and ran to the old stereo console she'd inherited from her grandparents that I had restored. A few moments later, Bing Crosby's *White Christmas* began softly playing.

David walked over and started petting the puppy as Gabe ripped off his Santa suit exposing his street clothes beneath. "So, Hawk, what you are naming her?" David asked.

"Hmm…I don't know." Just then, the name hit me. "Lucy…her name is Lucy," I said thinking about when my dad and I would sit in the living room and watch old reruns of *I love Lucy* together. One of the few precious memories I had with my dad.

After a homemade breakfast, Mom and Jennifer stayed in the kitchen preparing our noon Christmas dinner, while David read the morning paper on the sofa. Lucy needed walking, so I asked Gabe to join me as I hadn't really had a moment alone with him all that morning. I hooked the leash to her collar and led her out the back door. Soon she started exploring while I walked a few feet behind her. I shook my head at Gabe. "You really surprise me sometimes."

"What do you mean?" he asked.

"Just I wasn't expecting you to spend your Christmas morning with me. Aren't your parents upset?"

He bent down and picked up a stick. "No. Not at all. They understood you needed a friend this Christmas."

"I did." I felt myself getting emotional. Lucy stopped and so did I. I gazed into Gabe's eyes. "I don't want to get all emotional here, but I couldn't have made it through the past month and a half without you. Thanks for not allowing me to give up."

He smiled gently. "I'd never give up on you. You're my best friend, always have been."

I kept staring into his eyes and suddenly I felt drawn to him in a way that I'd never felt before. My skin tingled all over and butterflies fluttered in my stomach. Reactions I had only experienced for only one other person in my life. I leaned in closer, as her name popped in my head—*Shelby*. That name shook me from my trance, and I jerked my head back. Gabe's eyes searched mine. I knew he knew what I was about to do.

His eyes remained locked with mine, before pointing his finger at the ground. "She went."

"Huh?" I glanced down to a small pile of doggie-doo. "Oh."

He wrapped his arms around himself and shivered. "It's cold out here. Let's go inside." I could sense his uneasiness.

"Yeah...me too," I said, my voice filled with uncertainty.

After stuffing ourselves with turkey and dressing, green beans, corn casserole, and a variety of desserts, we all retired to the living room. Gabe left after dinner to go spend some time with his family. He volunteered to stay if I needed him, but I assured him I was fine.

After he left, I felt the need to do something I'd put off for too long. Making up a lame excuse to my family that I needed to fill up my car with gas, I grabbed Lucy in my arms and headed for the car.

Driving through the main strip of Pleasant felt like driving through a ghost town. Being Christmas Day, the only business open was the Jiffy Mart convenience store. I drove past it and kept driving until I reached the Pleasant Cemetery. I cut my wheel onto the paved little road that ran through the cemetery. Parking my car, I grabbed Lucy in my arms, and we headed to the newer section of the cemetery. Winding through the sea of headstones, I finally stopped at a mound of dirt with a small metal marker posted at the foot of the mound. Wilted flowers blanketed the ground, giving me an overwhelming feeling of sadness as the cold December wind chilled my body. Hooking the leash on Lucy's collar, I placed her on the ground, noticing a couple guys on the other side of the cemetery sitting on a bench in front of another grave.

Staring at the earth before me, a sense of loss washed

over me as I stood before the final resting place of my beloved Shelby.

"Hey, babe," I said, my eyes beginning to water, "I'm so sorry I haven't come to see you. It's just been…so hard." I looked up to the sky as a tear ran down my face. "This was the day we were to start our lives together, but I guess it wasn't meant to be."

Feeling overwhelmed, I moved to the bench at her grandmother's grave and sat down. "My Shelby, I miss you so much." I covered my eyes with my hands and let weeks of pent-up grief release itself in my flood of tears that seemed to last forever.

A hand on my shoulder, momentarily broke me from my cry. "I miss her too, Hawk." I glanced back as Shelby's brother moved around to sit next to me on the bench.

I immediately grabbed him in an embrace. "She was my everything, J.J."

"I know she was. She was the best little sister I could have ever asked for," he said, letting me cry on his shoulder. Rubbing my back, he began to speak, "Did she ever tell you about the time she and I skipped school to go to see *Beetlejuice* at the movie theater in Hot Springs?"

I pulled back, wiping my eyes trying and trying to pull myself together. "No."

He smiled at me. "In high school, I was kind of a goody-goody and almost never broke the rules. One morning, I was driving us to school and she joked we should go see *Beetlejuice* at the theater instead. I'm like 'okay, let's go.' She looked at me as if I had lost my mind." He laughed. "I drove past the school and straight toward Hot Springs.

Every fifteen minutes of the drive there, she'd look at me and say, 'I can't believe you're doing this.' I think she thought I'd suddenly get cold feet and drive us back to school. We saw the movie, I bought her lunch, and we even did a little shopping. We made a pact to never tell anyone of our skip day." He paused and wiped his cheek. "It's one of my most precious memories."

"She never told me that," I said.

"Sounds like she kept her side of the pact, as did I, until now."

"Shelby always kept her word," I said. Just then my eyes widened, "Lucy!" I started looking around frantically.

He put his hand on my shoulder. "It's okay," he said calmly, "Mason has her." He pointed across the cemetery to the bench where Mason sat holding her.

"Whew!" I grabbed my chest. "She was a gift from my friend Gabe, and I've only had her since this morning. I've got work to do on my parenting skills."

He chuckled. "Gabe sounds like a very good friend."

"He is. Honestly, I couldn't have made it these past few weeks without him," I said, thinking of him dressed in that Santa suit.

"You know...Shelby was the first person to openly accept me as being gay and my relationship with Mason."

"Yeah, she was your biggest advocate."

"You know, Hawk, you're still young and one of these days you're going to find love again. When you do, don't let gender be a barrier."

"Umm..." I stammered.

"It's okay, Hawk," he winked, "Your secret is safe with me."

My eyes widened. "How did you know?"

"Oh, I sensed it. I can usually tell with people. Bi?" He raised his eyebrows questioningly.

I nodded. "Yeah."

"Mason is bi. You and he should talk sometime."

"I'd like that."

I picked the red rose lying on the ground next to me and laid it gently on Shelby's grave. "I love you, Shelby."

Chapter Nine

The holidays were over, and my last high school semester had begun. It seemed impossible that in four short months, I would be graduating—with absolutely no plans for the future. College had been Shelby's dream for our future together, not mine. I absolutely hated school and couldn't see myself suffering through another four years of it. I scored well on my ACT, enough to qualify for a full scholarship to most in-state schools, but that fact had no bearing on my decision. My problem was bringing myself to tell my mother that I might be the first person in our family *not* to go to college. My father had graduated from the University of Arkansas with a degree in engineering. There is where he and my mother met. Jennifer would so be graduating from their alma mater with a degree in finance. The Keystones were an educated lot.

Gabe, on the other hand, had his future all laid out; or, rather, his father did. Mr. Sanchez had already set him up with a job in the parts department of his largest car dealership, where he'd be shadowing the parts manager for at least six months. From there, he planned on rotating him through his four dealerships in various positions, eventually shadowing Mr. Sanchez himself. Gabe planned on managing one of the dealerships in a few years. I knew he would be successful at it, assuming he learned to control his foot-in-mouth disease.

Shelby and Mel's deaths had not been forgotten by anyone at Pleasant High. The Student Council sponsored a project to set up a memorial wall in the main hallway of the high school dedicated to former students who had passed away while attending PHS. In the two months since her death, I attended regular therapy and my psychologist diagnosed me with something she called borderline "Dependent Personality Disorder". At first, I thought she was full of shit, but after she read the symptoms, I mentally checked off about five of the seven—symptoms such as behaving submissively, relying on friends or family in decision making, needing repeated reassurance, feeling isolated or nervous when alone, and the worst, fear of abandonment. She seemed to indicate that it stemmed from losing my father at a young age. It explained why I had centered my entire being around Shelby. Regardless, I vowed to never get so wrapped up in someone that my own happiness depended on them.

It was early January, when an extraordinary weather event occurred—Pleasant received a whopping six inches of snow on the ground. Snow in Southern Arkansas was rare; perhaps once a season would we receive any measurable snow, usually an inch or two at most. Most years we did not receive any. Most people not from the South couldn't understand how a few inches of snow could bring an entire state to a complete stand-still; Arkansas did not have the equipment for quick snow-removal from the roads, which made driving treacherous. Many people would remain snowbound for days. It just so happened that the snow event occurred on a Friday night and Gabe happened to be spending the night at my house; we woke up on Saturday morning to a winter wonderland.

"Holy Shit, dude!" I screamed as I pulled back my bedroom curtain.

"What?" Gabe rubbed his eyes from his position on the other side of my bed.

I glanced back at him, clad in just a pair of pajama bottoms like myself. "Come check this out." I grinned from ear to ear.

He got up, staggered over to the window and his eyes widened at the sight. "Holy shit! That's a lot of snow."

We both locked eyes like overly excited children, "You wanna go play?" I asked.

"Hell yeah!"

Quickly, we got dressed and out the front door. A snowball fight became the first order of fun. Using the vehicles in the driveway for cover, we pounded snowballs at each other. A direct hit to Gabe's face sent him spitting dirty snow out of his mouth. He then returned the attack with a machine-gun like volley of snowballs aimed at my head. Two of them hitting me in the chest and one on my cheek.

After about fifteen minutes of being bombarded by wet snowballs, I'd my fill of that game. "Okay, I've had enough." I said shaking the snow off my knit cap.

Gabe threw his hands up in victory. "I won!"

"You did not! It was a tie."

"You're the one that wanted to stop."

"Yeah, because I'm ready to do something else."

"Admit it, I'm just a better fighter than you." He puffed out his chest.

"You always got to be on top, don't you?" I asked.

"Always." He waggled his eyebrows.

I rolled my eyes. "My fault. I left myself open for that one."

He threw back his head and cackled. "Hey. I'm always open."

I rolled my eyes. "I get it, perv."

I'd always heard that in a gay relationship, one guy was always the dominant and the other the submissive. It seemed kind of fucked up to me. I mean, Gabe had a much more dominant personality that myself. But did that mean he'd expect me to submit to him? Arguably, in all the time I'd known him I'd let him have his way ninety-five percent of the time. Sexually, his jokes clearly indicated the role he expected himself to play in the bedroom and honestly, it *really* turned me on. With Shelby, I played the dominant role in the bedroom; but in therapy I came to the realization that I let her control most of the other aspects of our relationship and by that definition, I would have been the submissive one.

"Hey, Earth to Hawk," He interrupted my thoughts.

"Oh yeah, what?" I pulled myself out of my head.

"I have an idea." I immediately recognized the evil glint in his eye as he turned them toward the old '67 Chevy that my dad had parked in the pasture behind our house years ago with hopes of one day restoring.

"Oh no, I know that look. The last time I saw it, I

ended up covered in raw sewage." When we were kids, Gabe thought we could make our own zipline out of an old rope. To make it even more fun, he decided we should stretch it over the Murphystown City Sewer Pond.

He laughed. "Hey now, that wasn't my fault. You're the one that didn't know how to tie a proper knot." That reminded me of the terror I felt when half-way over the pond, the rope came loose from the branch of the weeping willow tree on which it was anchored.

"It was your dumb-ass idea to begin with." I laughed.

"If you thought that was a dumb idea, what if we took the hood of that old car," he pointed, "chained it to my jeep, and do a little off-road sledding."

The image of Gabe in the pasture beside my house, cutting donuts in the snow, with me holding onto that old hood for dear life flashed through my head, a very stupid and dangerous idea. For a couple of seventeen-year-olds, there was only one answer. The corners of my mouth pulled upward. "Let's do it!"

Gabe laughed manically.

Finding a chain in my father's old barn, we took the hood lying beside the car, flipped it upside down and chained it to the back of the jeep. Gabe's off-road vehicle easily handled the snow and mud.

After driving the jeep over the cattleguard leading into the cow pasture, I eagerly hopped on the metal hood and laid down. "Go easy!" I yelled.

Big mistake! As soon as I said the words, Gabe gassed it and the jeep leapt forward, spinning snow and mud everywhere, covering my face in a brown slush of snow, mud, and cow dung. "You asshole!" I shouted and wiped the mud from my eyes.

He stopped, looked back and covered his mouth. "Oops!"

"You just wait until it's your turn, buddy!" I adjusted my ponytail.

My vision finally clear, he yelled back at me, "You ready?"

I nodded. This time he took it more slowly and built-up his speed. Before long, I was flying across the snow like a rocket sled on wheels. Hitting the small hills, my make-shift sled leapt high into the air and landed hard on the ground; causing me to almost lose my grip. Adrenaline rushed through my veins.

Reaching the opposite end of the field, Gabe whipped the steering wheel to the right. With the sudden change of direction, the old hood slung out wide with momentum. Losing my grip, I rolled about six or seven times before coming to land flat on my stomach, my face pressed into the snow. Gabe stopped the jeep, opened his door, and leaned out just as I pulled myself up.

"You okay?" he yelled.

Brushing off the snow on my coat, I gave him a thumbs up and he nodded.

Getting back onto the redneck sled, I tightened my grip. Soon I felt like a mechanical bull rider as Gabe started cutting circles trying to sling me off, but I held on tight.

A few minutes later, we switched position. Of course, I had to give Gabe a little taste of his own medicine. As soon as I saw he was in position on the hood, I gassed the engine and covered him with a thick layer of snow and mud. With a smile, I gave him my most insincere apology.

A little over an hour later, I caught sight of my mother standing by the gate waving us to come back to the house. Although I couldn't see her face, being so far in the distance, I knew she would not be happy with our little stunt. I thought it best to drive Gabe's jeep back slowly as he clung to the old hood.

Pulling up beside her, I killed the engine and hopped out.

She stood with her hands firmly on her hips and a sour expression on her face. "What in the world do you think you two are doing?" she asked.

I glanced back at Gabe who was rising from the sled. "Umm…a little sledding." I gave her a guilty smile.

"Hawkins Keystone. Do you know how dangerous that is?" she asked, as Gabe walked up beside me.

"I'm sorry, Mrs. Keystone," said Gabe. "It was my idea."

She ran her eyes up and down both of us. I glanced to my right at Gabe, who was absolutely covered in mud from head to toe just like myself. "Just look at you two. You're absolutely filthy!" We both stood side-by-side like a couple of guilty toddlers, reminding me of the way we looked the day we stood in front of Gabe's mom after the sewer pond stunt.

We pouted hard, pushing our bottom lips out. Her demeanor softened and she giggled. "You two look so pitiful."

Gabe and I turned to each other and started laughing.

She shook her head. "Get inside, the both of you, and get a shower. I'm about to start breakfast…and pull those filthy clothes off in the laundry room. I don't want mud tracked through my house."

"Yes, ma'am," I said as she turned and trudged back to the house.

"At least she was cool about it," said Gabe.

"Yeah," I smiled, "a lot cooler than your mom was when I fell in the sewer pond."

"I learned a whole bunch of new Spanish swear words that day."

After we untied the hood and pulled the jeep form the pasture, we headed around to the back door of the house and entered the utility room, where I began removing my boots. I watched as Gabe did the same. Soon we had stripped down to our underwear. Scurrying down the hall to my bedroom, we covered the front of our underwear with our hands in case my mother stepped out of the kitchen.

Gabe closed the door behind us, "I feel like we're ten again." I laughed, feeling sudden déjà vu.

"I know, right."

I glanced toward my bathroom and waggled my eyebrows at him. "You wanna bathe together like old times?"

He rolled his eyes, "Oh God. I've rubbed off on you."

"So *that's* what you were doing under the covers last night." I winked.

"Shut up." He laughed and wrapped his arms around his body, hopping up and down to warm himself.

"Do you want to?" I nodded my head toward the bathroom.

It took him a moment to realize I was serious. While I felt a romantic relationship was out of the question, fooling around with each fell well within my comfort zone. It didn't mean anything. Every guy had physical needs and my it had been two and a half months since mine had been met. As far as taking care of those needs solo, it had been years. With Shelby, I never needed to.

His stared at me in disbelief. "Are you serious?"

I shrugged my shoulder, "Why not?"

"Because we talked about this, and we decided that we weren't going to let the fact that we both like dudes affect our friendship."

"Come on, Gabe. This isn't going to affect our friendship. It's just two guys showering together. I mean we shower in the locker rooms with other dudes all the time."

"Yeah, but this isn't the locker room and it's just us. Not to mention the fact that your mother is right down the hall." He pointed over his shoulder at the door.

"She'll never know."

He bit the side of his lip and glanced over his shoulder. I could see he was giving it consideration.

He lowered his eyebrows. "We can't."

"I'll wash your back if you'll wash mine." I winked.

"Would you stop it?" he said in frustration. It occurred to me how the tables had turned. He rubbed his arms with his hands, obviously freezing, yet unmoving.

"Fine," I said, slipping down my underwear. "I'm getting in the shower. Do what you want to do."

"Damnit, Hawk." He jerked his head away, but I knew he'd seen me in all my glory once again. I causally walked into the bathroom and turned on the water, adjusting the knobs to get at a nice warm temperature. I grabbed a washcloth, stepped inside, and pulled the shower curtain closed. Stepping under the shower head and letting the warm water flow over me, I pushed my matted hair back over my head. A few moments later, the sound of the shower curtain being pulled back startled me. I opened one eye as Gabe stepped inside. It was the first time I'd seen him in his full glory, and he was just as I had imagined— magnificent. As he closed the shower curtain and turned to look at me, I grinned. "I can't believe we're doing this," he said.

I chuckled. "You have a very nice body by the way," I said, grabbing the shampoo bottle from shower caddy.

He eyed me up and down. "So, do you." Both of us became excited, but I did not feel embarrassed. Seeing that I wasn't concerned, Gabe relaxed a little. He eyes focused downward. "Holy shit, *dude!*"

I focused back on him and laughed. "Holy shit is right!" While I held the record in my high school locker room, Gabe probably held the record for *all* high school locker rooms. *He did say he was a quarter black.* I laughed to myself.

I grabbed the shampoo and started washing my hair, as I moved back and let Gabe get under the shower head.

A minute or so later, we switched positions and Gabe watched me rinse the soap out of my hair. As I rinsed my hair, I deliberately arched my back like one of the models in a shampoo commercial, letting the steamy water wash down my body.

I heard the shower curtain being pulled back. "I can't do this," Gabe said, starting to step out.

"What's wrong?" I asked moving from under the shower head and wiping the water out of my eyes.

"This is going to fuck everything up."

"Gabe…it's just a shower."

He stepped out of the tub and grabbed a towel, covering himself, "You know where this is going and don't lie to me and tell me 'It's just a shower'," he mocked me.

I threw my hands up. "Fine! Okay. I'm horny."

He nodded toward my waist. "Well, no shit, Sherlock."

I looked down. "I mean…you scratch my back and I'll scratch yours, if you know what I mean?"

He let out a sarcastic laugh. "No."

"Oh, come on. Isn't this what you wanted since day one?"

Shaking his head, "Maybe at first, but not now.'

"And why not?"

He stared at me in silence several moments. "Do you seriously not get it, Hawk?"

I shrugged my shoulders.

"Obviously, you don't," he said before turning to leave. When he got to the door, he turned around one last time. "You know what I want. I told you months ago."

The bathroom door slammed shut.

I fumbled through my memories and recalled a conversation we had in my car the day I showed him Shelby's engagement ring and his words.

I wonder sometimes if I'll ever find a guy that loves me as much as you love Shelby. I want to marry and have a family just like you, but I can't because I'm gay.

Suddenly, I felt like a complete ass. He didn't want just a sexual relationship; he wanted a *real* relationship. With me? The idea of something more than a sexual relationship with Gabe was laughable at best. Being all lovey-dovey with each other, like me and Shelby, just wasn't something guys do. Was it? Shelby once told me that J.J. and Mason cuddled on the couch together...I mean both of them are very masculine guys.

I finished showering and wrapped a towel around my waist before walking out of the bathroom. Gabe sat in my desk chair, waiting for his turn to finish showering. "I'm finished if you want the shower."

"Thanks," he snapped.

As he walked by me, I grabbed his shoulder. "Wait."

He stopped and gave me an icy stare. "What?"

"I get it, okay? You want more than a physical relationship. Look, Gabe, this whole bisexual side of me is something I never thought I'd have to deal with. I don't even know if I'm capable of having a romantic relationship with a guy. It's only been two months since I lost Shelby and I'm not ready to get serious with *anyone*."

"I know," he sighed, "I shouldn't have reacted the way I did. I know you're still grieving. It's just our relationship is complicated. You know? You're like my best friend, but I'm attracted to you, more than any guy I've ever been attracted to in my life."

"I know, I feel the same about you."

"Fooling around together is just going to make it even more complicated and I don't want to lose my best friend, Hawk."

"I don't want to lose mine either."

He hesitated a moment before speaking. "I think maybe we've been spending too much time together. We're together almost every day...I think...I think maybe we need to spend some time apart."

I felt myself starting to panic. Thoughts of not seeing or talking to Gabe daily filled me with fear. He'd been my rock since the day Shelby died. It would mean me being completely on my own. "Time apart?" My eyes were frozen open.

"Yeah, Hawk, you told me that your therapist said you needed to work on being self-reliant and you can't do that as long as I'm around."

My initial reaction was to drop to my knees and beg him not to leave me alone, but that would go against everything I had learned about overcoming my dependency disorder. I had to fight with every fiber of my being not to fall to pieces in front of him. "Yeah, you're right."

"I only want what's best for you, you know that?"

"I know." I held back the tears.

He nodded. "I think the roads should be clear enough for me to drive home after breakfast."

"Yeah. It's melting pretty fast." I glanced toward the sunshine coming through the crack in the curtains.

The delicious aroma of pancakes began to pour in under the bedroom door. He rubbed his stomach and gave me a slight grin. "Let's get ready and go eat some pancakes. I'm hungry."

"Yeah, sounds good." I gave him a fake smile before he walked into the bathroom and closed the door behind him. As soon as I heard the shower turn on, I grabbed the pillow off my bed, dropped to my knees and screamed into it, "Fuuuuuuuuccccck!"

Chapter Ten

February 1993

It had been almost a month since I'd spoken to Gabe. For the first few days, I felt absolutely lost for the second time in three months. In my lonely state of mind, I decided to finally open up to my therapist about my sexuality and Gabe. She said that Gabe did the right thing and that I needed to work on myself as part of my healing. I knew she was right, but it didn't make me feel any better. I truly missed my best friend.

Not wanting to be alone, I started hanging out with my mother—helping her cook, do laundry, and other chores. At night, I'd sit in the living room watching television with her, although I didn't care for "old people" TV choices like *Matlock*, *Murder, She Wrote* and *In the Heat of the Night*. When she'd ask me about Gabe's obvious absence, I told her we decided we had been spending too much time together and needed some time to "pursue other interests". I don't think she believed me, but I wasn't ready to open up that can of worms.

At least my school life had improved. I was no longer seeing ghostly memories of Shelby and Mel around every corner The guys on the basketball team felt they needed to make it up to me for not being there and pooled their money to buy me a pair of Air Jordans. While I decided not to rejoin the team, I appreciated their efforts to make amends.

One Monday morning, I stood at my locker pulling out my Chemistry book for first class when a commotion from the other end of the hall caught my attention. I turned my head toward the source of the noise and observed several students gathered in a circle, while a boy in the middle struggled picking up scattered books from the floor. Principal Anderson appeared out of nowhere and began breaking up the crowd. As the crowd dispersed, I observed him escorting one of them away, leaving the kid alone with an arm load of books and disheveled papers. Just then, my friend Caleb walked by, having come from that direction.

"Hey, Hawk," he greeted, not stopping.

"Hey." I grabbed him by the shoulder and pointed down the hall. "What happened?"

He looked back over his shoulder. "Oh. A bunch of little seventh graders got into a fight or something."

"Ah, I see, do you know who that kid is?" I looked at the blond-haired, blue-eyed boy dressed in a pair of jeans and a striped, green pull-over. With a skater style haircut, he held his hair out of his face with one hand, while trying to hold the books and pick up a pencil at the same time.

Caleb shrugged his shoulder. "Nah, if he's not a fellow nerd, I don't know him." He grinned. I chuckled. "Hey, you wanna join us for lunch today? I promise we'll try not to bore you to death with sci-fi talk."

"Maybe." I smiled.

"Cool, I'll save you a seat."

"Thanks, man."

Watching the kid scrambling to pick up his belongings, I couldn't help but feel sorry for him. Closing my locker, I proceeded toward him.

"Fucking redneck assholes," the kid muttered under his breath as he managed to grab ahold of one of the many pencils on the floor.

I bent down and picked up a couple and held them out for him. "Here you go."

He cocked his head and eyed me suspiciously. It took a few moments before he finally grabbed them. "Thanks," he grumbled. Seeing him up close, I realized I'd seen him around campus. Being a small school, seventh through twelfth grades were all housed in the same building.

"No problem. What happened?" I asked as he bent down to pick up another pencil, his foot hitting it, causing it to roll under the locker.

"Fuck!" he cursed.

"Sorry," I said, noting his free use of swear words.

He groaned as he reached to the very back of the lockers and came up with his prize. "Sorry, dude. I'm not trying to be an ass. It's just been a shitty last two days."

"I see," I replied, "I'm Hawk, by the way."

"Yeah, I know who you are." I could tell his voice still held residual anger but softened a little when he saw that I meant him no harm. "I'm Jude."

"Hey, Jude," I said in a sing-song voice, unable to resist. He gave me a hard stare. "Sorry, I'm sure you've heard that one before."

"Only a few thousand times." He pushed his hair back over his head.

I glanced down the hall, catching sight of the group of students that had been bullying him.

He followed my eyes and yelled at them, "Assholes!"

I stared at him a moment, trying to recall where I'd seen him. "Wait! I've seen you. You play on the seventh-grade boys basketball team."

"Did play. I quit," he said, as he began stuffing his things back into his locker. I recalled walking through the gym once to see coach and spotted him playing with the other seventh grade boys. For a kid, I thought he handled the ball well.

I grinned. "So did I."

He stuffed the last of his books into the locker. "Why? I've seen you play. You weren't the worst player out there."

"Gee. Thanks."

"Sorry, dude. Sometimes whatever pops in my head comes out my mouth."

Gabe popped in my head. "Yeah, I have a friend like that too. Nah, I quit because I just lost interest." I didn't feel it necessary to go into any details.

"What about you?" I asked.

He shut his locker and turned around. "The players and the coach are all a bunch of douchebags."

"Agree with you about the coach," I said, recalling his stupid piece of team advice to "give me space". Just then, I noticed a sheet of spiral notebook paper with the words *Jason's Adventure in Atlantis (working title)* lying on the floor in front of the lockers. "Is that yours?" I pointed.

He aimed his eyes down and quickly snatched it up. "Oh. Yeah."

I thought back to when I used to write my stories in sixth grade. "You're a writer?"

"Sorta," he said, not offering up any more information.

"That's cool. I used to write too. Mostly adventure stories," I said.

His eyes flashed. "Really? Like sci-fi stuff?"

"Nah, not really sci-fi, more like fantasy adventures, I guess you would say."

"*Lord of the Rings* kind of stuff?" he asked.

"Yeah…God, I haven't read those books since I was in elementary school. I should read those again sometime. They're so good." Reading was another hobby I'd long given up.

"I have them, plus *The Hobbit* too, if you ever want to borrow them?"

"Yeah. I may do that," I said, scanning down the hall for the kids that had been bullying him and feeling the need to act as his bodyguard. "Umm…do you have a class you need to get to?"

"Yeah…English…Mrs. Keystone. She sucks," he said. Immediately, I recoiled my head. "I'm kidding, dude, I know she's your mother. She's actually cool."

I chuckled. "Most of the time, until she catches you doing something stupid like doing sledding on a car hood tied behind a jeep."

He laughed. "You did that?"

"Yeah. Me and my friend Gabe." For some reason, I felt the need to look out for him. I looked down the hall, which was starting to clear as people made their way to their classes. "My class is down that way too…I'll walk with you."

"Umm…okay." He scanned the hallway then fidgeted.

"Don't worry, if those assholes come back, I'll be ready for them," I said.

He puffed out his chest. "I can take care of myself. I don't need protecting."

At five-three and maybe a hundred pounds, I couldn't see him being able to take on five bullies. "I never said you did. I just was interested in hearing about the story you're writing."

"Oh," he seemed to perk up as we began walking, "yeah. It's about this boy that finds the remains of Atlantis and ends up getting transported back into time before it was lost."

"That's cool."

He shrugged his shoulder. "Yeah, I write these for myself, but I hope to one day get them published."

"I think I need to break out my old writing notebook," I said as we stopped in front of my mom's classroom. She waved through the window of the door, and I did the same.

He pointed over his shoulder. "Here I am."

"Okay. I guess I'll see you around."

"Yeah," he said as he walked into the class.

"Hey, Jude," He turned back around, "don't make it bad. Take that bad song and make it better," I said, unable to resist quoting one more line from the Beatles' song.

He pursed his lips. "It's 'sad song and make it better'. If you're going to make fun of my name, at least get the lyrics right."

"Won't happen again." I laughed as I started walking away.

At lunchtime, I exited the food line with a tray full of meatloaf and mashed potatoes. I stopped and scanned the two table options—the jock table or the nerd table. *God, I miss my lunches with Shelby and Mel.* Lunchtime was still the most difficult part of my school day. I couldn't help but look at the now empty table where I once sat with them. Since their death, no one sat at the table. It was if it had become a monument to their memory.

Shaking the memories from my head I tried to focus on my choices once again. Listen to a forty-five-minute conservation about *Star Trek* or jocks rating girls by boob size. Neither sounded fun. Then in the midst of the cafeteria jungle, I spotted a lone Jude sitting at a table by himself. I smiled and walked over.

"Is this seat taken?" I asked.

He looked up nervously. "Umm...no." he said. I noticed the only item on his plate that had been eaten was the meatloaf.

"How's the rest of your day going?" I asked, seeing that he looked bothered.

He shrugged his shoulder without saying a word.

"Is this your first year here at Pleasant," I asked, sitting down across the table from him.

"Yeah," he replied, picking up his small carton of milk and taking a drink.

"Where you from?"

"Gillette," he answered. I thought back to the only time I'd been to the small town in Southeast Arkansas known for its annual Coon Supper. The supper being a gathering of people from all over the state coming together to dine on various dishes made with raccoon meat. The event was a must-attend for local and state politicians campaigning for office. President Bill Clinton himself attended many times while governor of Arkansas.

"Ever go to the Coon supper?" I asked.

"A few times," he said, stirring his uneaten mashed potatoes with a fork.

He looked at his former teammates sitting at a table across the room. Obviously, something happened between them. Just then, a couple of them pointed and snickered at him.

"Bastards," he muttered under his breath.

"What's their problem?" I asked.

"They're a bunch of inbred bigots." He laid his fork down. "Look, dude. I know everybody likes you and if you want that to continue, you probably don't want to be seen with me."

I crinkled my brow. "Why would you say that?"

"Because you don't want to be seen hanging around with a little faggot," he said, his voice filled with anger.

"Dude. Firstly, I couldn't give a flying fuck what a bunch of seventh graders think about me and secondly, that name-calling shit just shows how immature they are. Ignore them." I picked up my fork.

"What would you say if I told you it was true?" He squinted his eyes at me.

"That you're gay?"

"Yep,"

I shrugged my shoulder and dug into my mashed potatoes. "Congratulations?"

He recoiled his head. "Seriously? It doesn't bother you?" I admit, it shocked me that two people had now openly admitted it to me they were gay, seemingly without reservations. Just thinking about announcing to the world that I was bi scared the hell out of me.

I decided to jump right to the question. "So, what happened with those guys?" I pointed at the table causing trouble for him.

"I told that bitch Leasa Greenwald in confidence that I thought Peter Lamb, one my teammates was cute. I thought she and I were friends and that I could trust her, but she went and told her friends and before you know it it's all over school. Then the guys on the team cornered me about it in the locker room. I denied it, but then a few days later I got caught checking him out by one of the other guys. God, if only I'd kept my head down. After that, shit hit the fan. They wouldn't have anything to do with me. I finally had to quit the team. That fucker Hadley didn't do shit. 'It will all blow over' he assured me. Bullshit."

Coach Hadley officially moved to the top of my most hated teacher list; stealing the spot from Mrs. Clark, my skinny-assed fourth-grade teacher, who seemed to take an instant disliking to all the overweight kids including me. "Hadley is a joke. Dude, I'm sorry."

"And now I'm a social pariah." He slumped in his chair.

Many times, I'd wondered what would happen if my secret was discovered. Seeing Jude only reinforced my worst fears. I would be a social outcast, not only at school, but in the community at large. J.J. and Mason were right to wait until they had moved away to come out. I honestly couldn't imagine the hell they would have endured if they had remained in Pleasant, including being avoided by the townspeople, local pastors openly condemning their lifestyle from the pulpit, and even acts of violence committed against then, just for being themselves. Being openly gay in the Conservative Christian South in 1993 would be social suicide. While I wanted to reveal my secret to Jude, I couldn't trust him, at least not yet, but I could support him and be his friend.

"I'm sorry, dude. If it's all the same to you though, I'll just finish eating here," I said.

He perked up. "You aren't worried people will think you're gay too?"

I chuckled. "I was going to marry the Homecoming Queen next summer. What do you think?"

A smile slowly formed on his face, "I see your point."

With Gabe and I taking a break from each other, I had absolutely nothing to do after school. Should I? What the hell, the kid needed a break. "If you're not busy after school, you wanna come over to my house and shoot some hoops?" I asked.

His face lit up. "Seriously?"

"Yeah, I miss play b-ball."

"Yeah, man, that would be great!"

"Cool. Meet me in the student parking lot after school."

I leaned against my Chevette, having removed my winter coat and thrown it into the backseat. Arkansas weather had to have some of the craziest weather on Earth. A few days ago, we had an inch of snow, today we were pushing seventy degrees. I sat down on the hood, just to make sure that Jude spotted me. The small patch of dirty snow lay beneath the oak tree a few feet in front of me became the focus of my attention while I waited. For some reason, it seemed so lonely to me, like the last vestige of an event that affected everyone's lives for a brief moment, but as with anything, time swept it away. My mind drew the parallels to Shelby and Mel's deaths.

"Hey!" I heard a voice, pulling me from my depressing thoughts.

Looking up, I spotted Jude walking my way, pushing the hair from his eyes. "Hey, man," I greeted.

"Hey," he said.

"You ready?"

"Yep."

I moved around my car and stepped into the driver's seat, and Jude flopped down in the passenger seat. Starting my engine, my CD began blaring Toad the Wet Sprocket and I turned down the volume, "Sorry. I like it loud." He looked around the inside of the car and back at the CD player. His face reflected his amusement, "I know what you're thinking, why do I have a CD player in this old piece of shit car?"

He laughed. "I was kinda wondering."

"I have my future brother-in-law to thank for that. This was my sister's car and he had a professional sound system installed where he could listen to his classical music in the 'clearest possible sound'."

"So, you can put lipstick on a pig, but it's still a pig," he shrugged his shoulder.

"Ooh…that was a low blow." I laughed, reversing out of the parking spot. He certainly was a sassy kid.

"I'm kidding dude," he said, pulling off his jacket.

"I know."

The car went silent for a moment. "I'm sorry about your girlfriend," he said, catching me off guard.

"Oh…yeah…thanks."

He turned his head to me. "I'm sorry, I shouldn't have brought that up."

"No, I actually appreciate you saying something." Since the accident, I noticed most people tried to avoid the subject of Shelby completely, and I hated that. At first, I thought they'd just assumed I'd forget about her, but after a while I realized they were afraid that by mentioning her name that I'd have some sort of emotional breakdown. Several times, I'd been with a group of friends at school, and we'd all be chatting, then I'd drop Shelby's name in casual conversation and everyone would go completely silent.

"It must be hard," he said.

"Sometimes. It's been three months, and I'm doing okay."

"My mom died when I was ten," he said, rubbing his hands on his legs.

"I'm sorry."

"My dad started dating again within three months."

"Really?"

"Yeah," he pushed his hair out of his eyes, "got married again within six months."

"That was fast! Are they still married?"

"Na," he said, "they got divorced last year."

"I'm sorry."

"Don't be. She was a bitch. She always made me feel like she didn't want me there. Not to mention she had a serious hoarding problem."

I chuckled. "Hoarding? Seriously?"

"Dude. You should have seen our house. She'd go to thrift stores and bring home shit and just pitch it down somewhere. There were bags of new clothes stacked in the corner of the living room that still had the price tags on them. She'd never wear them; she bought them just to have them. That's what ended their marriage. My bedroom was the only room in the house that didn't have her shit stuff piled from floor to ceiling. Oh, she'd try to put stuff in my bedroom when I was at school, but when I'd get home, I'd take it and throw it out the back door. Yeah, she didn't like that," he laughed.

"Wow. So, I take it you and your dad moved here after the divorce?"

"Yeah. Dad got a job at the chicken plant in Murphystown. We moved to Pleasant because my grandparents live here. We've been living with them since last summer."

"I see. It sucks having to leave all your friends and start all over here, only to have all this shit happen."

"It does. I guess if worse comes to worst, I can go to Murphystown school where no one would know about me."

"So does your dad know? About you being gay and all."

"He does. I pretty much had to tell him after all the shit went down here at school." He shrugged his shoulder slowly. "He seems okay with it. I'm sure it isn't what he'd wish for. I mean what parent wants a gay kid? But he's been cool about it so far."

"That's pretty amazing. I know Shelby's father had a hard time when her brother came out."

"That sucks, but at least he didn't throw him out."

"True." I thought about poor Mason, but Mr. Thompson was always an ass. He was the main reason I quit my part-time job at the hardware store, ordering me around like a drill sergeant.

Pulling into my driveway, I parked so as not to block the basketball net.

"Nice house," Jude said, as we both got out of the car.

I stared at our brick home. "Thanks."

"Try squeezing four people into a tiny house with one bathroom and a grandpa with a weak bladder. I have to schedule my shits."

I howled.

Walking toward the open garage, I pointed. "The

basketball is over there in the corner. I'm gonna run in and change clothes."

"Cool," he said.

I ran into the house and put on a pair of basketball shorts, some old Converses, and a tank top before returning. I saw that Jude had gotten the ball and was getting into position to shoot it, from about ten feet from the basketball net. Unable to resist, I ran up, stole the ball from him, and went in for a layup, making the basket. Almost immediately, he grabbed the rebound, ran back and shot a three-pointer, scoring.

"Nice," I said as I took control of the ball, dribbling it away from the basket. Suddenly, he came flying around me and swatted the ball from my hand. Grabbing it, he stopped a few feet from the basket and shot a two-pointer.

He gave me a wry grin as he walked away from the basket, leaving me to retrieve the ball. "Oh, so this is how it's going to be?" I ran after it.

On the next play, I made a two-point shot and scored. "Four-five."

He immediately grabbed the rebound dribbled back and made another three-pointer. "Four-eight."

"Damn, dude, what's with you and those three-pointers?" I laughed. He strutted around the driveway as if he were Michael Jordan. Over the next three minutes, he outscored me twenty-one to sixteen. He was a damn good player, much better than myself. I pulled off my tank, wiped my forehead with it and pitched it onto the hood of my car.

He stood beneath the goal dribbling the ball like some

sort of pool hustler waiting for his next sucker. "Ready for another?"

"I guess," I said. Fifteen minutes later, he had beat me again. This time twenty-one to ten. He'd worn me out "Okay, I need a break."

"How do you like having your ass handed to you by a thirteen-year-old?" He winked.

I pointed at him, thinking of Gabe. "You...sound just like someone else I know."

Walking over and grabbing a couple of folding lawn chairs from the carport, I set them up before grabbing a couple Gatorades from the fridge. We both sat down, my ponytail dripping wet with sweat, and I noticed that Jude kept cutting his eyes at me checking me out. I decided to rib him a little. "You enjoying the view?" I smiled, taking a swig of my drink.

"I...I..." He turned his head in the complete opposite direction, taking a drink.

"I don't care, dude. Look all you want."

He turned his head back around and gave me a good once over. "How did you get that ripped playing basketball?"

"I do weight-lifting too." I pointed to the house. "Got some gym equipment inside."

"I'm skinny." He looked down and pulled on his oversized shirt.

"Playing basketball burns a lot of calories. You need to eat more," I said.

"It's my grandmother's cooking. Most Southern grandmas are known for their great cooking. Not mine. She rolls her pork chops in cornmeal." He wrinkled his nose. "Who in the hell fries pork chops in corn meal?"

"I never heard of that. Mine always uses flour."

He threw his hands at me. "Exactly!"

Just then I spotted my mother's Buick pulling into the driveway. She pulled it up beside my car before getting out with her satchel full of schoolwork. "Hey, boys," she greeted.

"Hi, Mrs. Keystone," said Jude.

"Hello, Jude. I wasn't expecting to see you here."

"Hawk invited me over to play basketball," he said.

"I see." She looked to me and let out a sigh, which was her sign that she had a rough day at school.

"Bad day?" I asked.

"That eighth-grade boys' class. They're about to drive me crazy. They won't shut up. Laughing and whispering all during class. One of them threw a paperclip and hit me in the back of the head today while I had my back turned." She shook her head.

"Take them all outside and bust their behinds with Principal Anderson's paddle." I grinned.

"I wish I could…anyway…I am going to go inside, relax, and have me a cigarette and little toddy." She then pointed at Jude. "You didn't hear that."

Jude laughed. "Don't worry, miss. I won't tell."

After Mom went inside, I cocked my eye at Jude. "One more game?"

"Sure," he said and stood up.

A half hour later, we sat at the kitchen table with my mom eating Oreo cookies and drinking milk, while she sipped her drink. I glanced at Jude and then at Mom and remembered the story he had written that fell out of his locker earlier in the day.

"Hey, Mom, did you know that Jude writes short stories?"

"No. I didn't," she looked at him, "but I definitely think you have a talent for writing from what I've seen with your essays."

"Thanks, Mrs. Keystone," he said. "Hawk says he likes to write too."

She gave me a gentle smile, "Do you remember when you won that Easter basket full of candy in second grade for the best Easter story?"

I laughed. "Yeah, I wrote a take-off of *Goldilocks and the Three Bears* except there were three chickens and a bunny rabbit."

"It was so precious," she gushed. "I still have it in a drawer somewhere. Maybe you two should do a book together."

I moved my eyes to Jude. "That's an idea."

"Perhaps. Right now I need to focus on getting through the next five years of this school shi…. Sorry." He looked at Mom.

Mom reached over and patted his hand. "It's okay, Jude, I heard what happened and I think it's just awful. In fact, I'm close to telling a few of your teammates and Mr. Hadley off."

My brows lifted. I knew my mother was fairly liberal, but I never knew just how liberal. Even the thought of coming out to her as bisexual terrified me. Not that I believed she would ever throw me out or anything, but I loved my mom and I know I couldn't handle her rejection. At least now I knew she was open to it.

"It's okay. What's done is done," he said.

"If you ever need anything or just want to talk, my classroom door is always open," she said to him.

"Thanks, Mrs. Keystone." He smiled.

Just then I heard a vehicle pull up in the driveway and a car door slam. "Sounds like we have company, I'll see who it is." I got up to answer it, preparing to slam the door in the face of another vacuum cleaner salesman.

Opening the door stood a very fit blond-haired man in a button-up shirt and jeans. "Hello…umm…Jude wouldn't happen to be here, would he?"

"Umm…yeah," I said.

He held out his hand, "I'm Doug Campbell, Jude's father."

"Oh…Nice to meet you…I'm Hawk…Keystone." I shook it.

"Jude's grandma said I needed to come pick him up."

"I see. He's in the kitchen with my mom. We're having a snack." I ushered him in.

Leading the way to the kitchen, Jude looked up with surprise. "Dad, what are you doing here?"

"Your grandma said you called and needed me to come get you."

Jude sighed. "I called to tell her that I'm at Mrs. Keystone's house and that Hawk would bring me home later and not to fix me a plate for supper. She mixed it up… again."

He chuckled. "Yep, she certainly did." He then looked at my mom and his face lit up with recognition. "Livvy?"

"Doug!" She jumped up and ran to him throwing her arms around him in a hug. She then stood back. "My God. I haven't seen you in years! Where have you been hiding?"

"Wait," I interrupted, "you two know each other?"

Mom looked at me, "Doug and I went to high school together." She looked back at Jude's father, checking him out. "You haven't changed a bit since high school."

He rubbed his chin. "I don't know about that. Got more grey than blonde these days." He then ran his eyes over my mom. "But you…you haven't aged a day. Still the prettiest girl in Pleasant."

"Oh, now, Doug," she blushed, "you always were a charmer." Was my mother actually blushing? I'd never seen her blush in front of a man. I looked on with fascination as they both remained silent staring at each other like two lovestruck teenagers. Finally, my mom snapped out of it. "Tell me, where have you been all these years?"

Mom pointed at the empty chair between she and I, and Doug sat down. "After we graduated high school, I went to work for Tyler's Poultry. They moved me to their Eastern Arkansas plant shortly thereafter. Got married to a girl from Gillette and we had Jude, then she passed away three years ago. Got remarried, but we divorced about a year ago. Still with Tyler's Poultry. Last summer they moved me back here to be the controller of the Murphystown plant. That's pretty much the past twenty-five years of my life in a nutshell." He chuckled. "What about you?"

"So…as you know, I went to the University of Arkansas

to get my education degree. That's where I met my late husband. We got married, had a daughter, Jennifer, and Hawk, of course. Bob died when Hawk was five. I remarried a few years later, but it didn't work out. Been teaching English at Pleasant School for the past twenty-five years," Mom laid out her life story in about four sentences.

"Sounds like we've both had some losses in our lives." He frowned.

"Yeah, but it makes us stronger, I suppose," she said, still looking as though she was absolutely mesmerized by Jude's father. "I never put two and two together that Jude was your son. I should have guessed it with his last name being Campbell...I can see the resemblance now."

He chuckled. "Yeah. He's a chip off the old block."

"He's a great student, you should be very proud of him." She looked to Jude with admiration.

"I am." Doug followed her eyes.

The room fell silent as they looked back at each other and stared into each other's eyes. I certainly sensed some sort of connection. A few seconds later, they began talking about their former classmates. I looked at Jude and shrugged my shoulder. "You want to go play Nintendo or something?" I asked in a low voice.

He smiled. "Sure."

We both got up and went to the living room with neither of our parents even noticing as they chatted away.

Valentine's Day 1993
Sunday morning, I work up with Gabe on my mind. I

missed my best friend terribly. Jude and I had started hanging out more over the past couple of weeks, but it wasn't the same. Don't get me wrong, Jude was a hilarious kid and fun to be around, but Jude was thirteen and I was almost eighteen. I felt more like a big brother than a best friend.

I sat up in bed and ran my hand through my now shorter hair. Shelby always liked it long on me and never wanted me to cut it. In fact, it hadn't been cut since eighth grade, and it now hung all the way to my waist. Jude tagged along with me to the Hot Springs mall the prior day and helped me pick out a style and I walked out of SuperCuts with a medium-length skater cut—head buzzed on the sides, parted in the middle, straight locks hanging down just below my ears.

Reaching to my side, I gave Lucy a quick belly scratch and grabbed her leash off my nightstand to take her outside. She gave me a happy yelp as I picked her up and sat her on the floor, attaching the leash to her collar.

Pulling on my hoodie and slippers, I headed to the back yard. As I walked around the yard, I couldn't help but think about Gabe. Wondering what he'd been up to this past month. When he decided we should take a break from one another, he wasn't kidding. I thought I might get at least a phone call from him, but nothing. How could he forget about me so easily? It hurt. I replayed that last conversation with him in my head so many times. Admittedly, I completely misjudged him, thinking he wanted a "best friends with benefits" arrangement. He wanted a relationship and, at the time, I couldn't give him that. Even now, a month later, I still felt I couldn't give him that, though I felt I *might* be ready to give dating a try. Dating a guy? I didn't know if I was ready to face that side of me. I saw the shit Jude had to deal with on a daily basis being out—the jokes, the name-calling, the cruel things the other boys did to him like taping girls' panties to his locker with his name written on them. Mentally, I wasn't ready to deal with that if word got out about me and Gabe.

Walking back inside, I entered the kitchen, where Mom sat drinking her morning coffee.

"Hi, honey," she greeted me as I went to the coffee machine. I spotted an enormous bouquet of roses in a vase on the counter.

I pointed and grinned. "Doug?"

A few days after Jude's father and my mother became reacquainted, my mother called me into the living room for a talk. Doug had asked her out on a date, and for some reason she felt she needed my approval before she'd accept. Mom had not dated much since her and Bruce divorced. Her marriage to Bruce always seemed more like a business arrangement than a real marriage. I realized later, she probably married him because she felt Jennifer and I needed a father figure in our lives after our dad passed away. After Bruce, she became very picky on who she would go out with. Pleasant was not known for its wide selection of eligible bachelors. The ones that weren't married were either too old, had no job, or had substance abuse problems, with alcohol and methamphetamines being huge problems in our town. Of course, I approved. I wanted my mother to be happy. She then revealed to me that she and Doug had been high school sweethearts for a brief time. When I asked her why they broke up, she admitted it was her fault. She had it in her mind to go off to college and see the world, while Doug wanted to stay close to home. Ironically, she met my father in college and ended up back in Pleasant immediately after school, and it was Doug that left Pleasant.

She shook her head, sipping her coffee. "He sent those to me for Valentine's Day. He has the tendency to go overboard with the gifts."

"Are you complaining?" I took my cup and sat down across the table from her.

"Not at all." She grinned.

"I've never seen you like this." I blew on my coffee.

"Like what?"

"You know? In love."

"Pfft. Love. We've been on a few dates." She blushed.

I nodded. "Yep. I think your face says it all."

She reached across the table and slapped my hand playfully. "Now stop that. What are you doing today?"

I noted how she quickly she changed the subject. "I don't know," I replied.

"You and Jude doing something again today?"

"Nah. I think I may go for a hike or something,"

"You should invite Gabe to go with you. I haven't seen him around in weeks." I could see where she was going.

"He's probably busy."

"You never know unless you ask him. The phone is right there." She pointed to the telephone hanging on the wall.

"I'm good."

Her face became serious. "I know it's none of my business, but did you and Gabe have some kind of falling out that day it snowed."

"No," I snapped.

"Obviously, something happened. You two had been together nearly every day after Shelby's accident, then suddenly it just stopped. Did you two have a fight?"

I huffed. "I told you. He and I decided we were spending too much time together and neglecting the other parts of our lives, so we agreed it best to spend some time apart. That's it."

She cocked her head, eyeing me suspiciously.

"Mother!" I stood up. "Enough…I'm going hiking. I'll see you later," I said, stomping out of the room. I pulled on my hiking shoes and got in the car as fast as I could.

I parked my car in the gravel parking lot just below the dam. Being a Sunday morning in February, the area stood completely empty, just as I was hoping. A nice long hike to gather my thoughts was exactly what I needed. I grabbed Lucy from the passenger's seat and hooked the leash to her collar. Stepping out into the fifty-degree weather, I pulled the hood of my hoodie over my head and placed Lucy on the ground. The peacefulness of my surroundings calmed my anxiety.

I decided to hike along the trail that ran along the high banks of the damn spillway. That trail had always been my granddad's favorite because in one section the ruins of the old gristmill could be seen beneath the water of the riverbed when the water was low. As it happened, I caught it at a time when the dam was not generating electricity and stopped to study the hundred-year-old connected timbers lying on the bed of the river. I recalled the memory I had of mine and my granddad's last visit to this spot when I was eleven. Gabe came along and we snuck away to play in the waters of the spillway. Granddad almost had a heart attack when he saw us. *"If that dam starts generating you boys could drown. Now get out of there!"* Gabe and I just laughed as we trekked back up the bank, soaked from head to toe. That was the same day that the brakes went out on Granddad's '63 Dodge on the way home and he circled his yard until the car came to a stop, not phasing him one bit.

The sound of a car door slamming in the distance shook me from my thoughts. I glanced up to the parking lot, but could not see a vehicle behind all the trees. Focusing my attention back on the water, my eyes caught sight of a shiny object near the riverbank. Letting my curiosity get the better of me, I tied Lucy to a tree and scanned the area, noting the sign on the metal railing warning visitors of the dangers of wading in the waters of the spillway. Deciding to take a chance, I confirmed no one was around before I climbed over the railing and began hiking down the embankment.

Standing along the spillway bank, I reached into the frigid water, prying a shiny round metal object about six inches in diameter from the riverbed. Picking it up, I examined the embossed metal that read *Royston's Grist Mill 1869*. "Holy shit!" I said to myself.

Just then, a voice startled me from above, "If that dam starts generating you could drown. Now get out of there!" At first, I thought my grandfather's ghost was reaching out to me beyond the grave, but shooting my head up, I spotted the familiar eyes of a living being bent over the railing and peering down at me.

"Gabe?" I yelled, completely caught off guard.

"What are you doing?" he yelled back.

I held up the metal plate, twisting it in my hand, before climbing back up the steep embankment. Reaching the top, I stepped on the bottom rung of the railing and Gabe grabbed my hand helping me over.

"What are you doing here?" I asked.

"I don't know. I woke up this morning with the feeling you were in danger. Suddenly, the image of water bursting through a dam popped in my head. I just knew I had to get here, fast," he said, his face very tense.

My jaw dropped. "Seriously?"

The corners of his mouth lifted slightly. "Nah, dude, actually I called your house, and your mom told me you went hiking and I guessed you were here."

"Haha, very funny."

"You were always so gullible." He laughed. Obviously, his mood had made a complete one-eighty since we last spoke. "What did you find?"

I held up the plate. "Check it out."

He took it from me. "Oh man, this is old. Holy shit, 1869! Your grandad would have flipped over this," he said, examining the front and back of it.

"Yeah, he was so fascinated over this place."

"What are you going to do with it?" He handed it back to me.

"I don't know. It feels wrong just keeping it. I may see

if the Lewis County History Society wants it for their museum."

"Good idea." He spotted Lucy tied to the tree near behind me. "Dude, she's grown since I last saw her."

"Yeah," I went and untied her leash, "she's growing fast."

He bent down and stroked her head. "You're a good girl…aren't you, Lucy?" He looked up at me. "I like her new collar."

"Yeah, I bought that for her yesterday at the pet store."

"It's cool." He continued to pet her, obviously delaying whatever he wanted to say to me. I certainly wasn't in the mood for small talk after he abandoned me over a month ago. "How you been doing?"

"I'm good. You?"

"Good." He stood up. "How's school?"

"Okay," I said, my frustration building.

"Cool. Your mom doing okay?"

I huffed in exasperation. "Gabe. What is this?"

"What's what? I'm just catching up. It's been over a month since—"

"—you quit talking to me?" I completed his sentence.

"I was going to call you. I've just been busy working at my dad's dealership and just haven't had—"

"Don't bullshit me, Gabe." I cut him off.

He lifted his eyes and sighed. "Fuck. You're not going to make this easy, are you?"

"Why should I?"

"Okay. Fine. Maybe pushing you away wasn't the right

move, but you have to understand how hard it is for me to be around you and not be able to act on my feelings."

I crossed my arms in front of me. "And what feelings are those?"

He hesitated a moment before speaking. "These kind," he said before he rushed forward, grabbed the back of my head, and pressed his lips against mine. My initial reaction was to pull away, but I didn't. In fact, I pressed back with the same passion. God, his lips tasted so good. The hairs of his thin mustache tickled my upper lip, make me realize that for the first time in my life I was kissing a dude. Pulling away, he took in a deep breath. I stood blank, letting his actions sink in. "I shouldn't have done that."

I shook myself from my trance. "No...no...it's okay. It's just...I wasn't expecting it."

"I'm sorry I pushed you away. I...I had a dream last night that you had found someone else...another girl and I couldn't bear the thought of you with someone else." He shook his head, looking away.

"Gabe, listen to me. I don't know if I'm ready for a relationship at this point. Is there a certain amount of time I'm supposed to grieve for Shelby? Hell, I don't know. I feel like for the first time I'm not dependent on her for my happiness, and I take that as a sign I'm ready to move on, but I'm also scared of people finding out that I'm different...that *we're* different."

"I know."

"The only thing I do know is that I missed the fucking hell out of you."

He lifted his head. "You have no idea how miserable I've been."

"Good." The corners of my mouth lifted. "You should have been."

He smiled at me and I stepped forward, grabbing both his hands. Pulling him forward, I aimed my lips at his and gave him a gentle kiss.

"That was nice." He grinned from ear to ear.

"You want another?" I tilted my head.

"Please."

I gave him a longer one this time. He slipped his hands under the hood of my hoodie and pushed it down. As my hood fell, his eyes widened. "Holy shit! You cut your hair!" He stepped back.

I quickly flipped it over my head. "You like it?"

"Yes! It looks great on you!"

"Thanks." I looked up ahead at the trail. "So, you want to hike the trail with me?"

"Sure," he said.

As we started walking, he reached over and grabbed my hand and held it in his own. "Is this okay?"

I glanced down at our conjoined hands. "Yeah, it's fine. We're alone."

"Good. So, catch me up. How's life been going?"

"Where do I begin?" I chuckled as we walked along the trail nervously holding hands.

Chapter Eleven

March 1993

Spring had finally arrived. Warmer temperatures meant more time outside. I was once again hanging out with Gabe and his friends at Murphystown High. On the days he worked at his father's dealership, Jude and I hung out, playing basketball and video games. I'm sure people wondered why a senior would want to hang out with a seventh grader, but Jude was a cool kid. It felt good to be developing my own friendships and interests. Jude inspired me to get out my old writing notebooks and work on some of the stories I had started writing years ago. Of course, they read more like something a twelve-year-old would write, so I had to do a little updating; but the ideas remained solid. Sometimes Jude and I would write together, bouncing ideas off each other and sharing critiques.

A couple of weeks before spring break, my and Gabe's friend, Charlie, invited us to go Rabbit Hunting. One might think the activity involved shooting a loaded weapon at a furry animal, but one would be wrong. Rabbit Hunting was a game that involved the use of off-road vehicles and citizen band (or CB) radios. In the game, a group of sometimes twenty or more people in vehicles with CB radios installed would gather after dark and each vehicle would ante up ten dollars. Each vehicle representative would draw a straw and whoever drew the short straw would be the rabbit. The rabbit would go and hide their vehicle in the woods within a five-mile radius in the unpopulated forests that stretched for forty square miles north of Pleasant. It would then be up to the other hunters to find their vehicle using the signal strength meter of their CB radio on a designated channel. Once the rabbit had hidden, a hunter would say into their CB microphone the words "Where's the rabbit?" The rabbit, per the rules, must answer with "Here's the rabbit." This would allow the hunter to see on their CB, the strength of the signal from the rabbit. The stronger the signal, the closer they were to their target. I always thought of it like a submarine using sonar to locate an enemy sub. Whichever hunter found the rabbit first would win the pool of money, sometimes upward of three-hundred dollars from what I had been told. If no one found the rabbit within the specified time, usually an hour, the rabbit would get the pot.

On the day of Rabbit Hunting, I waited on the sofa for Gabe to pick me up. Lucy, who had doubled in size over the past three months laid on the sofa next to me with her head resting in my lap.

I looked up as Mom entered from the kitchen. "Hey, honey. I'm so glad that you invited Jude to join you guys tonight. Doug's been so worried about him after all that's happened at school."

"Sure," I said as she sat down in her recliner, "Jude's a cool kid."

"I know he's crazy about you. Doug said he's all you talk about." She laughed, before the room went silent. I noticed her fidgeting with one of the cloth-arm covers of the chair. That usually meant she felt anxious in talking to me about something.

"Is there something wrong?" I asked.

She looked down a moment. "No, nothing wrong... it's...just...umm...Doug invited us both to go with him and Jude on their annual spring break vacation to Florida."

My eyes lit up. "Really?"

"Yeah. I told him I would have to think about it...and of course talk to you about it," she said with uncertainty in her voice.

"It sounds fun to me!" I said, anxious for a trip to the beach. We hadn't been in several years, not since she had been married to Bruce, who insisted on us taking an annual family vacation, usually to some boring Civil War museum in the middle of West Virginia or some shit place.

"You know Doug and I have been dating for a few weeks now...this is a big step. You don't think this is too fast, do you?"

I'd noticed the spring in her step since her and Doug had been dating. She also complained less about her job and suddenly began wearing makeup and making weekly visits to the beauty salon. I was glad to see her happy. "Not at all. You do what you feel in your heart."

She slowly smiled. "Thanks, honey. I... this may sound funny...but since Doug and I have been seeing each other, it's as if things picked up right where we left them off twenty-five years ago."

"Doug seems like a good guy. I know he's a good father to Jude," I said

"He's a good man."

"I just want you to be happy, Mom."

"Thanks, honey. That means a lot to me." Her smile faded. "I know we haven't talked much in the last few weeks, but how you are doing?"

"I'm doing good."

"I'm so glad that you and Gabe worked out whatever problem you guys were having."

"Mom," I huffed, "there was no problem. We just needed some time to ourselves."

She paused, "Have you thought about you know... dating again?"

My body stiffened, asking me about dating right after mentioning Gabe. Did she know something? There's no way, but she did hit on a question I'd been wondering myself. Were Gabe and I dating? I wasn't exactly sure how to classify our relationship at this point. It occurred to me Mom could help me with one problem I'd been struggling with. "I've thought about it. Is that wrong? I mean do you think it's too soon after Shelby? It's been four months."

"Oh, honey, no, it's not wrong. Every person's mourning period is different. After your father died, I waited a year before I went out with someone. Looking back on it, I might have done it sooner, but I felt like everyone, especially your Grandpa and Grandma Keystone, would have judged me if I did. People in Pleasant love to gossip, and I could just hear them saying 'I heard that Olivia Keystone has started dating again, when her husband is not even cold in the ground.'"

"That's awful."

"That's Pleasant. I cared too much about what other people thought back then. I've learned since then that people are going to talk no matter what you do, and I really don't care anymore."

"Go, Mom!"

"Perhaps, you'll meet that special person when you go off to college next year. That's how I met your father, you know?" She had to drop the "c-word" in the conversation somehow.

I felt myself shrink. That college conversation was one I had been actively avoiding. Since she had started dating Doug, she hadn't been pushing me as hard about my education plans. I knew I was going to have to tell her sooner or later.

Just then I saw headlights in my driveway. "Hey, it looks like Gabe is here." I jumped up off the sofa and gave her a quick peck on the cheek.

"You boys be careful up there in those woods at night and tell Gabe to not drive fast down those dirt roads."

"I will," I grabbed my jacket from the rack next to the door, "bye."

Hopping into Gabe's Jeep, I gave him a once-over and burst out laughing. "What the hell are you wearing?"

He looked down at himself. "Camo."

From the camouflage cap to the camo shirt, pants, and shoes, he looked like a walking tree. "Seriously, dude, we're going to be hiding in a *bright red* Jeep."

"I know...I just like to be prepared." He smiled, looking me over. "Did you have to wear the brightest shirt in your closet?"

"Yes," I said sarcastically. "Besides, the chances of drawing the short straw to be the rabbit are pretty small."

I looked toward the house, making sure the coast was clear before I leaned in. He followed my lead and we met for a quick peck on the lips,

"Is your friend Jude still coming?" he asked.

"Yeah. I told him we'd pick him up at his house."

He groaned. "I'd rather it been just the two of us."

"Why? Jude's cool. You'll like him." I fastened my seatbelt. When I had told Gabe that Jude was gay, he was surprised. Then he teased me that I had a talent for sniffing out the gays.

"Have you ever thought I might want to spend some alone time with you? We haven't had much time together lately with me being busy working with Dad after school," he said, pulling onto the paved road.

"Why? We do the same thing alone that we do around others…hang out and talk."

He turned his head to me. "What's that supposed to mean? We kiss and hold hands."

"Yeah, we kiss and hold hands."

"Is that not enough? Are you saying you're ready to take this relationship to the next level?" he asked.

"*What* relationship? Dude, I don't know if we're best friends, dating, or just doing some kind of PG version of friends with benefits."

"I thought you wanted to take it slow," he said.

"I never said that!" I raised my voice, "You just assumed that."

"You haven't seemed too interested in going further."

"Have you asked me if I wanted to go further?"

"No, but I figured you were too afraid to." He gassed the Jeep.

"I'm not afraid of going further, I'm afraid of being outted."

He rolled his eyes. "I know. You have told me that more than once."

I grimaced at him in confusion. "I'm starting to think that you aren't as worried about this as I am."

He shrugged his shoulders. "Maybe it wouldn't be so bad if everyone knew we were together. I mean why shouldn't we be treated like any other straight couple?"

My jaw dropped. "What? Have you lost your ever-fucking mind? Do I need to remind you of the fact that we're living in homophobic, redneck Arkansas? We're going to have to pretend to be straight if we want to fit in. What are you thinking for our future? We gonna buy us an acre of land and build us a little house together? Wanna take bets how fast our house would be burned to the ground...a couple of faggots living together in their little love nest of sin. What would your parents think about that?"

He remained silent for several minutes. I could see the gears turning in his head. "Fine then. Let's take the relationship part out of the equation. I have needs and so do you."

"So now you're saying you want to fool around together? Unbelievable."

"God knows I'm not going to find another guy around here willing to do it. At least you've got girls to meet your needs. I don't. I want to have sex at least once in my life," he said.

The gears in my head began turning. Gabe was now agreeing to the friends with benefits plan that he so vehemently opposed two months ago. Maybe this was better in the long run. I could still have my best friend, with some relief that I *desperately* needed on the side. "Okay. Fine. On one condition, we do not let this affect our friendship."

"Fine by me," he said. Pulling up to Jude's grandparents' house, Gabe honked the horn.

"Hey," I said, "whatever you do, don't tell Jude you're gay. Okay?"

He looked at me puzzled. "Why not?"

"Because I don't want to take any chances of him telling someone," I said

"It's not really any of your business who I choose to tell. Is it?" he said in a clipped tone.

I felt a flash of irritation. "It's my business when it affects me."

"And how does me being gay affect you? Oh, wait…I know. He might think you're gay by association. I get it now. You're such a hypocrite. You tell me how sorry you feel for Jude because of the way he's treated at school and how you wish you could do something about it and when you have an opportunity to stand with him, you're too chicken to do it."

Anger shot through my veins. "Look who's talking! If you're so fucking brave, why don't you tell the guys tonight that you're a homo."

About that time, the front door opened, and Jude step out. "Let's just drop this. We're supposed to be having fun tonight," he said.

"Consider it dropped," I said, feeling a little hot under the collar.

A few moments later, the back door of the Jeep opened, and Jude climbed in behind me. "Hey," he said.

"Hey, man, how's it going?" I said as he shut the door.

"Good."

"Jude this is my best friend, Gabe. Gabe, this is Jude," I introduced them.

"Hey, Jude," Gabe said.

"Hey," said Jude as he buckled his seatbelt.

"It's cool to finally meet you. Hawk talks about you all the time." Gabe looked at him in his rearview mirror.

"Same here."

"Have you ever been Rabbit Hunting before?" Gabe asked.

Jude chuckled. "No. Hawk told me about it. It sounds like the stupidest game I've ever heard of. No offense."

I felt myself bristle knowing how Gabe took the game very seriously. I waited for him to let loose on him like he always did with me when I'd bring up that fact. Instead, Gabe returned the laugh. "That's what I said the first time my friend Charlie told me about it."

"So, if by chance we win this...hunt...or whatever, we are splitting the prize money three ways, aren't we?" he asked.

Gabe turned his head to me. "I like this kid."

Jude loudly cleared his throat. "My balls *have* dropped, so kindly do not refer to me as a kid."

I burst out laughing.

"You're thirteen, you're a still a kid." Gabe suppressed his laughter, opting instead to argue. What was up with him tonight?

"You're the one with Bart Simpson hanging on your rearview mirror?" Jude sat back, crossed his arms, and smiled.

"Hey! *The Simpson* is cool!" he said, turning the toy figurine to face him.

"Yeah, maybe if you're ten," Jude shot back.

I shook my head. It occurred to me in that moment how much Gabe and Jude were alike. "Is this how it's going to be all night?"

"What?" both asked me at the same time.

"Never mind," I sighed.

Meeting up with the guys, we drew straws to determine who would be the rabbit in our little game of hide-and-seek. I suppose luck was on our side, because Jude drew the short straw for our team. Gabe was ecstatic as he'd never been the rabbit and had been preparing a hiding spot for months. With twenty-four vehicles participating, they decided to up the ante to twenty dollars each which meant a shitload of money up for grabs.

Amid the miles of dark forests, Gabe's Jeep tore down the gravel logging roads at a breakneck speed. I put my hand on the dash.

"Gabe! Slow down!" I yelled.

"I can't," he said frantically. "I need to get to my spot and hide us before the hour is up."

"This is so cool!" a bouncing Jude said from the middle of the back seat, his hands gripping the back of my seat and Gabe's.

"It's cool until we hit a tree!" I said, as Gabe jerked the wheel to avoid a particularly large pothole in the road. I jerked my head to Gabe and yelled again, "Slow down!"

"Oh, come on, Hawk, loosen up," Jude said a few inches from my left ear.

"Yeah, Hawk. Loosen up," Gabe repeated.

Inviting Jude along made me feel like the odd man out. Gabe and Jude hit it off from the beginning and the two of them together brought out the worst in one another—sarcastic, crude, and bossy. "Quit telling me to loosen up. I already lost someone I cared about in a car wreck, I don't want to lose anyone else."

Immediate, Gabe hit the brake and we slowed to a crawl. He gave me a sympathetic gaze. "Sorry, dude."

"It's okay...just slow down, please." I gave him a reassuring smile as the car went silent. Obviously, the mood had darkened, and I needed to brighten it up again. "How did you find this hiding place?"

"Out exploring the roads one day, I found this abandoned deer camp. It's deep in the woods and the road is terrible. It narrows to just a trail and my Jeep just barely got through the thicket of vines and saplings. I figure that all the other guys' big pickup trucks will never be able to get through it."

Soon the road narrowed to just a trail.

Plowing through the thicket, the screeching sound of wood on metal, like fingernails on a chalkboard, gave me goosebumps.

"Dude. You're gonna need a new paint job." Jude chuckled.

Gabe patted the dashboard. "Nah, Old Red is tough."

"Old Red," I laughed, "that sounds like the name of a hound dog."

"Funny you should say that, I actually had a mutt named that," Jude said. "It used to roam around Gillette, breeding every stray bitch in town. I bet that dog sired at least a hundred puppies."

"Sounds like a good life to me." I grinned.

"Not to me." Jude curled his nose. "So, Hawk. Did you tell Gabe I'm gay?"

I looked at Gabe, who smiled and looked at him directly behind his right shoulder. "Yeah, he told me."

"Since when did you start openly admit that to everyone?" I asked Jude.

"I don't openly admit it to everyone, just people I think would be cool with it, and I trust Gabe because you trust him," he said.

"I'm cool with it," Gabe winked at me. I shot him a dirty look afraid he might spill the beans on himself.

"You're very hot by the way," Jude said to Gabe.

I turned my head back, my mouth agape. "Jude!"

He shrugged his shoulder. "Well, it's true. So, Gabe, you have a girlfriend?"

A small snicker escaped Gabe's lips. "No girlfriend."

Jude kept eyeing him. "You must work out a lot."

"Some." Gabe kept grinning.

"I bet you got a nice body under that shirt." Jude kept going, much to my irritation.

"Jude! Enough!" I shouted at him.

Jude shrugged his shoulders, and leaned back in the seat. "What? I was just making conversation."

Gabe checked Jude's reflection in the rearview mirror. "You know, Jude, you remind me a lot of myself."

My mind recalled the day in that boat when Gabe came out to me and then asked me to take off my shirt to check out my merchandise. Were oversexed guys just drawn to me for some reason? Or vice versa?

After another fifteen minutes of almost impossible terrain, the road opened into a clearing. Although forested, the undergrowth was not as prevalent as had been on the path in.

"We're here!" Gabe said as he pulled his jeep close to a grove of trees and parked. "Okay guys, I need your help." He hopped out of the jeep and Jude and I followed suit. He then went to the back of his jeep and pulled out a small hatchet. "Grab a hatchet or a saw and a flashlight and cut off some of these pine tree limbs and cover the jeep." He pointed with his flashlight at some of the low-lying limbs.

Jude grabbed the saw and I the other hatchet and went to work. "You came prepared," I said as I chopped a particular bushy limb off a pine tree.

"I've...been...planning...this...for...months," Gabe said between his chops.

"Is this big enough?" Jude yelled. Gabe and I shined our

lights at him standing next to a fallen pine tree, the three-inch round stump next to it.

"Perfect dude!" Gabe laughed.

Ten minutes later, we had completely covered the jeep in pine limbs, saplings, and vines. I had to admit the way Gabe had parked the jeep, we blended in perfectly with the surroundings. Even with headlights aiming right at us, we'd be hard to see. Inside the cab, Gabe focused on his watch. "Get ready, the hunt is about to begin."

"Can I handle the CB?" Jude asked like an overly enthusiastic kid.

"Sure," Gabe replied, and Jude leaned forward between us.

A few seconds later a voice came over the CB radio, "Where's the rabbit?"

Gabe handed Jude the CB microphone and instructed him how to use it. He held down the button on the mic and answered, "Here's the rabbit," grinning from ear to ear.

"That should have given everyone their first reading," Gabe said.

"How long do they have to find us again?" I asked.

"An hour and fifteen minutes," Gabe answered.

Another call for the rabbit came over the radio and Jude sent back the required response. The radio went silent as we waited for another call. "Hey, Gabe, did Hawk tell you we're going with our parents to Florida on spring break?" Jude asked him.

Gabe gave me a puzzled look. "No. I thought he and I were doing some hiking?"

"You never said anything about us doing something

together over spring break. You said you were looking forward to sleeping in all week."

"I think it was kinda a given since we had been talking about going hiking the other day."

"No, it wasn't a given. You should have said 'Hey, Hawk, let's do some hiking during spring break.'" I shook my head. Typical Gabe just assumed that I'd be available when *he* wants to hang out.

"That's just great!" He threw up his hands. "Now I'm going to be bored off my ass all week."

"Here's the rabbit," Jude finished answering the next request before turning his head to Gabe. "Why don't you just come with us to Florida?"

Gabe's face lit up. "Seriously?"

Jude shrugged his shoulder. "Yeah, I'm sure my dad won't mind. There's plenty of room in the condo. That is, if Hawk doesn't mind." He looked to me questioningly.

Of course, I was all for Gabe coming to Florida with us, but he and Jude together I wasn't too sure about. Just being with them a couple of hours, I had started to feel picked on. A week of it, and I'd snap. Not that I could say anything, of course. "Of course not. It'll be fun!"

"Cool! Just us guys! It's going to be a fucking blast!" said a giddy Jude.

Time seemed to tick by very slowly and what seemed like forever.

"How much longer until we win?"

Gabe checked his watch and frowned. "Thirty-five minutes."

I groaned.

Jude pointed out the window opposite the trail we came in on. "Hey, guys, I think I see a light."

Gabe and I quickly jerked our heads. "Looks like headlights but they're at least a half-mile away," Gabe said.

"Aren't they coming in from the wrong direction?" I asked.

"Yeah, no roads lead in here from that direction. My guess is they're looking for a way through, off the main road. As far as I know, the road we came in on is the only way in and out of here."

"What if they come tearing through the woods?" Jude asked.

"They'd never make it." Gabe shook his head. "There's stumps, ditches, and holes everywhere. Their truck would get stuck. We're safe."

Just then, we got another call for the rabbit and Jude replied. A few minutes later, the lights disappeared. "Looks like they've given up coming in that way," I said.

We sat in silence as the sounds of the crickets chirping and frogs croaking filled the cold night air. An occasional breeze through the dark forest caused the skeleton-like trees to creak and moan.

"It's kinda spooky out here," Jude said.

"Umm...I didn't want to tell you guys, but this is the old Denton homeplace. Back in the 1800s the Denton family lived in the old house that once stood just over there." Gabe pointed. "All of them died of tuberculosis."

Jude's eyes went wide. "Are you serious, dude?"

"Yeah," he answered. "There are four grave markers just on the other side of a mound of rocks over there." He pointed out the window about forty feet from us. Being so dark, we couldn't see anything.

"You're so full of shit," I scoffed.

"No. He's not. My grandma's maiden name was Denton and she told me the same story. These were some of her relatives and it's true," Jude said in a very serious tone. Chills ran all over me. I admit, I was getting a little scared, but I certainly didn't want them to know. "She also told me that the ghost of a little girl wanders around the place looking for her mommy."

"You're lying," Gabe said.

"No. I swear. It's the truth." Jude swallowed hard and made a cross sign across his chest. "Why didn't you tell us this before?"

"Because I didn't want to scare you," he answered, the scared look on his face making me wish I'd stayed at home.

"How much longer?" I asked Gabe again.

He checked his watch. "Twenty minutes."

"Fuck!" I felt more chills run down spine.

Suddenly, Jude jumped back in the seat, bringing his legs up with him, pulling them tight against his body. He pointed out the window toward the spot where the old house once stood. "Oh shit! Oh shit! Oh shit! I saw something!"

"What?" we both said in a panic, our voices low.

"A...a...a small white figure moving along the ground." He shivered.

I stared deep into the darkness. "I don't see anything," I said.

"Oh fuck! There it is!" said Gabe just above a whisper, his face frozen in fear.

I tried to discern figures, but all I saw were shaded silhouettes of the trees. "I still don't see anything."

Just then, Jude kicked the back of my seat with a force that knocked me onto the floor. I screamed as he and Gabe howled with laughter.

Anger flushed over me. "That was not fucking funny!" I struggled to pull myself off the floor.

"Yes…it…was," Gabe managed to say between fits of laughter.

"We got you!" Jude rolled over in the back seat.

"I nearly pissed my pants." I managed to pull myself back into the seat. While I wasn't one to scare easily, they were very convincing. "I'm not going to Florida with you two assholes."

"Aww, now. Come on, buddy," Gabe said.

"Don't buddy me," I folded my arms, turned my head and sulked, "I mean it, you two can go by yourselves. I'm staying here."

"It was a joke, Hawk." Jude stuck his head between us.

"I don't care. I don't think it was funny." I refused to look at them.

Gabe tried to touch my shoulder and I jerked it away. "Dude. I'm sorry. I thought you would think it was funny."

I refused to say anything more to them. After a few moments, Jude spoke in a genuinely concerned voice, "I'm sorry, Hawk, I didn't mean to make you mad. It was a joke." I remained silent.

"Yeah, man. I'm sorry," Gabe said in a similar tone.

I let them sit for several moments. I knew they were both looking at each other wondering what to do. Finally, I turned to look at them both, the corners of my mouth slowly rising. "Gotcha!"

"You asshole!" Gabe said and they both shoved me in the shoulder.

"Paybacks are hell." I laughed.

"Damn, dude. I thought you were really mad," Jude said.

"No. Maybe a little at first," I said. "When did you two have time to plan this?"

Gabe grinned, "While you were chopping limbs behind the Jeep."

"Whose idea, was it?" I asked, suspecting Gabe.

Jude raised his hand.

I rolled my eyes at him. "I should have guessed. And I agreed to a fucking week in Florida with you two. I must be crazy."

Jude let out a maniacal laugh.

"Shh." Gabe put his finger over his mouth and pointed down the trail.

"Oh no. I'm not falling for that again," I said.

"No seriously," he said. I looked and saw about a quarter of a mile away, another pair of headlights.

Being that close, they could have easily heard us talking and laughing. From the sound of their tires spinning, I knew they were having trouble navigating the road. Just then, they killed their motor.

"They're listening for us." Gabe turned the volume down on the CB. "Be very quiet."

Just then a call for the rabbit came over the CB. "It's them," Jude whispered.

Gabe picked up the microphone and answered the call in a low voice, "Here's the rabbit."

"They're close," I heard a male's voice say in the distance.

"Shit!" I whispered, "They're going to find us." I then saw two pairs of flashlights moving toward us.

Gabe grabbed my shoulder and held his breath as the beams came closer. Just then another call came over our CB from another team. "Here's the rabbit," Gabe answered. I only hoped they couldn't hear us answering through the forest.

About thirty feet away, they stopped. I then heard a voice say, "I don't see anything," Flashlight beams flashed through the cab of our jeep.

"They got to be around here somewhere," said a deeper male voice.

"This place gives me the creeps," the other voice said.

Just then, I saw one of the beams go out. "Dude, my batteries are dead," the first guy said before hearing him knock the flashlight against his hand repeatedly. "You go ahead."

"Are you nuts? I'm not going traipsing through these woods by myself!" said the other one.

"You're such a wuss!"

"Dude, there's no way Gabe would be able to get that Jeep down here. Let's go."

"Yeah, you're probably right."

Gabe pressed the button to light up his digital watch

and held up two fingers. A few moments later, we heard the truck start. I smiled at Gabe and gave him a low five. Jude removed his hand from my shoulder and did the same.

"Boys," Gabe began speaking in his normal voice, "We just won ourselves five-hundred smackeroos!"

"Woohoo!" Jude yelled from the backseat.

"Nice!" I said.

It took us about a half hour to get the jeep out of the woods and back to the meeting spot with the guys. Charlie and Steve were disappointed that they had come within twenty feet of finding us. Steve blamed Charlie for not packing more flashlight batteries, but the true hero of the night was Gabe. His meticulous plan had paid off.

The way back home we started telling dirty jokes. While originally, I wasn't sure how the evening would go with both Jude and Gabe together, I was having a blast with them by the end of the night. It had to be one of the best nights I'd had in months.

Chapter Twelve

Spring Break 1993

Lying on the beach in warm and sunny Florida, I sipped on my soda with a straw, listening to the sound of the ocean waves. Being the first time I'd ever flown, I admit I quite enjoyed the experience, though I cannot say the same for Gabe, who panicked at the slightest bit of turbulence. Jude's father had been generous enough to buy my and Mom's ticket, while Gabe's parents paid for his. Originally, it was to have been a road trip—a very long road trip—eighteen hours to be exact, but the thought of being stuck that many hours in the car all together did not appeal to me and, thankfully, Doug.

I glanced to my left at Jude relaxing in the sun. To my left, Gabe busily rubbed sunblock on his arms. Seeing Gabe in his short blue swim trunks *really* turned me on. Although we agreed to a "friends with benefits" plan, we had yet to do anything and my frustrations were growing. I think it came down to the fact that neither of us wanted to make the first move.

"This is the life," Jude said, adjusting his sunglasses.

I scanned the crowds of beach goers, mostly college students but a few adults mixed in. "Man, this place is crowded."

"It's like this every year," Jude said from his beach

blanket. "The partiers are further down the beach. This is the 'quieter' area."

Gabe peered off into the distance. "Why aren't we down there?"

"Because we're underage and have a"—I glanced at Jude wanting to say kid, but knew he would come unhinged—"set of parents with us."

Jude pulled down his sunglass and glared at me. "You were going to say kid."

"Never," I grinned at him, his eyes suddenly shifting away from me.

"Dude, check out the hot guy in the Speedo." Jude practically drooled.

While I tried not to show interest for the sake of maintaining my straight persona, I couldn't help myself. I followed his eyes and feigned disinterest, while whole-heartedly agreeing that the young frat-boy jumping to catch a Frisbee did look awfully good in the skimpy swimsuit. "Disgusting. I wouldn't be caught dead wearing a Speedo."

"Why not?" Jude asked. "I'd wear one."

"Me too," Gabe said. "It's not like I could wear one back home, but down here..." I could see where he was coming from, wearing a Speedo to a swimming hole in Arkansas, you might as well be waving a rainbow flag and inviting every redneck there to kick your ass.

"I'd pay to see you in one," Jude waggled his eyebrows at him.

"Jude!" I admonished him.

He shrugged his shoulder. "I would."

Gabe laughed, slathering more sunblock on his right

arm. He leaned closer and whispered in my ear, "I'd pay to see you in one, too."

"Yeah, when Hell freezes over," I whispered as he went back to rubbing lotion on his legs. "Do you really need *that* much sunblock?"

He stopped and lowered his eyebrows at me. "Oh, I see. Typical white guy thinking dark-skinned people don't sunburn."

My jaw dropped. "What? No, I didn't mean that…I just wanted you to save some for the rest—"

Gabe interrupted me, "I'm kidding, dude. I knew what you meant. We do sunburn, it just takes longer than you guys, but I'm not taking any chances. I've been burned before and it's not fun."

Mom and Doug were still at the condo getting everything unpacked for the week. The rest of us were anxious to get to the water, so we left them to do all the boring stuff. Luckily, this part of the beach was only a five-minute walk for us.

"Hey," Gabe elbowed me, "those girls keep staring at us."

"What girls?" I asked, lifting my head a moment to scan the beach.

"The ones just to the right of me, but don't look," he said turning his head to look at me instead.

Immediately, my eyes went to the cute brunette and the even cuter blonde with her. Most definitely college girls and most definitely hot. I couldn't help myself and smiled at them, brushing my hair back over my head. They grinned back at me.

"Damnit, Hawk. Quit smiling at them, they're going to come over here," he whispered in my ear so Jude couldn't hear him.

"Too late." I kept grinning at them.

Gabe groaned.

Jude must have heard him. "What's going on?"

"Oh, just a couple of hot girls in bikinis coming over here," I said.

Jude yawned. "Oh," he said, not moving an inch from his horizontal position to have a look.

As the girls came nearer, I couldn't help but examine the blonde's red bikini. Both qualified for the supermodel category. While I had classified myself as bisexual, I still didn't understand exactly where I fell on the scale. Allowing myself to explore those feelings had opened a whole new world for me and gave me time to reflect on my relationship with Shelby. Shelby had a very strong personality and I found I am attracted to those personality types, male or female. I realized Shelby controlled our relationship and whether it was healthy or not, I don't know, but she made me happy and that's all I cared about. As far as physical attributes of females versus male, I found them both equally attractive. The sex part, I couldn't say, as I'd never had sex with a guy.

"Hi," the blonde said with a smile, standing a few feet from me.

"Hi." I smiled at her; Gabe gave them a quick smile but remained silent.

She giggled, brushing her long hair back. "I'm Carly and this is Stacy."

"I'm Hawk, this is Gabe and Jude." I pointed to each one of them. Jude lifted a hand and waved, while Gabe gave them another nervous smile.

I had to admit Carly was even more of a knockout up close. "You guys down here in college break?" Carly asked.

Not wanting to sound like high school dweeb, I lied. "Yeah. Gabe and I are freshmen at the University of Arkansas." Gabe shot me a dirty look.

"Cool, we're Juniors from Temple University," she said, before looking at Jude.

"Oh, this is my little brother Jude. It's kind of a guys' road trip thing we're doing," I said, not exactly why I felt the need to lie to them about our relationship. Jude removed his glasses and leaned up on his elbows, giving me the evil eye.

"Do you guys want to go in the water with us?" She aimed her eyes at me and Gabe before turning her head back toward the ocean.

"Yeah, we'd love to," I answered and started to get up.

"I just got this sunblock on and need to let it soak in a little before I get in the water," Gabe said, turning his head aside, his anger blossoming.

"Oh...okay," she said. They seemed unfazed.

"Okay, I'm going," I stood up, "I'll see you guys in a bit."

Admittedly, walking off sandwiched between two beautiful girls, I felt my ego sufficiently soaked and my body aroused.

We swam out in the ocean, talked a little about music and college. Of course, I stole some of my sister's college stories to maintain my façade as your average college student; my age of course being eighteen; not seventeen. I found Carly to be a rather interesting person. Apparently, she was studying for a degree in political science, and we shared the same liberal beliefs. After a half-hour, I said my goodbyes to the girls and trotted back up to the beach to Gabe and Jude.

"Hey, guys," I said.

Gabe sat up and looked up at me, I couldn't see his eyes behind his sunglasses, but his face told me that he was not happy. "Did you have fun?" he snapped.

"Yeah, I did," I said. "Carly invited me for coffee."

"Well, good for you," he said, his voice laced with sarcasm. "I thought we came here to hang out…just us guys, but apparently that's not the case."

"It's just coffee and I'm not going to be gone *that* long," I said.

About that time, my mother and Doug walked up. "Hey, guys," Mom greeted.

"Hey," we all replied.

"You boys having fun?" Doug asked. Jude sat up and pulled off his sunglasses. "I am. Hawk's already got him a girl."

I gave a grinning Jude a dirty look. "I haven't got a girl…I'm just having coffee with one."

My mom put her hand on her hip, recoiling her head and smiling. "*Really?*" I knew she was happy to see me starting to be interested in dating again. "Who is this girl?"

"She a junior in college at Temple University and hot enough to turn a guy like me straight," Jude laughed.

I gritted my teeth at Jude. "Thanks, Jude."

Doug laughed. "You better watch out for those older women."

My face became flush. "Okay. I'm going to go back to the condo and get ready. I'll be back later."

I slipped on my sandals and started my trek back to the condo. I looked back to see Mom and Doug unfolding their beach chairs and settling in next to Gabe and Jude.

A few minutes later, I entered the condo and shut the door behind me. I made my way into the bedroom I shared with Gabe and Jude. Gabe and I took the bed, while Jude had the hideaway sofa bed on the opposite side of the room. The other bedroom was for my mom and Doug. Prior to Gabe being invited, the plan was for she and I to have one bedroom and Jude and his father the other, with me sleeping on the hideaway, of course. With Gabe coming along, it changed everything. The day before we left, she sat me down in the living room and asked me if I would be upset if she and Doug shared a bedroom. Of course, I told her it was the nineties and everyone was sleeping together, a bit of tongue-in-cheek humor she didn't appreciate.

I headed to the attached bathroom and took a quick shower. Wrapping a towel around me, I walked back into the bedroom to retrieve my clothes from my suitcase.

Bending over to grab a pair of underwear, I heard a door close behind me. I jerked my head around to see Gabe standing at the door. He did not look happy.

"What are you doing here?" I asked.

"I came to get my camera," he said in a clipped tone.

"Oh." I turned and went back to pulling out my clothes.

I heard him rummaging through his own suitcase. A few moments later, the sound stopped. "How long are you going to be out?" he asked.

I turned around, holding my shorts and tank in my hands. "A couple hours at most."

"I see," he said, his camera in hand. I could feel the heat from his anger across the room. "Are you hoping to score tonight? Is that the reason you're meeting her?"

I felt a slight irritation. "No! I thought she was an interesting person and would like to get to know her better."

"Have you told her yet you're just a seventeen-year-old high school kid?" he asked, using the word "kid" specifically.

"No…I was going to tell her over coffee," I said, which was the truth.

He folded his arms in front of him and lifted his chin. "Suuuure, you were."

His defensive posture told me that either he was upset I was spending time away from him or jealous that I was going on a date with a girl. "Do you have a problem with me having coffee with Carly?"

He stood silent. I could see the gears of his minds turning before his temper suddenly exploded. "Yes! I have a problem with it!"

"I told you it would just be a couple of hours. We'll have all week to hang out together," I huffed.

"Really, Hawk? I thought you and I had something going here," he said.

"What, Gabe? Please explain to me what this is? One minute you want a relationship, the next minute you want friends with benefits, then you get all jealous over some girl.

I don't know what you want anymore. Please tell me because I'd sure as hell like to know!"

Gabe started tapping his foot angrily, before dropping his arms and relaxing his posture. He turned his head away for a moment, before turning it back and staring deep into my eyes, "You, Hawk. I want you. You're all I've ever wanted since we were kids."

My eyes widened. "Really?"

Tears began to form in his eyes. "I love you, Hawk. I almost told you that day in the bus when we were twelve, but I was too scared. Seeing you again after all these years brought all of it back. Then when you lost Shelby, it wasn't the right time to tell you that my feelings for you never went away and being so close to you, sleeping in your bed, holding you. I couldn't take it anymore. It was killing me, so I had to step away and that was the worst month of my life.

I felt myself melting. I never knew he felt that way. He kept his feelings hidden and I never suspected they were that strong. I stood in silence, thinking of my response. I guess I waited too long because suddenly his face dropped.

"I shouldn't have told you. I'm sorry, I'm..." he turned toward the door, "I'm such a *fucking idiot*!"

With those words, he rushed out of the room, slamming the door behind him. I'd hurt him and I felt like shit for doing it. Never did I dream he was in actual love with me. My mind began flashing back to the time right after Shelby died—how he never left my side, how he held me when I needed consoling, how he saved me from my depression when all I wanted to do was die. Maybe what I took as friendship and sexual attraction went beyond that. He truly did love me, but did I feel the same way?

Standing in the middle of the room wrapped only in my towel, I contemplated my next move. I knew what I had to do.

A half-hour later, I strolled along the crowded beach with my head held high and a beach towel draped over my shoulder. A couple of girls winked at me and I smiled at them. In the distance, I spotted Jude and Gabe sitting on the beach under two large umbrellas. I picked up the pace as I headed toward them.

As soon as I walked up, Jude's eyes bulged at the sight of me. "What the hell is that?" He pointed at my new swimsuit.

I glanced down at my tight and rather low-cut red Speedo I had just bought from the beach store next to our condo. "My new swimsuit. You like it?"

"Umm…" he stared.

I glanced at Gabe, who sat up and slipped his sunglasses down his nose. His face frozen in shock. Finally, he worked his eyes up my body until they locked with mine. A grin slowly formed on his face as wide as the Grand Canyon. While I felt as if I were going to die of embarrassment, I needed to make a grand gesture to let Gabe know how I felt about him. "You can keep your money," I smiled at him in response to his statement earlier in the day that he'd pay to see me in a Speedo.

"Huh?" asked a puzzled Jude.

"Never mind, inside joke," I said to him.

I took my towel, spread it out, and sat down next to Gabe. I leaned over and whispered in his ear, "I love you too." I moved my hand close to him, discretely hooked my pinky finger with his and squeezed.

I looked back at Jude, who had his fist in his mouth like he was just dying to say something. "What's wrong with you?" I asked. He shook his head unable to speak. "What?" My voice went high.

He slowly removed his fist, grinning from ear to ear. "Dude…you *really* shouldn't be wearing that."

"Why not?"

"It's the…umm…" He balled his hand into a fist and covered it with the other hand then nodded toward my crotch.

"Huh?" I looked at him puzzled.

"What size is that Speedo?" he asked.

"A large," I said.

"*Large*?" Jude yelled. "Holy shit!"

I finally caught on to what he was saying and became a little embarrassed. Although there were other guys wearing them, obviously theirs didn't stand out like mine did. I didn't think about that when I put it on being more focused on my mission to show Gabe how I felt about him.

"I like it," Gabe said before turning to Jude and in typical Gabe fashion compared my reproductive organs to the reproductive organs of the Equus genus of mammals, and using certain common words of slang, telling him to deal with it.

"Gabe!" I yelled. "Don't tell him that!"

Jude started laughing manically and pointed down the beach. "Look who's coming, *this* is going to be fun." He then rubbed his hands together.

I peered in that direction and spotted Doug and my mother heading our way. In an instant, I realized that what seemed like a good idea at the time, was most definitely not. I grabbed my towel and covered myself. "I need to go back to the condo and change…now." Jumping up, I wrapped my towel around me.

"I'll go with you," laughed Gabe.

We both scurried away before they could see me in my almost naked state. Arriving back at the condo, I ran into the bedroom. Gabe, entering at a more casual pace, shut the door behind us. I looked at him and grinned, dropping the beach towel. He grinned back. "You wore that just for me?"

"I certainly wouldn't have worn it for anyone else." I kept smiling.

"You mean what you said to me?"

"I do." We walked toward one another, stopping when we were eye-to-eye. I reached up and pushed away the two twisted coils that covered his beautiful brown eyes, "You are so fucking handsome."

"You're not too bad yourself." He rubbed his hand over my cheek.

"I never told you, but I love your very dark skin." I ran my finger between the divide of his gorgeous pecs.

"I know," he shrugged his shoulder.

Our smiles faded, as we stared in each other's eyes, we knew exactly what we wanted. I intensified my stare, inviting Gabe to take what he wanted. He grabbed the back of my head and forced his lips against mine, relaxing into him; it felt so right as he turned me toward the bed. Yanking down his swimsuit, we kept our lips locked as I slipped out of my Speedo.

He shoved me onto the bed, and I climbed under the covers as he joined me. He laid on his back as I began kissing his neck, working my way down; ready to experience something I'd never experienced before with another guy. A few moments later his eyes lit up as I pushed him toward a pleasure I knew very well. It felt so nice to give something to my best friend that he'd been denied for so long because he was different.

Soon, I was doing something I had never done before and while different from my previous experiences, it was equally as satisfying. I had been preparing and felt absolutely no shame in letting Gabe use me in whatever way he wished.

Several minutes later, my head laid on his chest as I caressed the ridges of his tight abs with my finger. I moved my eyes up to him as he lay silent, staring at the ceiling.

"Wow…just wow." He ran his hand down my back.

"Fun, huh?" I said, grinning from ear to ear.

He tilted his head down. "You…holy shit…you were… amazing!"

I chuckled. "Yep, I've been told that a few times. Although never from a guy."

"I think you've definitely proven you're bi…if you had any doubt." He grinned.

"Oh, I think I pretty much knew it."

"Do you…um…feel that you could have the same

relationship with a guy that you could with a girl?" I could see some concern on his face. Truthfully, this was the final test I needed to confirm that I could have just as meaningful of a relationship with a guy as I could a girl. While different, as far as how mine and Gabe's relationship would be in comparison to mine and Shelby's, it felt right.

"For sure. I mean my role is different than before, but I like it." I laughed.

Gabe laughed. "True...but what about the other part. The emotional part."

I reached up and rubbed my hand on his cheek, "Gabe. You're my best friend. I love you as a best friend, but more than that. I've come to care deeply for you, and I just want to be with you. When you're not around, I feel lost. I want us to be together in *all* ways."

"I feel the same way about you, Hawk." He smiled tenderly. "In fact, I want to show you again."

He suddenly flipped me on my back and hovered over top of me; gently leaning down and kissing me. Just then the bedroom door flew open. "What are you guys...holy fuck!" I heard Jude's yell and the door slam shut.

Immediately, Gabe jumped off me and I pulled the blanket up to my neck. My heart racing, I whipped my head toward the door. Thankfully, Jude was on the other side of it. "Oh shit! Oh shit! Oh shit!" I panicked.

"Calm down, Hawk. It's just Jude," Gabe said, slowly getting up to get dressed.

"Just Jude!" I scrambled to my suitcase for a pair of shorts.

"So, he found out we're together."

"Gabe, don't you understand...what if he tells someone?" I grabbed a pair of blue running shorts and slipped them on.

"I don't know why you don't trust him. I've only known him for a couple of weeks and I trust him. You've known him for months."

I slipped on a tank top. "I know. It's just—"

Just then I heard a knock at the door. "Guys! Is this some sort of joke? Because I don't think it's funny."

I checked to make sure that Gabe was decent before I went to open the door. Grabbing the knob, I pulled the door back to a very upset Jude. "Hey," I started.

Jude interrupted me, "Are you guys making fun of me because I'm gay? Because if you are, it's a fucking cruel joke."

I shook my head vigorously. "No. Jude. I would never tease you about that. You better come in."

Jude entered and I shut the door leading him to the sofa. I motioned for Gabe to follow me as I sat down next to Jude. Gabe sat in one of the adjacent chairs. I wasn't sure where to start, so I just said it the simplest way I possibly could. "Gabe and I are more than just friends."

"I don't understand. You're both gay?" He looked at me with a puzzled expression.

"Gabe is gay. I'm bi."

He glanced at Gabe them back to me. "Why didn't you tell me? I thought I was the only gay kid in the entire school. You know how lonely I've felt?"

"I know, Jude. Gabe was right, I should have told you. It's all my fault," I said.

"Why, Hawk? I thought we were friends." He sounded so sad.

I let out a deep sigh. I knew I had hurt him. "I wanted to tell you, but I was scared. Scared what happened to you would happen to me if word got out. I was wrong and I'm so, so sorry."

"Why didn't you trust me? I wouldn't have told anyone." The hurt in his voice made me feel like the lowest form of life on earth.

"I should have trusted you, but I've been so scared to tell anyone. Gabe is the only person that knows my secret and I'm the only person that knows his. Look, Jude, I care about you a lot. You're like the little brother I never had, and I would never intentionally hurt you. I really am sorry."

He sat silent for a moment. "Little brother. I'm not little. Younger brother, that sounds better." The corners of his mouth rose.

"How about just brothers then?" I smiled gently and opened my arms for a hug.

"Brothers." He wrapped his arms around me.

Breaking away, he pointed at the two of us. "So, how long have you guys been together?"

Gabe looked up at the clock on the wall. "Umm...about forty-five minutes."

Jude wrinkled his nose. "Huh?"

I chuckled. "Just like hiding our secret from you, we've been hiding our feelings for one another for months. We just revealed them to each other about an hour ago."

"Wow! That must have been some kind of confession." He glanced toward the bed.

Gabe burst out laughing and I couldn't help but join him.

"I can't believe it. My two best friends are like me…this is…great!" Jude threw his arms wide. "Now we can talk about boys…you can explain to me how gay sex works…oh, can I watch you guys kiss? I've never seen two guys kiss before, especially two hot guys. I could totally get into that."

I rolled my eyes as he kept rambling. "Jude. Stop. You're making this weird."

"Oops, sorry." He grinned.

Gabe jumped in. "Listen, Jude, you cannot tell anyone…I mean *anyone*…about me and Hawk."

He began shaking his head. "Oh no. I would never. Your guys' secret is safe with me."

"Good," Gabe said. "Now that we have that out of the way…I'm ready to go have some fun on the beach."

"Me too!" Jude jumped up.

The next few days, Jude, Gabe, and I spent lying on the beach, swimming in the ocean, and exploring Ft. Lauderdale. Gabe's dad took us all deep-sea fishing on the third day. Jude caught one of the largest snappers the boat captain had ever seen. We all caught our share of tuna, mutton snappers, and kingfish. I felt rather bad about skipping out on the coffee date with Carly, but I suppose I didn't hurt her feelings because the next time I saw her, she was walking down the beach holding hands with another guy. As far as Gabe and I, we tried to spend time together as a newfound couple, but with Jude always around we never got any alone time.

On day four, Jude, Gabe, and I walked into the condo after a morning swim. Doug and Mom had gotten up early to go and do some shopping.

"Dude! Did you see all those hot college guys over by the fishing pier?" Jude said as he led the way to the bedroom.

"Yes, and they're way too old for you," I said.

"I like older guys." He entered the bedroom.

"Stick with kids your own age," said Gabe, who had fallen in behind me.

"Again, must I remind you not to call me a kid," Jude growled as we entered the bedroom, Gabe closing the door behind us.

Ignoring him, Gabe grinned at me before coming closer and laying a scorching kiss on me. I turned my eyes to Jude who stood mesmerized. I broke the kiss and arched my brow at Jude. "Why are you staring at us…again?"

He gave me an evil grin. "Because it's even hotter watching you guys kiss when you're both shirtless."

"You little perv." I threw my towel at him. I must admit every time I kiss Gabe, he turns me on. Over the past few days, not only had we done a whole lot more passionate kissing, we managed to do other things at night after Jude had dozed off. Now that Gabe and I were in a relationship, I began to realize how similar yet different it was from my relationship with Shelby. I had many months to analyze my relationship with Shelby. With Shelby, the roles of the relationship were clearly defined. She was my girl, and I was her guy. I felt a sense of protectiveness of her, and we showed our love for each other freely, especially in public. It was more of a warm and cozy relationship. Those were the positive aspects of our relationship, but in thinking back I realized I did allow her to control me just a little too much. Many times, I wanted to speak up about things I didn't like or did not agree with but remained silent for fear it might upset her and that she might leave me. I swore to myself that in my and Gabe's relationship, I would be more vocal about things I did not like. As far as my relationship with Gabe, it felt much different. Part of the time he was my buddy and part of the time he was my boyfriend. As a guy, it's very difficult to admit that I prefer to relinquish my stereotypical dominant male role to my partner. But with Gabe, it just felt right and honestly it had always been that way even back to when we were kids. Actually, it was nice having someone take care of me for a change.

"So, are you guys going to tell your parents?" Jude asked.

"I don't know," I said. I felt in my heart Mom would accept it, after all, she accepted Jude without question.

"Never," Gabe said, throwing his towel on the bed.

"Why not?" Jude asked him.

"Because my papa would probably throw me out of the house," he said.

I crinkled my forehead. "You really think he would?"

He shrugged his shoulder. "I don't know. My papa is very traditional." He shook his head, the new beads in his hair clacking together. "Hell, he might disown me over these braids and beads."

"Why would he? It's part of your Jamaican heritage. He should respect that," I said. When we had walked past the Jamaican hair salon while out shopping, Gabe commented he'd always wanted to try the style. I encouraged him to do it. They twisted his hair into small braids from his scalp to his shoulders and tied silver beads on the end of each braid. It was quite fascinating to watch the process and end result. I absolutely loved it!

"You obviously don't know my papa."

I could respect that, Gabe did run a big risk telling them, and I was certainly not ready to tell anyone outside Jude and my mom.

Just then we heard a door slam and a few moments later a knock on our bedroom door. "Hey guys, could you all come out here for a minute?"

"We just got back from the beach and are all in our swimsuits," I answered.

"That's okay, just come as you are," she said.

I looked at the guys. Something was most certainly up. I could tell from the tone of her voice.

I led the way into the main living area where Mom and Doug sat on the sofa next to one another. I took the adjacent chair to Mom and Jude to his dad. Gabe sat in a chair across the room. "What's up?" I asked.

They looked at each other and smiled before Doug took my mom's hand. She smiled at him, squeezed his hand and began to speak. "Boys, um...Doug and I have an announcement to make...we're getting married." One could have heard a pin drop. For the first time in my life, my mother had completely stunned me. "I know this seems sudden, but when something feels right—"

"You guys have only been dating for a few weeks," Jude interrupted.

"Actually, son, it's been about two months," Doug said in a calm voice.

"But, Dad, you married Candice three months after you met and look what happened," Jude said, surprising me with his boldness.

"Jude, listen. This isn't going to be like that," he said.

"She treated me like shit, Dad," he countered.

"You know Livvy…Mrs. Keystone…she's nothing like Candice."

"Hmph…I've heard that one before. Candice was nice to me too before you said 'I do', then she became the step-mother from hell." He crossed his arms in front of him and sulked.

"Candice had some issues I wasn't aware of when we were dating."

"Some issues?" He let out a sarcastic laugh. "You call her getting our house condemned because of her hoarding, 'some issues'?"

"Jude!" His voice became stern. "That's enough. "Livvy isn't like that, and you know it."

"Jude," Mom said calmly, "I would never do anything to cause you pain. I would love you like my own son." She looked at me. "As far as me and your father getting engaged so quickly, we have known each other since high school. In fact, we were in a relationship for almost a year. Your dad proposed to me before I left for college, and I turned him down. I wasn't ready for marriage at that time. I wanted to go to college and see the world outside of Pleasant."

I felt a little shocked at her statement. Mom had admitted they were in a relationship, but never told me that Doug had proposed to her. Jude looked at his father. "When are you guys getting married?"

Doug and Mom looked at each other. "Tomorrow," Doug answered.

"*Tomorrow?*" I said, my voice raised.

With that answer, Jude jumped up from his chair, ran to the bedroom and slammed the door behind him. I focused on the worried expression on my mother's face, "It'll be okay, Liv," Doug reassured her.

She then turned to me. "Honey...please say something."

I took a few moments to formulate my thoughts. "I just want you to be happy, Mom, and if Doug makes you happy, then you have my blessing. I admit I'm surprised it's so soon, but I trust you," I said. It was really a no-brainer. My mom never made rushed decisions. Hell, she took three months to decide on a new cutlery set for the kitchen. Also, she seemed happier with Doug than I'd ever seen her in my life.

"Thank you, honey." She stood up, came over, and gave me a hug.

After she sat back down, I pointed to Doug. "You better treat her right. I know you're bigger than me, but I do have youth on my side." A grin slowly formed on my face.

He smiled back. "I don't want to put it to the test." He got up, walked over, and extended his hand. I shook it.

"You're a good son to your mother," he said.

I nodded.

Gabe got up from his chair, came over, and offered his congratulations, "I hope you guys are very happy together," he said.

"Thanks, Gabe," Mom said.

Doug turned his eyes to the bedroom door. "I better go talk to Jude."

"No," I stopped him, "let me talk to him."

He hesitated a moment before nodding.

I knocked on the bedroom door, turned the knob and stuck my head in. "Can we talk?" I asked, spotting him sitting on the sofa bed, his head hung down.

He nodded. Walking over, I sat down beside him. "What was that all about?"

He sighed, "He always does this! Always! He makes some life-changing decision that affects me and doesn't even give me any say in it. He did this when he married Candice, and when he decided to take the job in Murphystown and move us halfway across the state. Then, instead of getting us our own place, he moves us into my grandparents' house where I don't even have my own room and I have to sleep on a cot in the laundry room." He turned his head to me, "Do you know what it's like to have to sleep with your grandma's underwear hanging on a clothesline above your head?"

I couldn't help but chuckle. "No, I can't imagine it's very fun."

"It's not. I miss our old house…our old house before Candice filled it up with all her shit."

"I'm sorry, bud. Have you told your dad how you feel?"

"What good would it do? He's going to do what he wants anyway. He always does." He hung his head again.

"I know…but your dad seems like a good guy. Believe me, if he wasn't, my mom wouldn't be marrying him. She can read people like a book."

He shrugged his shoulder. "I guess."

"You know, this time it may be a good thing," I said.

He looked at me questioningly. "What do you mean?"

"You're officially going to be getting me as your big brother."

He gasped. "Shit, I hadn't even thought about that. I was too busy being mad at my father."

"Just think. One big ol' gay family." I laughed.

He grabbed his chest. "What will the good, upstanding folks of Pleasant say if they knew? Why, it's downright scandalous."

"A regular house of sin."

"Eh," he waved his hand dismissively, "fuck 'em."

I nodded my head succinctly. "That's right, fuck 'em."

Just then, a knock came from the door, "I guess I know who that is," Jude said.

"Remember what I said…tell him everything you told me. Talk to him. Don't let this come between you guys."

He nodded. I got up to leave and made it a few steps before he stopped me. "Hey."

I looked back. "Yeah?"

"Thanks, big brother." He smiled.

"Anytime." I returned the smile.

The next evening on a moonlit beach before me, Jude, and Gabe, my mom and Doug were wed. I stood next to Gabe and couldn't help but discretely grab his hand and squeeze when they said, "I do." He squeezed mine and smiled back at me.

Chapter Thirteen

April 1993

With spring break over, it was back to the final stretch of my high school career. The trip to Florida turned out to be a life-changing event for all of us. I now had a new stepfather, stepbrother, and an official boyfriend. Gabe and I sealed our relationship and although we'd only been home for a week, I could see a big change in him—his typical sarcastic attitude had softened, he'd become much less bossy and much more physical. By that, I mean he would often grab my hand and interlock our fingers, he'd sometimes rub my back while we sat on the sofa, and he absolutely loved kissing me. It was a tender side of Gabe I'd only seen in my darkest days following Shelby's death.

Another big change as a result of Mom marrying Doug was the announcement that he and Jude would be moving into our house. Mom and Doug had talked about buying a house together, but Mom loved our home in the country and did not want to move. I couldn't have been happier because I did not want to move either, I did, however, have to give up my small weight room. Jude was to have Jennifer's old room across the hall from me, but my mother insisted on keeping one guest bedroom. That meant my weights being moved to the garage.

Jude had spent the night, in order to get an early start

on moving. We'd sat up rather late the prior evening playing *Street Fighter* on my Nintendo before we both crashed in my bed around 3:00 a.m.

Deciding to let him sleep a bit longer I rolled out of bed and got dressed in a pair of shorts and an old Poison tour T-shirt that I had cut the sides out of, leaving room for plenty of ventilation. In fact, I had gotten a little too carried away with the scissors and made the holes larger than I intended. I crept out of my bedroom, careful not to wake him. Mom sat at the kitchen table sipping a cup of coffee and staring out the windows. The sound of my entering startled her.

She gasped. "Oh, honey, you scared me."

"Sorry," I yawned.

"It's a nasty old day outside. We couldn't have picked a worse day to do this," she said.

I peeked out the window at the pouring rain. "Great. Just what we need." I headed for the coffee pot.

"Weatherman says it may be a stormy afternoon," she said. Immediately, I shivered at the word "stormy". Storms always terrified me, especially tornadoes. My fear began in fourth grade when Mr. Tapley, our elementary school principal, showed us a film on them. Looking back, showing a bunch of ten-year-olds a film on killer cyclones was not a good idea. My granddad didn't help either. When I stayed with him, if there was so much as an ominous cloud, he had us both in his old storm cellar, one that leaked and usually meant standing in a foot of water while the cloud passed.

"God, I hope not." I poured myself a cup of coffee, the strong scent making me feel human again.

"I told Doug we should postpone the move until tomorrow, but he said he's already paid for the moving van and that his friends would not be able to help tomorrow."

Doug had procured help from some of his buddies in Gillette to load their belongings from a storage unit into a moving van. He would then drive the van back to Pleasant for us to unload. Most of the things were Jude's, apparently Doug's ex had taken all the furniture except for an antique dining room suite that belong to Jude's late mother. It basically meant we had about four hours to get everything cleared out on our end to make room before they were back with the furniture. Jude had brought all his clothes over from his grandparents' house the prior evening.

"I think if he backs the moving truck as close to the garage as possible, we'll be able to get it in without everything getting wet." I walked over to the table and sat down.

"I admit I'm rather excited about seeing the dining room suite. Apparently, it was handcrafted by Jude's great-great-grandfather in Germany and is over a hundred and fifty years old." Her eyes twinkled; Mom always loved antique furniture.

"It certainly beats that cheap particle board shit from the seventies we have right now."

Mom chuckled. "It was the best we could afford at the time. I suppose I'll have you boys move it out to the barn until I can sell it."

"I'd say burn it." I smiled before blowing on my coffee.

Mom reached across the table and playfully slapped my hand.

"I know we haven't talked much lately. How are you doing?" she asked.

"To tell you the truth I'm happier right now than I have been since before Shelby died. Having Gabe back in my life as my number one best friend"—I really wanted to say boyfriend—"and my other best friend is going to be my little brother living in the bedroom, right across the hall from me. Things are really looking up. You know?"

"I know exactly what you mean." She paused a moment. "I'm going to share something with you that Doug told me and please don't share this with Jude."

"Okay," I said, suddenly feeling a little tense.

"Doug is trying really hard to accept Jude is gay. Jude is his only child, and he loves him more than anything, but he fears for his future…you know…this whole AIDS thing. He wonders if he'll ever find true happiness."

I sat my coffee cup down. "You mean find true happiness with another man?"

"Yes."

I shook my head. "So, wait, he thinks he can't find true happiness unless he's with a woman?"

"He hasn't said that in those exact words."

"Is that the way you feel?" I asked, feeling blood starting to rush to my face.

"No…I think he can find happiness with a man," she answered.

I could see the uncertainty in her eyes and bristled. "You don't seem too sure about that."

She reached over and grabbed my hand, seeing how upset I was becoming, "Honey...no...I think a person can find happiness in someone of the same sex. It may be the fact that Doug knows he'll never have grandchildren."

"Wrong. Gay couples can have children. It's called adoption."

"I know. Honey, please don't be upset at me. I'm working on him. The only reason I told you this is because I'm afraid Jude is going to pick up on how his father feels, and he may talk to you about it. I just want you to reassure Jude that his father loves him more than anything and wants him to be happy," she said in as gentle a voice as possible.

I tried to rationalize why Mom and Doug would feel that way. Maybe it was a generational thing or perhaps the intolerance taught to them by the church, which I seemed to have drifted further away from since Shelby's death. I decided telling her I was bisexual was not a good idea. Instead, I had a different bombshell to drop on her and for some reason I didn't feel the need to be gentle about it.

"Oh, I do have something to tell you...if you haven't figure it out already...I'm not going to college." I stood up and watched her jaw drop.

"Wait? What? What about all those college applications you mailed out?" she asked.

"I got accepted to every one of them. Even got a few scholarship offers. I just don't want to go. I hate school and I don't want to spend another four years in it."

"Wait...Hawk, I don't understand."

"Mom. I don't want to go off to school."

"You don't have to go off to school. You could live here

and commute to college in Arkadelphia. It's only a half-hour away."

"Don't you understand? Going to college was Shelby's dream. All I ever wanted was to get a regular job, get married, buy a house, and start a family. *That* was my dream."

"Why didn't you tell me?"

About that time, Jude entered, clad in the pair of shorts he fell asleep in the prior evening. "Hey," he said, rubbing his eyes and yawning.

"Hey," I returned.

"Good morning," my mother put on her best act of not appearing frazzled, "can I...um, get you some breakfast?"

He pointed to the box on top of the refrigerator. "Can I have some of those Froot Loops?" he asked.

Mom got up, while he took a seat at the table. "Coming right up," she said.

"What are you guys doing?" he asked me.

"Oh, just talking," I said.

"Oh." He nodded, glancing out the window and sighing. "Oh, great! It's raining."

"I know, right? It sucks."

Mom came back with a box of Froot Loops, a bowl and spoon, and a carton of milk, setting them on the table in front of Jude. "Would you like a cup of coffee with that?"

Jude wrinkled his nose. "Coffee? I'd take some orange juice if you have any."

"It just so happens I do," Mom answered and headed to the fridge.

I had to tease him. "Coffee will put hair on your chest."

He glanced down at his smooth chest and smiled. "Somehow, I don't think it would help."

While Jude ate his cereal and I ate a muffin, Mom would occasionally catch my eye. I knew she was itching to continue our discussion about my future, but thankfully she was not going to broach the topic in front of Jude. As soon we finished eating, Jude got dressed and we made our way across the hall to my sister's old room.

I turned the knob of the door and introduced Jude to his future space. His eyes absorbed the surroundings. "Damn! Your sister has a lot of stuff."

"Yeah, she does." I glanced at all the boyband posters hanging on the dark wood-paneled walls, along with a canopy bed, dresser, chest of drawers, and cedar chest.

He then looked at the floors and walls and laughed, "Green shag carpeting? Dark paneling? I feel like I've stepped back into the seventies."

"Yeah, my dad built this house in 1972 and Mom has never really updated it. If you love the carpet, you're going to love your Harvest Gold bathroom complete with swag lights and marble gold mirrors over the sink."

"Your room doesn't look this dated."

"It's because I ripped up the old carpet to reveal the hardwood floors and I painted the paneling. Actually, Shelby and I did. We can do the same to yours sometime if you like."

"Nah, I actually kind of dig it. I've always been fascinated with the seventies. Love disco. Be kinda cool to get some vintage 70s décor in here. You know some blacklight posters and lava lamps. It'll go great with my waterbed."

I laughed, "You have a waterbed?"

"Yeah. It was my parents'. Best sleep you'll ever have." He grinned.

"Groovy," I stared at my sister's canopy bed and mentally traced through the steps of dismantling it.

"Dude," he went over and sat down on it, "you don't know how happy I am to finally have my own room again."

"I bet," I said, before pausing and staring at him.

"What?"

I shook my head, "It still seems so weird that you're going to be living here. I mean...hell, you're *really* my little brother now. Just think if I had never come over that day to rescue you from those bullies, you and I would have never met, and our parents would have probably never have married."

He smiled at me. "I know, right? You know, I'm glad we met because I'm looking forward to having an older brother, especially one that understands what it feels like to be different."

"True." I thought back to the conversation with Mom regarding Jude's sexuality.

"You know, I'm getting braver with my sexuality since everyone knows now." I glanced at the index fingers on each of his hands, painted with blue fingernail polish and his bold clothing choice of a pink half-shirt.

"I'm happy for you, but don't get too brave. This is Arkansas and there are lots of homophobes that would like nothing better than to put you in the hospital...or worse."

"Oh, I know. I'm not going to go all RuPaul. At least not yet." He winked.

A sudden clap of thunder shook the house before a torrent of rain began pounding on the roof. "God, I hate storms."

"Yeah. This weather is crazy," he said.

I glanced out the window, the storm making my anxiety grow. "I wish Gabe would hurry up and get here." I had to admit I had become worried about him driving in the downpour.

Just then I felt a set of hands slip through the two holes in my shirt and tickle my belly, "Guess who?" I felt my body relax.

"Umm…Manuel?" I heard the clacking of the beads in Gabe's hair.

He began tickling me from behind. "I'll show you Manuel."

"Stop! Stop!" I finally broke away and twisted around. "It's about time you got here. We got a lot of work to do."

He stole a kiss from me, "I know, babe." I noticed Jude staring with interest. "You guys could have started without me. You know? Hey, Jude."

"Hey," said Jude, standing up.

Gabe ran his eyes over him, then me. "What is this, Gay Pride Day with the skimpy shirts, with him showing his navel and you flashing your nipples to everyone?"

I scowled at him. "Very funny."

He focused his attention back on the room and clapped his hands together. "So, where do we start?"

I glanced out the window, "It looks like the downpour

has stopped for the moment. Let's start with moving Mom's old dining room furniture to the barn and get that out of the way. Then we'll focus on moving my weights to the garage and the stuff in this room to the new guest room."

Gabe laughed. "Will that dining room table make it to the barn without falling apart?"

I chuckled, "I know, right?"

After clearing out the dining room, moving my weights to the garage, and tearing down my sister's bed, my mother came to the doorway. "You boys ready for some lunch?" she asked.

"Yes, ma'am," said Gabe.

For lunch, Mom prepared tuna sandwiches, potato salad, and homemade pickles she'd canned the previous summer. As we sat down to eat, Mom looked to Gabe. "So, Gabe what's your plan after you graduate?"

I immediately became annoyed. She refused to let it go.

Gabe spoke, "I don't know if Hawk told you, but I'm working in the parts department of my dad's dealership in Nashville, learning the business. I hope in a few years to be managing one of his car lots and perhaps, eventually all of them." He dug a pickle from the Mason jar.

"I take it college isn't an option?" She asked.

"Nah. Honestly, Mrs. Campbell, I *hate* school." He laid the pickle on the plate.

"Apparently, you're not the only one." She glared at me, placing her napkin in her lap.

I gritted my teeth. "Mom. I do not want to discuss this now."

She innocently shrugged her shoulder. "I'm asking Gabe *his* plans. You've made your plans quite clear."

Just then a clap of thunder shook the house causing me to jump. "Looks like it's starting up again. I hope Dad gets back soon," Jude said, before taking a bite of his sandwich.

"So, Gabe, do you have a special girl in your life?" Mom asked.

I glared at her, "What is this? A Spanish Inquisition?"

"I thout you werem Mesican," Jude looked to Gabe his with his mouth full.

I lowered my eyes at Jude.

Gabe smiled at her. "No, ma'am. No girl."

Jude swallowed his bite and reached for his can of Diet Dr. Pepper. "Yesterday in your class, Clint Wagner kept smiling at me. You think he's gay like me, Mrs. Keystone?" he asked.

Mom, who had taken a sip of her iced tea, started choking before coughing once and clearing her throat. I caught Jude's eye, and he winked at me. *Way to go, new little bro! See how she likes being put on the spot for a change.*

"I…um…I wouldn't know, Jude," she stuttered.

"It would be great if he is. He's *really* cute," Jude said. I noticed my mother's face had become flushed.

A familiar intermittent screeching sound from the television in the living room caught my attention, the sound of a severe weather alert. "Uh-oh," I said with a concern in my voice, "that's never a good sound."

Jude jumped up from the table and ran into the living room and then returning in a flash, "It's just a tornado watch for the Southern half of Arkansas," he said, sitting back down as if it weren't a big deal.

Growing up in Arkansas, spring usually meant lots of tornado watches, but rarely a tornado. Even when a tornado warning was issued, nobody really panicked. Admittedly, at one time I did, right after I saw that film in fourth grade, but over the years I'd learned to control it. Sure, I'd get anxious, but I didn't run to my mother crying whenever I heard thunder like I did when I was ten. Occasionally a tornado would touch down, and you'd hear about it on the news the next day of it taking the roof off a chicken house in some small town in Arkansas you've never heard of. I had never seen an actual tornado. Mom had told me the story of a town near Pleasant that was literally wiped off the map back in the fifties, and the strange story of how the funnel destroyed a family's house completely and somehow transported an infant in a carrier to the top of a large oak tree leaving it unharmed.

I supposed Gabe noticed my anxiety, "It's okay…ba…dude. It's just a watch. The chances of a tornado actually hitting here are basically like me winning the lottery."

"I don't know," I said, biting my lip. "I don't like storms and the weather just feels off today." Not only had I felt the humidity in the air, but I had also noticed the low-lying, fast-moving clouds as we moved the dining room furniture to the barn behind our house.

Just then, the phone hanging on the kitchen wall rang, and my mom got up to answer it. I heard lots of "yesses" and "okays" before she hung up. "That was Doug, he said they're about an hour away."

"Oh crap," Jude said, "we've just gotten started on your sister's room."

"We better get to it," I said, and we all jumped up to get back to work, except Mom, who stayed to clean up the kitchen.

Forty-five minutes later, we had most of her bedroom items packed in boxes and piled into my old weight room along with her furniture. The only piece left to move was her cedar chest.

"God, it's hot in here," Gabe removed his sweat-soaked T-shirt, wiped his forehead and threw it into my bedroom.

"I'll adjust the air," I said and went into the hall to adjust the thermostat lower. Just then, I heard weatherman on the television in the living room and stuck my head around the corner where Mom sat on the sofa, her eyes glued to the TV. "Is everything okay?"

I could see the worry in her eyes. "I don't know. There're tornado warnings popping up everywhere west of us. They're calling this an outbreak, and Doug's out there on the road," she said.

"Shit," I said, feeling some butterflies in my stomach.

"Are you boys about finished?"

"Yeah. We just need to move the cedar chest and do the vacuuming and we'll have Jude's room cleared. Jennifer may not like the way we just threw her stuff in boxes and crammed it all into the spare bedroom."

Mom pursed her lips, "She'll just have to get over it."

Mom and Jennifer had not been on the best of terms

since Mom's marriage to Doug. I could see it from both their points of view. Mom was in the wrong in waiting until the night before the wedding to inform Jennifer of her and Doug's plans, but Jennifer was wrong in lecturing her on jumping into a marriage with someone she had been with less than two months. Seeing as she and David were engaged less than two months after they met, she didn't have much room to talk. She should know our mother wasn't the type of person to make rash decisions. I knew it would all blow over within a few weeks.

Just then, the television began flashing a red banner across the bottom of the screen. I shot my attention to the map or Arkansas and the big red blob directly over us. *"I repeat, a tornado warning has been issued for Lewis County until 3:45 p.m. Central Daylight Time. At 2:55 p.m, weather spotters confirmed a large wedge tornado on the ground five miles west of Pleasant moving to the northeast at forty-five miles per hour. If you are in, or near, the town of Pleasant, take cover immediately."*

Suddenly, things got real. Chills ran all over my body and I began to shake. "Oh God, Mom, that's us."

Mom jumped up from the sofa. "Get Jude and Gabe."

I ran into the bedroom, where Jude and Gabe were sitting on the cedar chest, Jude explaining to Gabe his plans for his new room. "Guys, come on. We're under a tornado warning."

"How many times have we been under a tornado warning, and nothing happened?" Gabe asked, as if it were nothing to be concerned about.

"No, the weatherman said for Pleasant to take shelter immediately. There's one on the ground!" I said.

"Oh fuck," Jude stood up.

Just then Mom came up behind me. "We need to take shelter. Now!"

"Where's the most interior room of the house?" Gabe instantly switched modes. Being in tornado alley, we were taught from a very young age what to do if one was coming our way.

"Umm...the master bathroom," Mom answered.

"Come on." Gabe quickly led the way out of Jude's room.

Just then, Doug burst through the front door. "Get under cover. Now!"

"The master bathroom," Gabe yelled at him from the dining room, before turning back leaving the rest of us scrambling toward Mom's bedroom.

"Where you going?" Jude yelled at him.

"My shirt, it's in Hawk's bedroom."

Just then, the electricity went out. "Fuck the shirt! Come on!"

The loud thumping sound of a tree limb hitting the roof stopped me in my tracks just inside my mother's bedroom. I completely froze in terror. My legs would not move. No matter how much I willed them to, I was glued to the spot.

Gabe came running up from behind me, immediately he saw the absolute terror in my eyes. "Babe! Come on. We need to get in the bathroom." He put his hand on my shoulder.

"I...I...can't...move," I stuttered. Just then I heard another limb hit the roof, followed by the sound of glass breaking. Suddenly, I felt Gabe's strong arms left me from the floor.

"Hold on," he instructed me.

I reached around his neck, pressing my face into his naked shoulder. He turned me sideways to get us through the bathroom door. Raising my head, I spied Jude in the bathtub while Mom and Doug huddled against the wall opposite it.

"What's wrong with Hawk?" Jude asked Gabe.

"I don't know. He's having some sort of panic attack," he answered.

"Get him into the bathtub," said Doug.

Gabe stepped into the bathtub with me still in his arms, I felt him slip once, but maintain his hold me. We huddled in the opposite end of the tub from Jude. I clung to Gabe for dear life. Just then I heard the sound of wood cracking. I screamed as tears began pouring from my eyes. "I can't do this, I got to get out of here."

"Babe, we're going to be okay," he said, as my tears continuing to flow.

"We're going to die." I screamed as the sound of large hail hitting the roof drowned out our voices. Then everything went completely silent.

I held onto him tighter. He began stroking the back of his head. "Shhh...babe...it's going to be okay." He kissed me on the forehead.

"I'm so scared, Gabe," I cried and pressed my nose against his chest.

"Shh…it's okay, babe." He stroked his hand down my back. "Just hold onto me. I'm not letting you go."

Then the sound of a roaring wind like I'd never heard in my life deafened me. "Oh God, it's coming!" I tightened my grip on him. Just then I felt another set of arms wrap themselves around me and Jude pressing his face against my back.

My ears popped from the sudden air pressure drop in the house. This was the end. My short seventeen years on earth cut short from a house falling on me. "I love you, Gabe."

"I love you too, Hawk." He said and rested his head against mine.

I closed my eyes waiting for the inevitable. My mind spiraled into that dark place I never wanted it to go ever again. *What is it like to die? Do you feel anything? What did Shelby feel when she saw those headlights coming at her with no way to escape? Did her life flash before her eyes? Did she look away, unable to face her inevitable death? Or did she look to Heaven and smile, embracing that bright light ushering her to some form of an afterlife?* I wanted to believe the latter with all my heart. *Please, God, help us.*

As soon as it all began it was over. I felt Gabe's tears soaking my hair. I slowly turned my head and saw Doug cradling Mom in his embrace as Jude recited the Lord's prayer in my ear. Everything was eerily silent.

Jude lifted his head slowly. "Are we dead?"

"No," said Doug. Jude scrambled out of the bathtub and to his father, who put his arms around him.

"I love you, Dad," he said.

"I love you too, son," he cried.

Gabe continued cradling me as I lifted my head and we locked eyes. Immediately, we began kissing each other frantically. We were both alive and at that moment I didn't care who witnessed our love for each other.

Breaking away, my eyes went immediately to my mother, whose jaw rested on the floor. A few moments of awkwardness followed. "Um…Hawk. Is…there something you haven't told me?"

"Yeah, Mom, Gabe is more than my best friend, he's my boyfriend and I love him," I said with no shame whatsoever.

"But Shel—" Mom started. I knew what she was thinking.

"I'm bisexual, Mom. I've known it since I was ten, I just never explored that side of me until I reconnected with Gabe," I answered.

"Oh." She nodded, although I could see it had not all sunk in yet.

Doug pulled himself up. "Let's go see if there's anything left."

The rest of us followed his lead, me refusing to let go of Gabe's hand. As we journeyed out of Mom's bedroom into the living room, I noticed the blown-out windows and all the wall-hangings scattered and broken on the floor. The carpet was soaked, but the rest of the room remained intact. Mom split into the kitchen, while Jude headed to the back door. Doug stepped out the front door leaving Gabe and I alone in the living room. "You okay, babe?" he asked, gently rubbing his hand down my arm.

"Yeah. I think so," I said. "I thought we were dead."

"Me too, honestly."

I studied his handsome jaw and strong muscular body. "You know you're really good at taking care of me." My mind flashed back to the time after Shelby's death.

"I'll always take care of you...because...well...you're my guy." The corners of his mouth crept upward.

I laid my arms over his bare shoulders, "And you're mine." I smiled and leaned in for another kiss. I pulled back and looked down. "You lost your shirt."

"Yeah...I better go find it." He shrugged and gave me another quick peck before sprinting down the hall.

Just then, Doug came through the front door. "There's a few trees down, and hail damage to the cars."

At that moment, Jude came tearing into the room panting, "The barn is gone!" he said frantically.

"What?" I asked in disbelief.

"The barn. It's completely gone! Caput! No more!" Jude motioned for us to follow him.

Standing in the back yard, my eyes beheld the empty piece of ground where once stood a two-story barn. The tornado came within forty feet of the house, enough to take the barn but leaving the house relatively undamaged, albeit a few missing shingles I saw lying on the ground in front of me and several blown-out windows. Luckily the only thing of value in the barn was a few old tools that belonged to Bruce and the old broken down '67 Chevy, which was thrown half-way across the field.

Just then, Mom gasped. "Oh no, my old dining room

suite!" she said, referring to the shit furniture we'd moved to the barn earlier in the day.

I repeatedly clicked my tongue and shook my head. "Such a tragedy."

"Oh, you!" She playfully slapped my arm.

Just then, Gabe appeared on the other side of me, no longer bare-chested, "Holy shit. The barn is gone."

"Yeah," I said, grabbing his hand in mine and interweaving our fingers.

"So, guys. There's nothing we can do about the barn and being there's no power, we better get the house cleaned up by dark," Doug said. "Livvy, do you have any candles? We're probably going to need them later. It may be a while before the electric company restores the power."

"I have some in the kitchen," Mom said.

Before dark, we unloaded the moving van so Jude would have a bed to sleep in. Luckily, there were no broken windows in mine or Jude's bedroom. Neighbors came by to offer help in cleaning up our property, which we gladly accepted. The tornado wiped out a couple of barns and one chicken house, but luckily no injuries or deaths.

For dinner, our meal consisted of cold tuna sandwiches and chips, since there was no electricity for cooking in the all-electric kitchen. Later, we all sat around the new antique dining room table, playing Monopoly by candlelight.

"That'll be…two-thousand dollars please," Jude held out his hand as Gabe groaned and handed him the last of his money.

I glanced down at my final fifty dollars and then to Jude's large stack of five-hundred-dollar bills. "Remind me never to play this game with Jude again."

"I learned that lesson years ago," laughed Doug, who'd already gone bankrupt.

Mom, distracted by her newly acquired antique dining room table, ran her finger along the decorative edge. "This table is absolutely gorgeous. The craftmanship..."

"You know, I was named after my great-great-grandfather who built this table," said Jude.

"I thought you were named after The Beatles song," I said, sorting my property cards into color groups.

"Nope. Isn't that right, Dad?"

"Yep. Jude's mother chose that name and I liked the song...so that's how Jude got his name."

"You never told me where your name came from, Hawk?" asked Gabe.

"Yeah," said Jude, "I've never heard anyone named that before."

"It's actually Hawkins," I said. "I'm named after some friend of my dad's. Isn't that right, Mom?"

"That's right. Ben, my late husband, named him after his best friend growing up, Granbury Alastair Hawkins. He died the year before Hawk was born Hawk's father wanted to honor him."

Jude gave me a scrutinizing stare. "You mean your full name is Granbury Alastair Hawkins Keystone?"

"Yep." I smiled at him.

"No wonder you prefer Hawk." He grinned.

Gabe chuckled. "Sounds like the name of a murder mystery writer."

"Hmm… you may be on to something there. Maybe I should try writing those kinds of stories instead of adventure stories."

Doug let out a yawn. "So, guys, I think I'm done for tonight."

"Yeah, I'm pretty tired myself," I said. "Doesn't look like the power is coming back on anyway." From what we had heard on the radio, it might be a couple of days before power would be completely restored. Many power poles had been laid to waste by the twister. "You ready to turn in?" I asked Gabe.

"Yeah," he said.

I pushed my chair back and grabbed one of the candles.

"Does Gabe want to sleep in Jennifer's bed tonight?" Mom asked me.

I gave her a puzzled looked, "Why would he want to sleep in there?"

"I just thought he might be more comfortable in a bed by himself," she said.

I rolled my eyes. "Seriously, Mom?"

"I just don't think it's very appropriate for you two to be sleeping in the same bed…seeing that you're…you know? Together. What do you think, Doug?" She put her new husband on the spot.

"I…um…" he stuttered.

"Gabe can sleep in my bed with me," Jude grinned from ear to ear.

"No!" Mom and Doug both said at the same time, much to Jude's amusement.

He snapped his fingers. "Darn."

"This is ridiculous, Mom." I felt anger rising up my collar. "Just because you know Gabe is my boyfriend now, it doesn't change anything."

"It just doesn't seem appropriate. It would be like me letting you and…never mind," she said.

"I know what you were going to say…you were going to say me and Shelby. I don't understand why you're making such a big deal about this. Believe me, if Gabe and I wanted to do something we'd find a way to do it."

"Livvy, he's got a point," Doug spoke up.

Doug's statement surprised me after Mom had revealed to me that he had difficulty in accepting Jude's sexuality. "Thank you," I said to him.

She rolled her eyes. "Fine. Just go."

"Come on," I said to Gabe, leading the way down the hall with my candle.

After we got to my bedroom, we both took turns getting ready for bed using the single candle to brush our teeth and use the restroom. We stripped down to our underwear and climbed into my bed. Lying on my back, Gabe stretched his left arm, and I cradled my head against his chest and rubbed his pecs with my hand.

"You're quiet, babe," he said.

I huffed, "Can you believe my mother?"

"It will just take her time. Her finding out about us the way she did…I mean it wasn't the ideal way, for sure."

"Amen to that!"

We lay in silence a few moments before Gabe spoke. "You scared me today. The way you just froze up like that."

"Yeah. I know. That's never happened to me before, but I've never been that scared in my life...if it weren't for you...anyway...you saved me once again."

"I'll always be here to save you no matter what." He smiled at me.

"I know." I smiled back at him.

"I do see you as an equal in this relationship," he said.

I lifted my head and wrinkled my brow at him. "Where did that come from?"

"I don't know...what you said about me taking care of you. I know it's probably not what you're used to in your previous relationship. I mean...a male-male relationship...I mean...the roles aren't as clear-cut."

"I know. I've thought about it. Shelby had a strong personality like you, and in some ways our relationship wasn't that much different. I felt like I had to play the role of the 'protective boyfriend' but with you I don't feel that way," I explained.

"I just don't want you to ever feel like I'm controlling you or anything."

"Believe me, I'll let you know when you've stepped over the line." I chuckled. "Been doing that since we were kids."

Gabe laughed. "True." He paused. "I'll tell you what... I'll take care of you, and you can take care of me. We'll take care of each other."

"It's a deal!" I nodded and glanced toward the door. "Say, you wanna do what my mother's afraid we'll do?"

"I thought you'd never ask!" He laughed.

Chapter Fourteen

May 1993

A few weeks had passed since the tornado struck our homestead and took out our barn. Luckily, none of us suffered any physical injury from the twister, but the emotional damage I suffered had taken its toll on me. My fear of storms had only intensified, so that any approaching rain cloud I was immediately on edge, glued to the television monitoring the weather. Gabe tried to reassure me that the tornado was an isolated event, and we would probably never be that close to one again in our lifetime.

The storm had brought Gabe and I closer together. He'd spend every weekend at my house and I was always happy to see him, but I sometimes felt my mother was not. In fact, for the first time in my life, my relationship with my mother had become strained. We communicated less and I found myself doing things I knew would get under her skin, like cuddling with Gabe on the sofa, sometimes kissing him when she walked into the room. While she never said she opposed our relationship, she certainly did not embrace it.

One night, Gabe and I sat on the sofa watching *Quantum Leap* after he'd put in a hard day of school and work. He removed his arm from around me and reached down to rub his calves.

"My legs are killing me. That parts manager, Jerry, has me running all over the warehouse pulling parts for the mechanics. I bet I climbed up that damn ladder a hundred times this afternoon getting down boxes," he said.

"You want me to rub them?" I asked.

He grinned and quickly pulled off his socks and stretched his legs across my lap.

I chuckled at him. "You knew I'd offer, didn't you?"

He coyly shrugged his shoulder.

I began working the left calf, his shorts coming just above his knee. Even after all these months of us being together, I still got a sense of awe being able to touch another guy in such an intimate way. Our relationship had progressed to the point where our bodies no longer held any secrets from one another, and no parts were off-limits. I felt as comfortable touching him as I once did Shelby, and I knew he felt the same way. He was my boyfriend as much as Shelby was once my girlfriend.

"I love your hairy legs." I rubbed my hand up from the bottom of his shorts down to his ankle.

"I love your hairy pits," he said, making me shake my head at one of his little weird fascinations. Wearing a tank top, I put my arm behind my neck and grinned.

"Nice," he said.

As I moved to massage his toes, Mom walked into the room just as Gabe closed his eyes and moaned, "You're so good at that, babe."

Mom frowned at me. "Doug just got home from work and has brought pizza if you boys want any."

Gabe, upon hearing my mother's voice, opened his eyes

and sat up, yanking his legs from my lap. I grabbed them and pulled them back, causing him to flop back down on the couch. "Okay, after I finish giving my boyfriend a foot massage," I said defiantly.

She nodded and left the room.

"You're just being a little shit, aren't you?" He laughed.

"She shouldn't be so homophobic. She never complained when I gave Shelby a shoulder massage in front of her."

"Cut her a little slack, she's used to seeing her son with a beautiful blonde white girl, not a black Mexican boy with braids," he joked.

I rolled my eyes at him. "Please."

"I'm just saying, she might kick you out if you're not careful."

"I don't care. I've been thinking about moving out, anyway," I said.

His eyes went wide. "Wait? What?"

"It's always been my plan. I've been thinking…what if we got our own place and moved in together?"

He pulled his feet back and sat up. "Are you serious?"

"Yeah. Why not? You've known that's always been my dream…get a job, move out, get married, and raise a family."

"That was your dream with Shelby."

"Yes, but Shelby isn't here anymore. There's no reason it can't happen with someone else." I cocked my eye at him.

He shook his head. "Woah…wait. You want us to be together like…a married couple?"

"Not right now…one day." Although in my mind, the sooner the better.

"Hawk, two dudes can't be married."

"Well, duh. I know that, but it doesn't mean we can't *act* like a married couple. We could have like some sort of commitment ceremony with rings and all. I have read that Eureka Springs has ministers that will do that for same-sex couples."

He scratched his head. "How would that even work? With our friends and family?"

"As far as everyone would know, we're just a couple of best friends who decided to get our own place and split the expenses—in other words roommates."

Gabe started chewing on his lip. "You know, we could pull it off if we're careful about it. I mean we'd have to get some place with two bedrooms to pull off the illusion we had our own rooms. You know how the guys are always teasing me about not having a girlfriend. How we gonna explain that?"

That was most definitely a problem, my period of "mourning" would be over at some point and people were going to start asking me why I wasn't dating. "I don't know. Hell, we'll figure that out later."

"Dude! It's a crazy idea!" he said, a grin widening across his face. "But I love it!"

The next day at school, the wheels in my mind were spinning. Gabe and I had started building a map for our future together. Sure, it still seemed a bit crazy to me, but I firmly believed we could be a very happy same-sex couple. Shelby would have wanted me to be happy with someone, and I know the gender of that person would not have mattered to her.

By third period, I had already planned the way I would propose to Gabe. I would suggest going hiking up to the Little Missouri Falls near Albert Pike Recreation area, one of our favorite places. It would be both beautiful and most importantly, it would be private.

I had just closed the door to my locker when I heard yelling from the other end of the hall.

I yanked my head toward the sound, spotted Jude sitting on the floor crying, covering his right eye with his hand, while a blond kid with a camo jacket stood over him. My face contorted in rage. I threw down my books and shoved my way through the crowd of students.

"Faggots!" I heard the bully taunting Jude and the other boy that stood behind him.

With absolutely no hesitation, I rushed at the bully, shoving him against the lockers where I proceeded to give him a punch in the stomach. I then grabbed him by the shoulders and pinned him against the locker "Don't you ever call my brother that!" I yelled and punched him in the jaw. The smacking sound of my fist against his face echoing down the hall. Just as I pulled my fist back to hit him again, I felt someone grab my arm from behind.

"Hawk!" It was Coach Hadley's voice. "Stop it! Now!"

I struggled against him to resume my assault, but he grabbed my other arm and pulled me away. My anger clouded my vision, but I could clearly see a bruise on the bully's face. While I would never strike a kid, this guy wasn't a kid. He was in my grade and loved nothing better than to pick on those he considered weaker. One of his favorite tortures was taking his senior ring, flipping it around, and whacking seventh graders on the head.

"Greyson!" Hadley yelled at one of the bystanders. "Get Chad to the nurse."

I struggled against Coach's overpowering grip. "Let me go!"

"Calm down, Hawk." He held me as I tried to wiggle out of his arms. The man was much stronger than he looked.

"Let…me…go! My brother is hurt."

Finally, he released me as I rushed to Jude, squatting beside him. I put my hand on his shoulder. "You okay, buddy?"

He sniffled. "Yeah."

I gently took his arm and tried to ease his hand away from his eye. "Let me see." As I pulled it away, I saw the black and blue, but inside, all I saw was red. "What happened?"

The black-haired boy standing behind him answered, "Jude and I were talking, and Chad came up and started calling us names. Jude spit at him and called him an inbred piece of white trash and Chad hit him."

Hadley put his hand back on my shoulder. "Okay Hawk, he's fine. I need you to go to Principal Anderson's office."

I glared up at him. "I'm not going anywhere until he says he's okay."

"Are you okay?" I asked Jude.

"Yeah," he said, just barely audible.

"He's fine, Hawk, it was just a little scuffle," Hadley said very calmly.

I stood up and pointed at Jude's eye. "You call that a 'little scuffle'? He punched my brother in the eye and call him and his friend…that word. I want Chad expelled!"

"I don't think that's up to you, son," Hadley said evenly.

"I am *not* your son, asshole!" I spat. I heard gasps from the crowd of students.

His beady eyes flashed red. "Listen, you need to calm down. You're in enough trouble as it is," he said.

I scanned the crowd of dumbfounded faces, seeing the ignorance, prejudice, and intolerance in their eyes. "Why didn't anyone try to help my little brother?" I yelled.

A bunch of them shrugged their shoulders before I heard a voice in the back of the crowd yell, "Because we don't want queers in our school."

"Who said that?" I searched for the owner of the voice. It was then I saw the face of one of my former teammates. "Kyle Proctor. You dumb shit! You think everyone in this school is straight?"

The crowd parted in front of him. "Everybody but those two sissies!" He pointed at my brother and the boy behind him.

I laughed, my adrenaline pumping. "Sissies huh? You think all queers are sissies. I'm a queer. Do you think I'm a sissy? How about you come over here and I'll show you how a 'sissy' can kick your motherfucking ass."

The crowd gasped. I scanned the dumbfounded faces.

"Yeah. That's right. Your former Homecoming King is a queer. So, look at your friend, the teammate you shower with in the locker room, the person sitting next you in class...because believe me there are a lot more of us in this school!"

Just then I heard a clapping coming through the crowd. My eyes lit up at the sight of my mother coming closer as the students parted to let her through. She walked up and stood beside me.

"Well said, son," she said loud enough for everyone to hear her.

"Thanks, Mom," I said.

She reached down to help Jude to his feet. "I'm taking Jude to the nurse."

I nodded.

"Hawk," Coach Hadley pointed, "to the principal's office. Now"

I looked to my mother. "Don't worry, honey, I'll be down there after I'm sure Jude is okay. I'll straighten it out." She leaned in and whispered to me, "I love you and I'm sorry how I've been behaving at home."

"Thanks, Mom. I love you too." I smiled at her.

Later that evening, I stuck my head into Jude's bedroom. "Hey," I said. He lay on his bed with a notebook and pen in hand. "You okay?"

He looked up and rolled his eyes. "Yeah, for the hundredth time, I'm okay. It's just a little black eye." He then smiled.

"Okay." I paused. "What are you doing?"

"Writing."

"Oh. What are you writing about?" I entered and sat down on the side of the bed.

"It's an idea I got for the adventure of this gay teenager who gets transported to a parallel earth where everyone is gay and all the straight people are the minority," he said, placing his notebook on the bed.

I chuckled. "Sounds…interesting."

"It's kind of a social commentary story."

"I see." I examined his black and blue eye. "Does it hurt?"

"A little." He touched his finger to it. "Thanks for standing up for me today."

"It's part of my job as your new big brother." I ran my eyes around his room. True to his vision, Jude had decorated his bedroom in a seventies theme with bean bag chairs, beaded curtains, and blacklight posters. "You got some groovy new stuff in here." I pointed to the lava lamp sitting on his nightstand.

"Yeah, last weekend my friend Clint and I went through his parents' attic and found a bunch of this stuff."

"Is that the kid you were talking to today?"

"Yeah, that's him." I could see his eyes had lit up as soon as he mentioned his name.

"Do I sense a little something going on here?" I grinned.

He playfully punched me in the shoulder. "I don't know…maybe. His name is Clint Wagner, he's in my grade. He used to play sports when he was a kid but doesn't anymore. We played one-on-one basketball on the back court the other day and he's actually pretty good at it. He likes to draw comic books, which I think is cool. He says he likes girls, but thinks he likes boys too." Jude blushed. "He told me this morning he thinks I'm cute...right before douchebag Chad showed up."

"Go, little bro!"

"Thanks."

I frowned. "Sorry Chad ruined the moment."

"It's okay. It was worth it to see you kick his ass." He smiled then hung his head. "I'm grateful for what you did for me, but I wish you hadn't have outed yourself. You see how I'm treated, now everyone's going to treat you the same way."

I waved my hand dismissively. "Eh. I'm not worried about it. I graduate in two weeks, anyway."

"What are you going to do after graduation?"

"Hell, if I know." I chuckled.

"Are you going to move out?"

I shrugged my shoulder. "I don't know. I've been thinking about it. Mom hasn't been too crazy about me and Gabe being together. She stood up for me with Anderson today and got my punishment down to three days of detention, but I don't know if her actions mean she's ready to accept me and Gabe." I had to give Mom credit, when Coach Hadley pressured Principal Anderson to expel me for calling him an asshole on top of the fighting, Mom threatened to resign on the spot if that happened. I guess Anderson felt sympathetic toward me after all I'd been through and the fact that he didn't want to lose one of the best teachers in the school, so I got the same punishment as Chad.

He sighed. "I know. I was going to see if I could invite Clint for a sleepover next weekend, but if her and Dad find out he's bi, then they're going to be all weird about it, like she is with you and Gabe."

"You're probably right. I suppose having one teen son in the house with a boyfriend is hard to accept, imaging having two."

"Yeah." His face drooped before he raised his pleading eyes at me. "Please don't leave, Hawk. I don't want you to go. I never thought I'd have a big brother and now I have the best one in the world right across the hall from me."

His words felt like they reached in and twisted my insides, putting me in a position I didn't want to be in if my plans with Gabe came to fruition. "I'm not going anywhere right now, I've just been thinking about it. Regardless, I love you, and I'm always going to be here for you."

He reached out and put his arms around me. "I love you too, big brother."

"What's going on here? Am I interrupting a *Family Matters* tender moment?" Gabe's voice came from the doorway.

Jude pulled away and I looked toward the door. "Yep…you did…Urkel."

"Did I do that?" Gabe pulled his pants up high and did his best Steve Urkel impression. Just then he saw Jude's eyes and pointed. "Woah! What happened to you?"

"It's a long story," said Jude.

"Yeah, you better come in. We need to talk," I said.

"Oh no, this can't be good." Gabe came closer.

I caught him up with everything that happened, including the moment I outed myself in Jude's defense.

Gabe stood up, put his hand on his forehead and began pacing, "Fuck, Hawk, you came out to everyone at your school?"

"Not everyone, but I'm sure by now everyone knows, but I don't give a shit. I'll be out of there in two weeks anyway."

He stopped and locked eyes with mine. "No, Hawk. Don't you understand? This is going to spread beyond Pleasant. It's just a matter of time before someone at my school finds out...then the guys will find out...then my parents, and then how am I going to explain this?"

I really hadn't thought about the repercussions of my actions and how it would affect Gabe. Murphystown and Pleasant are fifteen miles apart and both small towns. Although the schools were big rivals, lots of the girls at my school had boyfriends at Gabe's school. "Tell them it's none of their fucking business."

"You don't understand, Hawk. My father will forbid me to be see you. Not to mention the fact, he may already suspect I'm gay. It's not like I have a track record of girlfriends you know?"

Jude joined the conversation. "I'm sorry, Gabe, I didn't mean for any of this to happen. It's my fault."

He sighed. "It's not your fault, Jude. Hawk was just standing up for what's right. I would have done the same thing if I'd been there." He walked over and sat down on the bed. "I just don't know what I'm going to do if this gets back to my parents."

"Have you ever thought of just telling them you're gay? I didn't think my dad would accept it, but he has," Jude said.

"You don't understand. My family is Roman Catholic. Homosexuality is a sin…a *big* sin. Accepting me means them rejecting the teachings of their church. Fuck! I knew I was going to have to deal with this someday, just not while I was still in high school." He bowed his head and covered his eyes with his palms.

I rubbed his shoulder. "I'm sorry, honey."

"It's okay." He put his arm around me, pulling me close. "If I have to tell them, I will, and I'll deal with the fallout."

"I love you," I said.

He put his hand on the back of my head and pulled my head down kissing me on the forehead. "I love you too, babe. It's going to be okay."

It took just two days for the news of my sexuality to make it to Murphystown and to the ears of our friend Adam, who cornered Gabe in the parking lot and asked him if the rumors were true. Gabe confirmed them, per my permission, of course. I felt there was no use in denying it, the words came directly from my own mouth in front of at least thirty Pleasant High students. According to Gabe, Adam just turned and walked away. Charlie was the next to confront him and when Gabe confirmed it, he followed it up with asking him if we were together. Apparently, Charlie had seen Gabe's hand on my knee under the table at the

Dairy Barn after one of our Saturday morning football games. When Gabe admitted we were, he just laughed and said, "I knew it!" At least he was cool with it. Out of our six mutual friends, only two did not have a problem with it.

Gabe and I had many discussions about the situation and he ultimately made the decision to come out to his parents. I questioned if he felt he was truly ready to take this life-changing step, but after a lot of soul-searching, he said he didn't want to live a lie the rest of his life. Being with me, he said, had convinced him that he was doing the right thing and that he didn't want to fight his father to see me.

He chose the day after his graduation to tell them. Being the first high school graduate in his family, his parents had planned a big party afterward. His mother had been preparing it for weeks, and he didn't want to ruin it by dropping his bombshell on them. As it so happens, Pleasant High's graduation was held the same Saturday as Murphystown's. Jennifer and David came from Fayetteville to witness me walk across stage and receive my diploma. Both got to meet Doug and Jude for the first time. While Jennifer wasn't happy at first with my mother's decision to marry so quickly, she accepted it and her and Mom reconciled.

I sat in our living room a nervous wreck. I wanted to be with Gabe when he told his parents, but he thought it best that he does it alone. He joked that when his family got upset, everyone starts speaking Spanish, so I'd be completely lost anyway.

I glanced up at the clock that read 12:45 p.m. *They're just back from church*, I thought to myself. Everyone in my family knew it was happening, and I had asked Mom and Doug to prepare for the worst-case scenario, that being Gabe's parents throwing him out of their house. I turned my head to Jude who, like me, kept checking the time. In the chair to my right sat Jennifer. In the kitchen, I could hear Mom, Doug, and David sitting around the table talking.

Just then the doorbell rang, causing me to nearly jump out of my skin. I glanced at the clock again. "Surely, he hasn't told them already," I said.

"No," Jennifer said, jumping up to answer it, "I sent for reinforcements."

I gave her a puzzled look. "Huh?" A few moments later, two muscular guys in jeans and T-shirts entered the room. "*J.J.? Mason?*" I stood up.

"Hey, big guy." J.J. smiled as he came over and grabbed me in a bear hug. Mason did the same.

"What are you guys doing here?"

"We just happened to be in town this weekend when Jennifer called and let us know what was going on."

Jennifer bit her lip at me, "I hope you don't mind me telling them about you and Gabe. I just thought you guys could use the support."

"Umm…no…it's fine." I looked to J.J. Seeing as I was about to marry his little sister and now, seven months later, I had moved on to someone else, I wasn't sure how he would feel about that. "I hope."

"Don't worry, Hawk, Shelby would have wanted you to be happy and so do I."

"Thanks, J.J. That means a lot to me." I paused and

looked to Jude. "J.J., Mason, this is mine and Jennifer's new little brother, Jude. I guess you could say he's one of us, too."

"Hey, Jude. Cool name…and hair color." Mason walked over and extended his head.

Jude chuckled at the platinum-blond hair color they shared. "Yours too."

"Have you heard anything from him yet?" J.J. asked me as Jennifer offered them both chairs. I sat down.

"No. He should be telling them now."

"How do you think they'll react?" Mason asked.

"Not good, I'm afraid." I anxiously wrung my hands.

Mason shook his head. "Been there, done that."

"How you been doing, Hawk? I haven't seen you since Christmas," J.J. said.

"Good, I guess. I mean the scars are always going to be there, but it's better. Thanks to Gabe and this guy right here." I patted Jude on the knee, who turned to me and smiled.

"How about you…and your parents?" I asked.

"I'm doing okay. Mom and Dad, not so good. Mom feels better when we talk about Shelby, but Dad doesn't want her name even mentioned. I'm trying to come home more often now. I do worry about them. Mom has made a shrine out of Shelby's room and goes in there and sits for hours."

I frowned. "That's so sad."

"She wanted me to tell you that if there's anything special you would like from it, you could have it."

It didn't take but an instant for me to know what item I wanted. I had wanted it for a long time, but emotionally I felt I couldn't have handled it until now. "There's a giant stuffed gorilla sitting in the yellow chair in the corner of her bedroom. I won it for her at the fair and it has a special meaning to me."

J.J. gently smiled. "I'll bring it to you tomorrow."

About that time, the doorbell startled me once again. This time I knew it had to be him. I wasted no time in jumping up and running to the door. Grabbing the knob, I yanked it open. Standing before me was a teary-eyed Gabe with a duffle bag in hand. I immediately knew what it meant; he had prepared it ahead of time and put it his jeep in case of the worst.

"Oh no, honey." I grabbed him in an embrace.

"What am I going to do?" He crumpled into me, gripping my shirt with his fingers and burying his face into my neck. I knew it had to be pure torture to hold it in long enough to drive to my house. My heart ached for him, and I just wanted to comfort him like he had comforted me in my time of need.

"It's going to be okay, honey." I held him tight.

"No, it's not," he cried. "They don't want me anymore."

"We're going to make it through this. I love you."

"I...love...you, too." he returned, between sobs.

"Come on. Let's go sit down." I ushered him further inside. As soon as I entered the living room, I discretely shook my head at everyone, letting them know it did not go well.

Jude leapt up from the sofa and grabbed Gabe in a hug. "I'm so sorry, Gabe."

"Thanks, Jude," He sniffled before breaking away and

sitting down on the couch. I sat beside him. Jennifer walked over with a tissue in hand for him. Thanking her, he wiped his face and looked around the room.

"Gabe. This is J.J., Shelby's brother, and his boyfriend, Mason. They're here because they've both gone through what you're going through," I said.

He nodded at them.

I put my arm around him and pulled him close to me. "What happened?"

He wiped his nose. "After church, I asked them to sit down with me at the kitchen table that I had something I needed to tell them. I didn't know how else to say it, so I just said the words, 'Papa. Mama. I'm gay.' Immediately Papa pointed at the door and told me to get out, and Mama immediately stopped him. Then they started arguing with each other. Miguel and Maria came into the room from hearing all the screaming and began crying. Then...then..." he began crying again, "Papa ran over and grabbed me by my shoulders and pushed me out the door."

My eyes bulged. "He didn't hurt you, did he?"

He shook his head. "No. I didn't resist him...I got in my Jeep and left." His desperate eyes met mine. "Hawk, I've never seen him that angry in my life."

"Gabe. I know this is difficult, but you sure he didn't hurt you?" J.J. asked.

"No. I'm okay," he said. "What am I going to do?"

"You're going to stay here. I've talked to Mom and Doug about it and you can stay here as long as you need to," I said.

"How can he do this? I thought he loved me. I love him." His hopeless brown eyes stared into mine.

"Gabe," Mason said, "my father did the same thing to me five years ago, but my parents never loved me, and the feeling was mutual. If your mother was fighting for you and if you love your dad like I know you do, hope is not lost. It may take time, but I feel they'll come 'round."

"Mason's right, Gabe," J.J. said. "My father had a hard time accepting it at first. We barely spoke for months, but my mom worked on him and eventually we mended our relationship. They love Mason like their own son and their grandson just as much."

My eyes lit up. *Grandson.* I had no idea they had a son together. It gave me hope for me and Gabe. I had to know more, but now was not the time.

Gabe nodded, just as the telephone rang. I could hear my mom in the kitchen answering it. A few moments later, she came into the room. "Gabe, your mother is on the phone and would like to talk to you."

His eyes went large.

"It's going to be okay," I said.

He rushed to the kitchen as Doug and David exited to give him privacy.

"I take it things didn't go well," Mom said.

"No. They didn't," I replied.

The minutes seemed to drag by, eventually I got up and moved closer to the kitchen door to see if I could get a clue as to how it was going. Jennifer caught my attention and whispered, "Anything?"

I shook my head. "I don't know, I don't speak Spanish."

A few moments later, he hung up the phone. I backed away from the door as he entered. "Well?"

"Mama and Papa had a big fight, and Mama left with Miguel and Maria and are staying with my abuela tonight. She said she doesn't care if I'm gay and that she loves me, no matter what." I could see a slight twinge of hope in his eyes.

"I knew your mother couldn't let you go. I've seen how much she loves you." I grabbed him in my embrace.

"I couldn't do this without you," he whispered into my ear, words meant for only me to hear.

Later that evening, after everyone left, I laid in bed, my head on Gabe's chest. I played with one of the beads in his hair. "You keeping your braids?"

"I don't know. Papa doesn't like them. He says they make me look too 'black'."

"I didn't realize how bigoted your father is. I mean he never seemed like it to me," I said.

"I never told anyone this, but I think my father is ashamed of me because my skin is so dark. In my culture, lighter-skinned Latinos are looked at more favorably. It's so wrong." He shook his head.

"Right. It's not like you can control your genes," I said.

"Exactly! I have no more control over that than I do over the fact that I'm gay."

"Obviously, I don't care if people know that I'm into dudes. I practically shouted it to the entire school with a bullhorn." I chuckled.

"True." He looked at me. "Do you regret it? I mean, you could have just as easily chosen a girl to be with and no one would have ever known. Your life would be so much easier."

I lowered my eyes at him. "Gabe, you got it all wrong, I didn't 'choose' to fall in love with you, just like I didn't 'choose' to fall in love with Shelby. It just happened."

"I guess it's just hard for me to understand a person who is bisexual."

"I know, it was hard for me to understand, too. I mean, there's things I like about girls: their delicate features, the smell and soft texture of their hair, boobs." I chuckled. "Then there's things I like about guys: pecs, abs, a nice bulge in a pair of jeans. I don't know, I get this giddy feeling when I'm around a person I like, whether it be a girl or a boy."

"Yeah. You're the only person that I've ever got that feeling around."

My eyes widened. "Seriously?"

"That night we ran into each other again after all those years…I got that feeling for the first time in five years. Then to see how hot you'd become…well, I wanted you…*bad*." He chuckled.

"Oh yeah, I know. You made that very clear that day in the boat." I laughed. "I told you that I couldn't handle you coming on to me because I wasn't gay. That wasn't the truth. The real reason I pushed you away is because you were too big of a temptation for me, and I was afraid that I might do something I'd regret."

"So, out-of-sight, out-of-mind," Gabe said.

I shrugged my shoulder. "It seemed like a good idea at the time."

"I understand." He stroked my hair, looking deep into my eyes, "Shelby was one lucky girl to have you. While I hate the circumstances that brought us together, I'm so happy you're mine."

I smiled gently at him, "I'm happy you're mine too. I love you, honey."

"I love you too, babe." He leaned in and kissed me on the lips.

Chapter Fifteen

July 1993

Two months had passed since Gabe came out to his parents. It had taken a week for his father to speak to him and another week before he allowed him back in the house. All of which, drove a wedge between his parents. His mother came to visit often over the two weeks he stayed with me and would sometimes bring his little brother and sister along as well. Gabe's father agreed to allow him to move back home, but their relationship was not the same as it was before. Gabe's father said he would try and accept Gabe's sexuality, but from what Gabe had told me, he wasn't trying very hard. He remained distant and cold.

Gabe's mother seemed genuinely okay with Gabe and I being together. His mother had always liked me, and I her. I loved Gabe with all my heart, and it pained me to see his relationship with his father virtually destroyed. He continued to let Gabe work in the parts department of one of his dealerships, but no longer took him under his wing to teach him the family business. Gabe said he felt like just another employee that put in his forty hours for a paycheck and nothing more.

As for me, the college discussion with my mother came up once again a few days after graduation. I argued the same points with my mother as before, but it took Doug to convince her to let me decide my own future. He gave me a job working in the chicken processing plant he managed in Murphystown. While deboning chicken would not have been my first choice of jobs, it paid above minimum wage. Doug said he saw lots of potential in me and thought within six months, if I continued to work hard, I could be line supervisor. He said that's how he started with the company and eventually worked himself up to plant manager. I was thankful for the job and so far, Doug had impressed me as a stepfather to the point I honestly liked him. He seemed to accept my and Jude's sexuality. I think after seeing how Gabe's father treated him, he decided that he didn't want a relationship like that with his son and stepson.

It was a warm and sunny summer afternoon when Gabe and I decided to head up to the Little Missouri Falls to do a little hiking and swimming. Gabe pulled his jeep into the gravel parking lot and killed the engine. We both grabbed our backpacks containing water, snacks, and other supplies from the back seat. With temperatures climbing into the nineties, we knew it was going to be a hot one. I pulled my shirt off and threw it into the back seat.

"Shirtless hike, huh?" He grinned at me from the opposite side of the vehicle.

"Yep, I like to show a little skin." I winked.

He did the same. "I'm always ready to see that hot bod of yours."

"Sexy," I winked and picked up an excited Lucy from the back seat. I put the leash on her collar and placed her on the ground. "Come on Luce, let's go." I led her toward the head of the trail.

I glanced around and noticed quite a few people swimming in the river and picnicking near the banks. "It's busy today."

"Yeah, I guess because it's such nice weather."

We hiked the trail that wound up the mountain, the warm breeze caressed my skin. I loved Arkansas during the summer. We passed a couple with a young child coming back down the trail that greeted us with a "hello". It made me think of J.J. and Mason and the fact they were gay parents. In the past year, they had bought a house together after Mason's young son Dylan came to live with them. Apparently, Mason had gotten a girl pregnant in high school and she allowed Mason to be a part of Dylan's life. Things went South when she became mixed up with an ex-con and got arrest for manufacturing and distributing methamphetamines and was serving a two-year prison sentence. Child Protective Services took Dylan from their unfit home, a run-down mobile home with no running water or electricity and gave him to the girl's parents to raise. When Mason got wind of it, he sued for custody of his son and won.

Gabe looked back at me. "Do you still want children someday?"

"Of course. The sooner the better." I laughed. Most young adults would not be thinking about starting a family so young, but I wasn't like most. With Shelby, it would have been easy to get married and have a baby, with Gabe, not so easy. Mason fought for over a year to obtain custody of his own son. The fact that he was in a same-sex relationship was not looked upon favorably by the judge.

Coming to a fork in the trail, I stopped. "Here. Take Lucy, I need to tie my shoe." Gabe took her leash from me as I bent down.

"Let's go up the mountain rather than down to the falls. I have a feeling it will be crowded down there," he said.

"Sounds good to me." I raised up and cocked my head at him. "Are you fidgeting?"

"No. Why?" he answered quickly.

"You're anxious."

"I'm not anxious," he said a bit defensively, "I'm just not in the mood to be around a bunch of people is all." He turned to face the trail ahead of us. "Come on." He tugged on Lucy's leash, leading her in the right direction.

About a half-hour later, the terrain became much steeper as we ascended the rocky slope. A few times we had to stop and pick up Lucy and carry her over a few boulders. I looked ahead and saw no one. Same behind us. "We may have to turn around. Lucy's not going to be able to climb this trail if it gets much steeper," I said.

"Yeah, we've probably gone far enough," Gabe scanned the surroundings. "Let's take a break before we start back down." He pointed to a group of boulders clustered together beneath a tall hickory tree.

Sitting down beside one another, I adjusted my ponytail. "This hair is hot. I need to get another haircut soon."

"Yeah, I know what you mean." He shook his head of long box braids.

I pointed at his head. "Don't you dare cut your hair. I really like it like that."

"Charlie's sister did a good job of it. Papa hates it of course."

"Of course," I said. Gabe's father had made it clear that he did not like Gabe sporting traditionally black hairstyles. As if he should feel ashamed of his African heritage. Growing up in the South, I'd seen displays of racism firsthand from members of my extended family. When Gabe and I had shown up together at my cousin's birthday party together a couple of weeks prior, I overheard my great-aunt, Stella, referring to Gabe with a derogatory term that I don't care to repeat. Rather than cause a huge scene like I wanted to, Gabe convinced me to let it go. He said he'd dealt with that kind of ignorance all his life. Racist old bitch. I always hated that woman.

I reached into my backpack and pulled out a Gatorade, handing it to him before getting one for myself.

"Thanks, babe," he said, unscrewing the top.

He moved his head around, taking in the beautiful surroundings. "Arkansas is such a beautiful state."

"Yep. It is," I said, taking a sip of my drink. We sat in silence for a few moments taking in the sound of the birds and crickets and letting the warm breeze wash over us as it rustled the leaves on the trees. "You know, I've been wanting to talk to you about something."

"Me too," Gabe said as he turned up his bottle, guzzled, then wiped his mouth, "but you go first."

"So, it's about...college. I've been thinking about taking Mom's suggestion and going to Henderson next month. It's only a thirty-minute commute and I could still live at home to cut expenses."

Gabe's eyes widened. "Really? I thought you said you would never go back to school."

"I did, but I don't want to be deboning chicken the rest of my life. I figured out Mom and Doug's little scheme to show me what kind of life I'd have without a college education...and as much as I hate to admit it," I laughed, "it worked."

Gabe chuckled. "You know I'll support you in whatever you want to do, babe."

"That's why you're such a good boyfriend." I leaned over and kissed him.

He smiled at me. "So, I have something I want to talk to you about as well." He took a deep breath. "I'm quitting my job working for my father."

"Okay," I said evenly. I was a bit shocked, since his dream was to one day take over his father's car dealership business, but I understood why he would want to quit.

"I don't know," he shrugged his shoulder, "he's never going to let me run the business. Not now. He's already taken Miguel to work with him a couple of times and introduced him to everyone. I'm not stupid to know what he's doing."

"Oh, honey, I'm so sorry." I rubbed his shoulder.

"Every time he looks at me, I can see the disgust in his eyes. The only reason he tolerates me is because of my mother. It's fine. I don't need him. In fact, as soon as I can find another job, I'm moving out."

"Move back into my room with me? My mother won't care."

"I was thinking. What about us getting our own place together?"

It took me by surprise that he suggested it before I did. I had been thinking a lot about it myself. "Let's do it. My scholarship will cover my school expense, so I was planning on quitting my job, to focus on school, but I'd rather keep it if it means us moving in together."

"No. If you go to college, that would be your job. I'd take care of all the living expenses."

I frowned. "Gabe. You can't afford to do that by yourself, and I wouldn't expect you to."

"No. I got toys to sell. I got my jeep and about ten thousand dollars in childhood savings bonds. I mean it's a start anyway." He gazed deep into my eyes. "I want to take care of you."

"Honey, you already do. I'm okay. Don't worry about me," I said, as he grabbed both my hands and placed them in his.

He squeezed my right hand before reaching into his pocket and pulling out a small black velvet box, my heart skipped a beat. Opening the box, he presented me with a beautifully sculpted wood ring. "Granbury Alastair Hawkins Keystone. Will you marry me?"

I gave him a puzzled look. "Gabe. You don't have to do this. I know I've told you this was my dream, so don't do this because you feel like you—"

"Hawk," he stopped me. "You've always known my dream to run my father's business, but that dream has changed. It changed the day you walked into my bedroom after Shelby died and asked me to hold you. I held you in my arms for two hours while you slept. I knew in that moment I just wanted to take care of you always."

I felt a tear fall from my eye. "You are the sweetest guy I have ever known in my life." I looked down at the ring. "Yes."

His face lit up. "Yes, you'll marry me?"

I wiped my cheek. "Yes, I'll marry you." I smiled.

"Holy shit!" He laughed then looked up to the sky. "He said 'yes'!" he screamed, then grabbed me in an embrace, kissing me all over my face. "I'll be the best husband to you."

I pulled back. "Wait. I thought I was the husband. How's this work?"

"We're both husbands!" he shouted, then pointed at Lucy, "and that's our baby…at least for now." He shrugged his shoulder.

"You're so corny, but I love you anyway." I kissed him on the lips again.

"I love you too." He grinned.

Epilogue

January 1994 (Six months later)

I finished spooning my enchilada mix into the tortilla. Carefully folding it, I placed it seam-down in the casserole dish. Looking up at the clock, I realized I should have started on the refried beans fifteen minutes ago.

"Shit!" I cursed, knowing my little planned dinner was less than an hour away. My timing could not have been worse, as I waited for the small oven in our mobile home to rise to the required temperature. Sweat gathered on my forehead as I ran the few feet to the front door and opened it, letting some of the cold winter air inside. I cursed at the broken thermostat hanging on the wall, before running back and opening the oven door, placing my dish inside. After Gabe and I were joined together in a small commitment ceremony in Eureka Springs, we lucked out and got a really good deal on a 1970s model mobile home that Mom and Doug helped us buy. We had it moved onto a piece of property my mom owned that lay about a quarter of a mile from them. Although we were just a five-minute walk from my family's place, it was private enough so that we felt like we had our own lives.

Just then, I heard a vehicle pull into our dirt driveway. My face lit up, knowing my husband had made it home from another hard day of work at the chicken plant. A few moments later, I heard him ascend the wooden steps and come inside.

"Hey, babe," he greeted, stopping as I bent down to pull out a saucepan from the cabinet.

"Sorry, hon. Running behind." I ran to him, gave him a quick kiss before rushing back to start on the Mexican rice.

He came up behind me and put his arms around me, kissing me on the neck. "Shirtless cooking tonight, are we?"

"Stupid thermostat is broken again. It's eighty-five degrees in here!"

"I'll take a look at it after dinner." He started swaying me in his arms. "You look sexy in that apron."

"Thanks," I said, trying to read the directions on the box of rice. Although Mrs. Sanchez had shared all her best recipes with me, I still wasn't the best cook and had a lot of learning to do. Making the rice and beans homemade was the original intent, but one homemade dish a night was all I could handle, settling for premade items instead.

He started moving his hands up my naked torso, feeling each ridge of my abs before rubbing my pecs. "So sexy." He kissed my neck again.

I turned around to face him and frowned. "Hon, please, we don't have time for this right now. Jude and Clint will be here in a little over an hour and I still have to shower and get dressed."

He pouted his lips. "Maybe just a quickie?"

"Babe, you know any other time I'd say yes but I really want this night to be special for Jude. This is his birthday present." When I asked my stepbrother what he wanted for his fourteenth birthday he said a double date with me and

Gabe to a Mexican restaurant and a movie afterward. Unable to afford a night on the town, I suggested I'd cook dinner and a movie rental at home. He agreed.

"I know, I do too," he said. "How was school today?"

"Eh," I grabbed a can of refried beans and the can opener, "business classes are so boring."

"Mi pequeño contador." He smiled.

I tapped my finger on my chin and then pointed at him. "My little accountant."

"Sí," he replied. "See now. Aren't you glad I talked you into taking that basic Spanish class last semester?"

"Sí," I replied. "At least now I'm not completely lost around your family."

While Gabe's relationship with his father was basically over, the relationship with his mother had strengthened. She even came to our commitment ceremony and referred to me as her "otro hijo" or "other son". Unfortunately, the relationship between her and her husband had deteriorated to the point they were now separated. Gabe carried a lot of guilt, feeling he was the cause of it, but she assured him that there were other factors involved and that Gabe's coming out only made the problems even more clear.

"How was training today?" I asked him. Doug had been kind enough to pull a few strings to get Gabe a job as a security guard for the chicken plant. The job required three weeks of training before he would be put on the overnight shift. While we weren't crazy about the hours, it paid well and beat the heck out of handling raw chicken.

"I got to shoot a gun today." Gabe aimed his finger like a gun toward the furnace and mimed pulling the trigger.

"Mi vaquero Mexicano."

"Very good." He laughed at me calling him "my Mexican cowboy".

"Oh," I said as I stirred the refried beans, "J.J. called today and invited us to Austin for the annual Gay Pride Parade."

"That sounds fun," he said as he began unbuttoning the shirt of his security uniform. I glanced over my shoulder as he unfastened the last button and pulled his shirt open, revealing the white T-shirt underneath. I slyly glanced back at him as he slipped the T-shirt over his head, distracting me from the beans.

"You're going to burn those if you don't watch it." He stood shirtless, reaching for a soda from the fridge, deliberately taking his time bending over to show me one of his best features.

"I know what you're doing, and it's not going to work." I went back to the task at hand.

"I'm just getting a soda." He turned around to face me, a soda in hand, playing all innocent. He sat the soda on the counter as I turned the burner down to let the beans simmer. Next, I heard his belt buckle rattle. I refused to turn my head, smiling to myself.

"Whew, it's hot in here," he exclaimed in that deep voice of his.

I checked the remaining time for the enchiladas—fifteen minutes. "Are you standing behind me in your underwear?" I asked.

"No," he said.

"You're lying, I heard you taking off your belt," I said, setting the Mexican rice to a back burner.

"I'm not standing in my underwear," he said coolly, "turn around and see."

I swung around to a smiling Gabe in his birthday suit. "Gabe. The front door is open!"

"Oops," he chuckled, casually leaning his hand against the refrigerator.

I ran to the door and closed it, then pointed at him. "You are trouble." I grinned.

"So," he motioned his head toward the bedroom, "you...um...wanna go play a quick game of Truth or Dare...you know? For old time's sake?"

I tapped my finger on my chin. "Are you going to dare me to kiss you?"

"Probably." He winked.

"Well in that case," I ran to him, grabbed his hand, and pulled him toward the bedroom, "let's go!"

About S.W. Ballenger

Shawn Wesley Ballenger is an Arkansas native. A computer programmer/analyst by day and a writer by night, he lives with his boyfriend and their three cats. He enjoys collecting American Top 40 shows with Casey Kasem, restoring vintage electronics, hiking, and geeking out over classic Doctor Who. A proud nerd since 1983.

More by S.W. Ballenger

A Gay Polyester High School Romance
A Gay Polyester High School Romance 2
A Boy Remade
Hunting Rabbits in the Dark

More From Deep Hearts YA

The Mixtape to My Life
Jake Martinez

Justin has always been comfortable in his skin, even if the world around him wasn't. A junior simply counting down the days for when he can leave for college, Justin's life is thrown for a loop when the one thing that helps him feel like himself suddenly slips away from him. But an unexpected blast from his past puts summer on a new and exciting path, one as random and unexpected as a mixtape.

Gay Love and Other Fairy Tales
Dylan James

What starts with a surprise kiss leads to a year of shared secrets, hidden love, relationship troubles, and broken hearts. For football captain Benjamin Cooper and his secret boyfriend, cheer co-captain Jordan Ortiz, there's only one thing standing in the way of their love—Ben's intense need to stay closeted, a need that just might tear them apart.

L.I.F.E.
Felyx Lawson

Rider is a closeted high school student and would be happy to stay that way, if not for two obstacles in his path: an assignment about love, and Cameron Walker, a new student who is so much more than the jock he first appears to be.